ESCAPING THE

Twilight

SIGRID WEIDENWEBER

arnica
PUBLISHING, INC.
Portland, Oregon

Library of Congress Catologing-in-Publication Data

Weidenweber, Sigrid, 1941-
  Escaping the twilight / Sigrid Weidenweber.
     p. cm.
Includes bibliographical references.
  ISBN 0-9726535-5-4 (trade pbk. : alk. paper)
  1. Girls--Fiction. 2. Mothers and daughters--Fiction. 3. Female
circumcision--Fiction. 4. Sudan--Fiction. I. Title.

PS3623.E425E83 2003
813'.6--dc21

                                                        2003007346

Arnica Publishing
620 SW Main, Suite 345
Portland, OR 97205

"*People and their cultures perish in isolation, but they are born or reborn in contact with other men and women, with men and women of another culture, another creed, another race; if we do not recognize our humanity in others, we shall not recognize it in ourselves.*"

—CARLOS FUENTES, *The Buried Mirror*

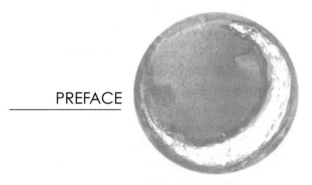

PREFACE

I learned about Female Genital Mutilation (FGM) while studying medical anthropology. When exploring the subject of spirit possession among different cultures, the writings by Janice Boddy, University of Toronto, were most relevant in explaining the antecedents of this phenomenon. Her beautifully written documentation of the practice of pharaonic circumcision and the often occurring Zar possession in Sudanese women haunted me for years until I decided to free myself from the nightmare by giving a face to the victims of this practice—a face with eyes through which the rest of us may perceive what their lives are like.

The voices that proclaimed the subject unpublishable as a novel proved correct for many years, and so now I am thankful that Arnica Publishing, Inc., decided to take a chance and allow you, the reader, to decide whether the life of Amina, the heroine of this story, deserves attention and consideration.

It is my fondest hope that this book might contribute to the discussion of how FGM can be stopped. The Islamic villages of Sudan are enclosed, hidden worlds. They languish in poverty and the rejection of outside ideas, untouched by thoughts of women's freedoms and rights.

Although the apologists for cultural integrity and tribal rights are entitled to their views, I believe certain cultural practices are affronts to humanity and must cease. There are no incentives within these cultures to stop the practice; therefore, education and encouragement for change must come from the outside.

Let us remember that the abolitionist movement spread to America via the London Committee for the Abolition of the Slave Trade, and was rooted in the teachings of religious humanitarianism by the English politician and philanthropist William Wilberforce (1759–1833). Likewise, the binding of Chinese women's feet did not end until Western-educated Sun Yat-Sen, influenced by Western doctors, decried the practice.

I have been asked why I chose such an unusual and affecting subject for a novel. Did I not know that such a subject held little hope of becoming published, never mind becoming widely read?

To those posing the question, I have only one answer: "I did not choose the subject, it chose me."

THANKS AND ACKNOWLEDGMENTS

Thank you, Ellen Joseph, for believing in my ability to write, and for your time and teaching. Thanks to Don, my husband, for all his support and the pronouncement that this book allowed him to understand women's thoughts and emotions better than before. I am grateful to Professor Lawrence Hammer for his suggestions and assistance when I began this project, and to Jessica Morell for her help toward the end.

Janice Boddy, a professor of medical anthropology at the University of Toronto, inspired me. I used her impeccable research with its rich cultural detail as a template to create the life of Amina. Her description of dances, rituals, clothes, food, spirit possession, sheikahs and feki Islams, family interactions and her interpretations of the meanings of rituals essentially allowed me to see through the eyes of a Sudanese woman, helping me to better explain her culture.

I also want to pay tribute to I.M. Lewis and his book *Ecstatic Religion*, which explores the cultural relevance of possessions and ecstasy as a spiritual and healing part of religions.

I am indebted to Robert Simon, M.D., founding chairman of

International Medical Corps who believed in my ideas on a previous project and went to great length to help me.

Last, but not least, thank you to Ross Hawkins, Gloria Gonzalez, Jennie Chamberlin and Aimee Genter, the staff of Arnica Publishing, Inc., for making publishing such an enjoyable experience.

GLOSSARY OF
ARABIC TERMS

adat	the rules, laws and codes of a culture
agal	a piece of embroidery or twisted rope
ahmar	red
aish	to marry (literally to make a nest for, or to nest)
angareeb	pallet, mattress
'aqel	reason, control over self-interest
asfar	light of color, white
asrag	dark
ayam el tahur	season of purification
benidj	anesthetic
Circassian	native of Circassia, a region of Southern Russia bordering on the Black Sea; also the language of the region
dilka	cleansing dough, made from millet and powdered, aromatic wood

El Asraq	the Blue Nile (beginning at Lake Tana in the high Plateau of Ethiopia it flows through the Sudan until, at Khartoum, it joins the White Nile to form El Bar en Nil)
El Bar en Nil	the Nile River in Arabic
el-khalla	the desert, the emptiness
feki Islam	religious doctor who cures with prayer and charms
gabeela	Muhammad's closest circle—his family and friends
Gehenna	Islamic hell
gulla	small, rounded pottery jar used to add water when making kisra
haboba/habobat (pl.)	grandmother
haboob	sandstorm blowing from the desert of the Sudan
harr	hot, painful
harr ceremony	circumcision
hashishin	one who uses the drug, hashish
hosh	courtyard, enclosed by a high, earthen wall
infibulation	term given to the procedure in which the vagina is partially closed by approximating the labia majora in the midline
jannat	heaven, paradise, closeness to Muhammad
jinn	spirit (soul) unable to attain entry to heaven that lurks on earth to cause mischief and seeks to possess a human body through which to experience earthly pleasures or to torment
kaffiyeh	Arab head-dress made of a a square piece of cloth and the agal
kaftan (caftan)	long (to the feet), loose long-sleeved shirt
kisra	flat bread made from sorghum flour and water
kofta	dumpling made from meat or flour

Mahdi	Islamic title (esp. Shiite) for a spiritual and political temporal ruler destined to establish Islamic righteousness throughout the world
mogren	confluence
nafs	uncontrolled passion, animal lust
Nubian	inhabitant of Nubia, a region once extending north of Khartoum from the Nile to the Red Sea
palau	rice dish (Afghan)
qismat (kismet)	fate
salaam	peace (often used in greetings)
shamla	tightly woven blanket of camel hair
sharmuta	prostitute
shawatin	black devil (black jinn) that brings illness and death
sheikha	woman spirit healer who communicates with Zairan jinn
souk	shops clustered into one or more streets, enclosed or open
Sufi	member of ascetic, mystical sect
surah	prayer section of the Qur'an
tahir	clean, pure
tob	garment worn by Somali women
washkhan	dirty, unclean
Zairan, Zar	red jinn (one of the four mentioned in the Qur'an)
zir	a pottery water container that cools water through evaporation on its porous exterior

CAST OF
CHARACTERS

Amina	Sudanese girl, heroine
Abu Assad Bakr	Amina's father
Assiza	Amina's mother
Umma Reha	Amina's grandmother
Hamida	Amina's cousin and best friend
Mahmood	Amina's youngest brother
Karem	Amina's middle brother
Khalid	Amina's oldest brother
Zahra	Amina's sister
Zaina	Amina's aunt
A'isha	Amina's aunt and Hamida's mother
Zainab	Amina's aunt
Sasat	Amina's aunt
Halim	Sasat's husband, brother of Abu Assad Bakr
Khurshid	Sasat's daughter

Rehana	Amina's aunt
Zora	Amina's aunt
Mansoor	Zora's son
Abate	Zora's daughter
Abdul Hakim	chauffeur
Feki Islam	a religious doctor
Sheikha	a spirit woman; healer
Hadija	midwife and exciser
Rishana	Amina's cousin
Shirin	Amina's cousin
Meme	Amina's cousin
Nazila	Amina's cousin
Ahmed Baqr	Amina's cousin
Farida	sister of Umma Reha
Fatima	Ahmed Baqr's bride
Majid	A'isha's husband and brother to Abu Assad Bakr
Fahid Mahdi	Hamida's husband, A'isha's son-in-law
Yussuf Nasredi	Amina's husband
Zajid Nasredi	Yussuf's father, Amina's father-in-law
Amna Nasredi	Yussuf's mother, Amina's mother-in-law
Zaynab Mahdi	wife of Yussuf's brother
Meriame Nasredi	wife of Yussuf's brother
Bashira	Meriame's cousin
Aziza	servant woman
Abdullah	brother of Zajid, Yussuf's uncle
Sophia	Abdullah's wife
Marie Latourelle	doctor, gynecologist
Hassan Nasredi (Abdul Hassan Majid)	Amina's/Yussuf's first son

Fahim Nasredi	Amina's/Yussuf's second son
Maryam Nasredi	Amina's/Yussuf's daughter
Madam Thibodeau	wife of the French Ambassador
Nahid	wife of Yussuf's youngest brother
Nuredin	trusted servant of Madam Thibodeau
Etienne	French doctor, Amina's second husband
Estelle	Sophia's daughter
Claudine	Sophia's daughter

CHAPTER *One*

To my grave I will remember the day my happy life ended and my twilight life began. The year was 1979. I was nine years old approaching ten. Occasionally I was still allowed to play with the other children, but I could sense that my childhood was ending. For weeks my mother, aunts and female cousins had been hinting somberly, threateningly, that I had reached the age of transformation. Although I was curious and excited because their hints meant I was joining the women's ranks, fear of the unknown gripped my soul, killing small joys and happiness, and stripping from me the careless freedom of my childhood.

Once declared marriageable, shroud-like wraps would hide my body, my face, all of me, except for my hands. I would be forced to live in the adult women's quarters, forever separated from the other children.

And as I sit here in my cozy Paris apartment and recall those days, I once again hear the women's grating voices; I feel my body heated by the remorseless sun, and I am transported to my childhood home: my feet glide over the dark earthen floor, smoothed to a shine for uncounted years by the bare feet of generations. As I walk past my aunts, cocooned in their tobs, they smile, "Amina, it looks like your time has come."

It frightened me when they spoke like that. I had already noted a subtle change in my body; two small nubbins, like those on a young goat's head, sprouted on my chest. They were so small that I paid little attention to them, but the women surely spotted them when I bathed and changed my clothes.

I never knew solitude in the village. It was a place where prying eyes followed my every move. At night, I slept with my younger sister and female cousins, and during the day every room in our house swarmed with people.

Hofryat was a village where time flowed as lazily as El Bar en Nil, the mighty one, the Nile. There were times when the days slowly seeped into each other like water stains spreading through the mud walls of our brownish houses. There, the rooms facing the outside had shaded verandas leading to the court-yards. Entire complexes were enclosed by walls high enough to protect those inside from curious observers. The wall prevented us from seeing or partici-pating in the interesting happenings along the River Nile, such as travelling foreigners and men running amok while possessed by shawatin. My brothers never missed the exciting events, but barricaded inside the walls, the females experienced little.

We mostly lived outdoors in the courtyard, the hosh. Only the smothering heat drove us inside, into our homes thatched with reeds cut at the Nile's edge during the dry season. It seldom rained so our houses were open and airy, a fact I fondly remember.

Children freely roamed throughout the house. Childhood gave us license to explore the parts of our compound forbidden to the women—gave us license to visit with our fathers, on the few occasions they were at home. The women only entered a husband's divan when called, modestly dressed as always, to serve food.

My father's divan was a large room, its stamped earthen floor was covered with reed mats overlaid with fine carpets. Along three walls high, cushy mattresses covered with heavy, black Egyptian cotton invited you to rest. Bolsters and cushions covered in blue, brown and ochre cotton, and even silks dotted the divan and the carpets. The fourth wall was a large, wooden, double door leading onto the veranda. I never saw this door closed.

My father, Abu Assad Bakr, ate, slept and received my uncles, his friends, traders and his children, my three older brothers, my sister, Zahra, aged five and me, in this room. Of my three brothers only Mahmood, eleven, regularly visited the women's hosh, while my two older brothers, Khalid, eighteen, and

Karem, seventeen, rarely visited our mother. Until last year my cousin Hamida and I stealthily followed Mahmood and his playmates the moment they sidled up to the solid wood gate set into an arched opening of the wall—the divide separating the male and female section of the hosh. We followed them in hopes of spending time with our father or the uncles, but then Hamida became tahir, a woman, and then only seldom did I creep to Father's divan with Zahra, my younger sister.

The men congregated on one another's divans to eat, drink tea or fruit juice, smoke and talk. They sat in a circle on the carpet with their cups and utensils in front of their crossed legs, sometimes reclining on the cushions.

If luck favored us, our father acknowledged our presence and motioned us to sit to his right, slightly behind his back. On those days when no motion invited us closer, Zahra and I knew to sit silently back, outside the circle, like shadows on the wall. Mahmood and the other boys grinned and filled the empty spaces between the men. They received friendly shoves and cuffs, signs of affection from the older men. The men teased them and told much antici-pated stories of huge Nile crocodiles pulling men under water if they fell over-board from a vessel, and stories of camel fights and bandits laying in wait for the traders. Yet, I too, loved to hear their tales of places far from our sleepy village—enticing tales so unlike the dull repetitious lives of the women.

They spoke of Khartoum, the big capital city, of Port Sudan and Kassala, and of crowded bazaars where hundreds of shops offered a perplexing array of fine jewelry, artfully chased copper, metal tools for the farmer or the fighter like daggers, knives and spears, leather goods, pottery, tempting gossamer fabrics, and useful household goods. They told of heavily loaded barges plying their trade along the Nile and of caravans providing the cities with fruits, vegetables and grain.

During a few blissful hours, released from my daily chores, I played with Hamida in the walled-in courtyards that surrounded our compound. Sometimes we were brave enough to venture outside on the road. But not after Hamida had to leave her childhood. Wherever I went the shrill voices of my grandmother and my aunts pursued me. It seemed I was always needed for something.

"Amina, Amina! Come hither, you worthless girl. Where are you hiding your lazy body now?" Those screams followed me relentlessly.

I loved to escape into the dry, dusty road which, hemmed in by ochre courtyard walls, wound its way through the village like a fat snake slithering gracefully through tall grass. On this road we raced to the village's boundary. I was fleet of foot and faster than other children, faster even than Mahmood who often jealously tripped me whenever possible. Running, I felt my white sleeveless shift slapping against my calves as my bare feet stirred up the gray dust hovering in the air behind me. The hot air, pungent with the smell of dry dung and decaying vegetation, filled my lungs until they stung.

Where the road ended, the desert began, leading onward to the east, to the horizon, seemingly forever. To the west, cultivated fields followed the bed of El Bar en Nil. We call the desert el-khalla (the emptiness). Repeatedly Mother warned us: "There are jinn in the desert, and it's filled with serpents and scorpions and is not a place for children."

Heeding her warning, we always lingered where its vastness began, gazing longingly into the void. No matter how often my eyes beheld el-khalla, my awe remained for this terrifying, seemingly dead and endless expanse—Allah's creation.

Approaching the river, the desert was dotted with clumps of dry, thorny acacia scrub. The boys brought their families' camels to feed here because camels can extract food from even the poorest plants. We frequently met the boys by the thorny girdle of scrub, shouting at them while they yelled back happy for the distraction during their otherwise tedious chores. Together, we sniffed the air, pungent with the moist odors of the river, or, when the winds changed, with the smell of alkaline from the ashy heat of el-khalla.

Growing up hemmed in by walls upon walls, I felt frightened and yet exhilarated by the expanse of the desert with its clay soil bleached ash-white and mostly covered beneath yellow sands. My sight was lost upon the dreadful, barren sameness, my eyes unable to fix on objects for the comfort of reference. All life seemed to have been scoured from the desert's surface by the hot breath emanating from the interior sending sand storms like immense caresses.

Contrary to feeling cowed by el-khalla's melancholy and terrifying isolation, I was gripped by an overwhelming desire to run into her unfenced freedom; even if it meant death. I wanted to run free toward the horizon until my lungs gave out and my feet faltered. I never flew into that void, though the intense longing never yielded.

When the aunts began to speak of my time, I knew it was too late. They talked about becoming pure, but I sensed there was more behind the word tahir (pure) than their cryptic words revealed. Some secret rite was connected to becoming tahir. Something dark and haunting that was never talked about. This secret frightened me, for I was awake at dawn when they came for Hamida. They came early one morning, three women and Haboba (my grandmother). Hamida's mother was among them. They surrounded her and I heard their solemn words, "Come with us. Your day has arrived."

Gripping her tightly by her arms, they led Hamida away. Days passed before I saw her again. I knew she now slept with the young women. She was tahir. When I met her in the courtyards I wouldn't have recognized her but for the silver and lapis lazuli ring glistening on her left hand. Our grandmother gave her that ring when she was five, which was supposed to restore health during a grave illness. I spotted the ring and ran to her.

She was covered in white from the crown of her head to her naked feet with the shroud the women wear, the tob. She seemed shrunken somehow, as if the garment weighed down her head, crushing her spine. Perhaps it did, for the tob was nine meters long. Her ringed hand held the wrap tightly in front of her face, exposing oddly old, hurt eyes—eyes that I did not recognize. If it hadn't been for her exposed hands and an occasional glimpse of the toes or soles of the feet, a ghost could have been moving her garment. Her life-light dimmed, she walked in twilight.

"Hamida! Hamida, why are you wearing this? Where have you been?" I cried out, clinging to her. "What have they done to you? Why did you not come back to me?"

I had pestered my mother with these questions and she answered that Hamida was now grown and would no longer sleep with children. But I wanted Hamida to explain. I needed to hear from her lips what had changed her so drastically.

"Tell me all that happened to you," I begged.

She seemed exhausted and the words spilled from her mouth like teardrops rolling down a cheek. "Don't bother me," she snapped hoarsely, as if her throat was raw from sobbing. "You will find out soon enough for yourself."

She left, leaving me feeling confused, hurt and alone. I hid in the hosh's corner behind an old kerosene barrel, and wept and wept. Older by a year, Hamida had been my closest friend since I learned to walk. What had they done to her who was dearer to me than my sister? How could she push me away and say, "Don't bother me?" How could she dismiss me with such cold indifference?

Before they enshrouded her, we looked after the younger children together, swept the courtyards with reed brooms, and were scolded and cuffed on our heads by the aunts and older cousins. We wept in each other's arms, comforted one another faithfully, and picked thorns and stickers from each other's feet, and now she wanted me no more.

What terrible thing had they done to change her so? Had they stolen her very soul? Where was that cherished heart that had loved me? What was the terrible secret that went with the shroud they called tob?

Each time I thought of Hamida terror seized me. I knew that soon they would come for me—secretly, very early in the morning when all the other children slept. What would they do to me? I already knew that I didn't want the wrapping of the shroud. Who would be able to run swiftly, move freely, encased so in the tob?

"You must grow up," the women laughed and looked at me with their dark, mocking, secretive smiles when I proclaimed I wanted no women's wraps, that I wished to forever remain a child.

Meanwhile, I walked every morning with my younger sister to the hosh enclosing the school for girls. The school was a circular, open-air structure with a thatch roof. Its walls reached halfway up the support posts, allowing the hot desert winds to vibrate the reeds of the roof, producing a hissing, monotonous tune. Here, we learned to read, write and count a little, but mostly we memorized surahs, prayer sections from the Qur'an. The boys were schooled in another building.

• • • • •

When summer blazes in from the desert, the intense heat dries the last of the farmers' fields and the reeds at the edge of El Bar en Nil; remorselessly it steals the last traces of green from sorghum fields, turning them rust brown, leaching millet stalks and blackening cotton brush, leaving a world colored brown, gray, russet and golden wherever stubble and sand reflect the sunlight, a world of harsh brilliance. Summer is so fearsome that the mighty river retreats protectively into its cradle. Wading birds with long beaks explore the drying mud flats abandoned by the river's retreat. Then the stench of decaying algae, river vegetation and dead fish hangs over the village until the desert sends her cleansing winds. Daily, the angry jinn of the desert whip sand storms across the plain and shower our village. The school closes. This is the season of ayam el tahur, the season of purification.

It's a season to rejoice, although it is harsh and vexing because the wind we call haboob cunningly deposits sand in minute places and openings, and annoys my people, irritating their eyes, ruining their food and abrading their homes. Yet, we rejoice because this is the time the village becomes whole once again. It is the season when those fathers forced to work in cities far away, the trader caravans and the artisans come home for their yearly vacation bringing prosperity and gifts for their families.

Aunt Zaina, who more than anyone hated the sandstorms showering misery upon women trying to prepare food, greeted that ayam el tahur with ululations, our women's joyous exclamations of personal triumph. My mother whispered of Zaina's wish to become a mother again. There was a saying in our village, "A woman without children is an empty husk." Aunt Zaina had borne only three little ones, all girls. This was an unforgivable state bemoaned by Umma Reha, our grandmother, many times each day. Zaina rejoiced loudly because that ayam el tahur would bring back her husband from Port Sudan where he worked as a stevedore. It is also the season when fathers swell with pride because their boys become men through the rite of circumcision. Oh, what great feasts the boys are given. Feasts, so enormous that only weddings compare to the pomp.

I loved the ceremony and feasting, but I sensed, ominously, that the day of my own ceremony of purification was drawing near.

Some of the men returned home often while most visited only once a year. My father traveled from village to village along the Nile, often going far beyond Khartoum, along Bar El Asraq, the blue Nile into Ethiopia. He traded in goods and farm produce. Once, when we sat with him he explained to the boys, "As a trader you must be clever; you buy low-priced goods here and sell for a profit in another place. Most of all you must be fair and bring the people needed products, and you must never cheat them. If you live by this principle, people will be glad to see you arrive at their villages and Allah will bless you."

He taught us that our village was part of a much greater place which they call Sudan.

"If you travel some two hundred miles upstream from Hofryat, you come to Khartoum, the big city. My brothers and cousins work in Khartoum as laborers. Some own small shops filled with cloth, others sell sorghum, millet and rice. Another group provides services to offices, carrying important messages about town, things too delicate to relate by telephone."

I always wondered how these telephones worked. There were no telephones in the village, nor did we have electricity.

In the morning's coolness it was my task to carry water and clean the kitchen hosh. Sweeping yards was a Hofryati obsession. We were obsessed with creating purity and order; our brooms were weapons in our war to control our bland environment. Mounds of sand deposited by the haboob became targets to be demolished by us, the possessed.

One morning as I raked up the refuse with my stiff broom, my eyes circled the yard. By the huge iron griddle knelt A'isha and beside her knelt Hamida. Mother taught daughter the art of making kisra; more so, she taught her what to look for in a husband.

"We shall look for a cousin for you, sideways to our lineage; that keeps family together," A'isha proclaimed. "And, of course, we hope he will be rich. I want for you to have servants."

I listened attentively, without attracting their notice, following every syllable of their never-resting mouths. From their conversations I gathered that it would be more advantageous to marry an ugly, wealthy man if he had a good disposition, than a handsome, poor man.

Nearby, cross-legged upon a pillow sat our haboba, Umma Reha, blue worry beads sliding through her gnarled fingers as she took charge of the marriage conversation.

"Don't scare Hamida," she admonished A'isha who tried to impress upon Hamida the problems of finding a good marriage prospect. "Our girls do not have to worry about finding a man. Every one knows that our women are of superior purity."

Why, I wondered, were the women of Khartoum less pure? Were they sharmuta? Prostitutes?

At that, Mother and the aunties entered into the fray. While their quick hands performed a hundred tasks, their mouths ran on and on. Sometimes they thought we girls didn't understand certain things, sometimes they forgot we were present, and so we listened and learned.

An example was Aunt Rehana. She sat across from me, leaning her round back against a wall, her fat legs, spread like giant tongs, held a shallow basket into which her nimble, sausage fingers dropped the peas she shelled.

"Mansoor will go to school in Khartoum," she proudly announced. "He is a man now, a man of reason, who can be trusted to live away."

Of course, we all knew that she was referring to the belief that men have 'aqel, reason, and women do not. Mansoor was her oldest son; one who visited seldom. I hardly knew what he looked like.

"Ah, boys are easy," Rehana continued. "Abate will be married two years come harvest time and there are no children yet. The worry that she might be barren is killing me." Rehana's jowly face shook with the horror of this possibility; the other women commiserated, eyes softened by pity, for they all knew the consequences of barrenness.

All day, going from chore to chore, I thought about such women's talk. Of course, marriage must be followed promptly by birth. I already knew the importance of bearing male children soon after marriage. Who could forget what happened to barren women in our own family? Poor unfortunates. Some were divorced by their husbands and forced back into the fold of their families, and so disgraced, they never wed again. Unable to bear children, they were declared worthless and treated like slaves. If the husband didn't divorce, it was the fate of such poor souls to carry the household's burden and watch another wife's happiness.

Thinking weighty thoughts made me drowsy and I soon fell asleep wedged tightly behind the kerosene barrel. I awoke with a start. The twilight of night softened the shapes of all things familiar; the barrel, the griddle, the grinding stone, the wall—all looked velvety smooth.

A great commotion ensued in the street beyond. Camels cried their harsh plaint, a woeful sound of a donkey's bray and a dying man's moan. Men's shouts echoed between the hosh walls; metal clanked, leather creaked and a horse whinnied shrilly. An old, beat-up truck's engine whined pitifully, as its wooden flanks heaved and moaned in an effort to contain the overflowing goods stuffed into its belly.

They had returned. They were back—the fathers, uncles, brothers and cousins from Khartoum.

A giant eagle owl flying river's way, silently cast her shadow over the hosh, making me shiver with unknown dread.

• • • • •

I felt with every new month invisible ropes binding me tighter and tighter to the women. Their grown-up problems filled my head, and yet still, they kept many things secret from me. I watched with horror and little empathy when terrible things began to happen to my aunt, Sasat.

Sasat was the youngest mother in our house. Her shoulders bent, face pinched, she moved, as her chores dictated, from the common room to the hosh and the kitchen—week after week, growing more sad and depressed. She was so thin that her hip bones showed angular through the heavy tob when she bent down, and her eyes were permanently glazed by worry about her youngest child's ailments.

My mother whispered in Zaina's ear, thinking she couldn't be heard, "Who in this house doesn't know that Halim stays in Khartoum year round. No one has seen him here in almost two years. And so, there is poor Sasat with two girls, one of whom is always sick with something, and no boy child."

Even I understood that Sasat desperately needed to bear a boy, for with the birth of a male child came position. The pressure from family was great, and only added to her misery. Whenever a husband neglected his wife the rest of the family added the sting of disdain. The most malicious ones tormented her like dirty hens who peck on the weakest in the farmer's yard.

"Sasat, what did you put in his food to make him stay away so long?" asked the haboba, or, "Did you ruin his sleep with your animal passion when he was here last time?"

Her degrading words were greeted with howls of laughter, sounding to my ears like the fiendish laughs of desert hyenas. Sasat's errant husband was one of Haboba's sons and therefore the fault for the bad marriage was placed in full measure on Sasat. Burdened thus, it was inevitable that Sasat would eventually become ill.

The rains came in November, dropping the temperature twenty degrees to a comfortable ninety degrees fahrenheit, as A'isha informed us with overt pride. Her husband owned a thermometer and gloried in the knowledge of temperature degrees and such—the rest of us never cared to know numbers. Who needed numbers when one felt the difference?

The first rain fell amidst thunder and lightning. All night long the booming thunder kept me awake. I listened as the rain beat the rushes on the roof, creating a sighing, rustling song. Every few moments a lightning bolt lit up the upper part of the inside walls. In the morning Sasat called out "I can't get up.

My joints are on fire."

Grandmother, Umma Reha, clucked her tongue and said, "Nothing is wrong with her; she just doesn't want to work."

Although Sasat struggled to rise, she clearly couldn't move. In the end her bitter tears softened the hard hearts of the aunts, and they placed small, sand-filled hot bags on her painful joints. Sasat's symptoms changed daily; from head to toes every part of Auntie's body seemed to develop a different affliction. The aunts tried different remedies to relieve the pain, herb tea, cool, moist compresses, cushions for the aching back and rich soups. It was a mystery to me why they were so patient with her when in days past they had acted so unkindly.

However, despite the women's best efforts the pain so severely disabled Sasat that in time she could not even hold her comb. Mother, hearing her wails, surmised that Sasat's soul was on fire, not her body.

"It is not natural. It's not her body, but her spirit that ails. The Zairan will find it easy to conquer her," my mother predicted.

The aunts agreed, "She might be possessed already."

Possessed? Zairan? The words were familiar but they meant nothing to me, and yet they sounded full of secrets and intrigue. I wanted to unveil their meaning.

Whenever I needed to unravel a puzzle, I asked Umma Reha. Grandmother was revered for her wisdom because she had borne seven sons and two daughters and knew many passages from the Qur'an by heart. Once she became frail and too old to work, she began to sit on the women's veranda contemplating her life. A life which had been defined solely by her domestic activities, constantly seeing to the wishes and commands of men—facts she would never acknowledge. Perhaps stimulated by her contemplation she also became deeply religious. For hours she would sit in the afternoons listening to her young grandsons recite from the Holy Qur'an.

It was difficult to sneak away from the kitchen yard to Grandmother's veranda. My mother's eyes saw everything. One day I hid the ragged broom I'd been using to sweep the hosh with one quick motion behind my trusty kerosene barrel, and slunk like a cat along the house wall. A moment later the curving wall concealed me.

Mahmood sat on the veranda step below Grandmother who was enthroned on a pile of cushions. Mahmood's head was well within the reach of her knuckles. I was glad that it was Mahmood's turn to be a sacrifice to Umma Reha's whims, for her victims were forced to read loudly to the nearly deaf women, and besides, they received a hard knock on their heads whenever they made the slightest mistake. Many times I burst out laughing at the wretched whine of the boys trying to imitate the sonorous voice of a mullah. To me, they sounded like donkeys braying for food. On those occasions I was happy that I didn't have to read to her.

Mahmood, a sly grin on his face, put out a foot to trip me as I came closer, but I avoided him with a small jump. There were days when I felt like an agile cat, always ready to spring or pounce. I wondered about Mahmood, wondered why he picked on me. Perhaps because the women spoiled him.

"Here, Mahmood, have a little dumpling...Try these almonds they are delicious...Put a little honey on your kisra, Mahmood, you are a growing boy," so chirped the aunts, as he greedily devoured everything they offered.

The haboba was particularly annoying in the way she pampered him. She interspersed her knuckle raps with offerings of sweet figs, which went straight from her hand to his mouth, and pistachios, which she shelled for him.

Mahmood was tall and well made for his age. He had skinny arms and legs, large, narrow feet with long, oddly separated toes. His head was more round than the women liked, but he had big, black eyes that made up for his shortcomings—or so Mother believed. Behind Mother's back, the aunts said that he was a shade too dark for our family, but the haboba liked him for that because her skin was deep brown too.

A faint odor of old person and cloves emanated from Umma Reha's body and fused with Mahmood's boy smell of sweat and animal. The haboba, unhappy to have her leisure interrupted by a female child, did not invite me to sit. Her voice was harsh and querulous and without preamble, she launched into her explanation about the Zairan.

"Zairan belong to the jinn; they are spirits of which the Qur'an speaks. They are formed of fire, water and air." Her arm, heavy with bracelets and charms gestured in a wide arc. For a moment she forgot that she was angry with me for interrupting and her voice became low and ominous.

"The souls of unfortunate dead, those not called into Allah's presence, are doomed to drift in the desert winds. They mingle with the shawatin, the devils. They crawl into humans, possessing them at will."

She grew suddenly pensive, focusing inward on old memories. "Live by

Allah's words, Children, because if a shawatin possesses you, sickness will rage in your body so fearsomely that it may kill you. Our neighbor, Abu Bakr, you never knew him, he died because a black devil crept into his body and ate his entrails. Oh, he died horribly."

I shivered, though the afternoon's sun blazed fierce. Haboba's small, black eyes were fixed on mine as if measuring my response; then she shifted her weight and continued.

"There are white jinn too, but they are benign." She pointed her finger, curved like a striking talon, at me and said, "But you, girl, you must fear the red jinn or Zairan for they possess women."

Mahmood who looked glum during her early recital, now smirked and snickered when she mentioned the possession of women. Grandmother's hand shot forward, connecting hard with his head. He winced, and I smiled inside, marvelling at her quick reflex. Satisfied, the haboba took up her thread again.

"Red Zairan seek pleasure. They are capricious and must be pleased." She popped a date in her mouth and turned to me, "Now, leave me so I can hear Mahmood read."

Grandmother's abrupt dismissal left me in a quandary. I was plagued by the thought that a red Zairan could enter my body. How would I feel? What could I do? It sounded so horrible. How could I rid myself of such an undesirable spirit?

So next morning, while I knelt beside Mother pouring water for her wash from a big zir, she explained that some Zairan can be exorcised, but that exorcism angers the red Zairan.

"Once a red Zairan inhabits a body of its liking, it can experience once more the physical pleasures missing in the spirit world. Naturally, it violently resists any attempt to deprive it of having fun. No, contrary to removing them, possessed women must mollify them, submitting to their wishes no matter how bizarre they might seem."

Sasat's misery continued for three weeks. Then our clan decided that her illness had to be treated with the only effective cure they knew for Zairan. A desperate summons was sent for my uncle, informing him of his wife's illness. He did not come. Sasat, hearing that her husband didn't care about her illness, withdrew and lay silent on her bed for many days.

• • • • •

Hamida, her tob dragging in the dust, swished through the hosh. The noon heat made all of us sluggish. Glancing around for prying eyes she sidled up to me and whispered, "Come with me. I want to show you what the Zairan can do."

She took me by the hand and whisked me into the older women's bedroom. It was a large room because the women sleeping here still had young children requiring their attention. A stack of small mattresses in the corner attested to the many nights sick children slept beside their mothers. The auntie's beds were arranged along the walls leaving a square in the middle. Ostrich eggs, signs of perfect fertility, strung and clustered, hung in the corners. Pillows and colored blankets were the only bright spots in the otherwise drab room.

On her narrow angareeb among a pile of pillows, Sasat, thin in a white cotton shift, was rhythmically rocking back and forth. Her hair hung wildly about her head and shoulders, her eyes were large and angry. As she rocked she moaned and chanted crazily. I was frightened, and I wondered if she might leap from her bed and lash out at us in anger.

"Look at her," murmured Hamida, "see how the jinn is shaking her."

"How do you know it's a jinn? It could be fever," I whispered reasonably.

"No, no it's a jinn all right. I know! I saw my mother when her jinn shook her. See, how her eyes are turned up and unfocused, and listen to her. Have you ever heard such howls?"

Sasat's chant had grown loud and shrill until it was a steady, piercing wail, and at last, the entire village knew of her illness. I was dismayed, for I was truly fond of Sasat. Feeling sad, I attended to my never-ending chores with a pain inside me as sharp as a toothache. There was little I could do for Sasat, but I decided to look after her girls. The older one, Khurshid, was a delightful child. I liked having her around me. But, the three-year-old was a sickly one and a spoiled pest, and I resolved to change that.

It was one thing to hear tales of jinn and shawatin but quite another to live with a possessed person. It was pandemonium. The men complained that no peace could be had in this house, that something must be done.

Fortunately, the aunts knew what to do. Many of them had Zairan in their lives, since a jinn, once possessing a body, resides within its victim forever, showing its power whenever displeased.

The unusual excitement was a welcome interruption from our

predictable, mundane lives, and so Hamida and I watched with gusto the unusual, comical procession leaving our gate. As dawn crept over the hosh wall Hamida found me in the kitchen and pulled me, shaking with suppressed excitement, into the yard. We stood beneath a giant fig tree watching expectantly as the event unfolded. Our fig tree was an anomaly. It was the only tree in the village inside a compound. It was planted into the corner of the kitchen hosh by my grandfather, a trader like Father, who had fallen in love with fig trees during one of his many travels. Despite dire forecasts, the tree prospered. Daily draughts of wastewater were enough to sustain it.

The procession consisted of my father and an uncle in the lead, followed by two aunts and my mother who helped poor Sasat, in fact, almost carrying her. Behind them ambled three elderly, male cousins at a proper distance, ensuring that the women were not approached. As they progressed down the road the sun came up and brightened their white garments and turbans. Father was distinguished by a bright turquoise headdress made of folded silk which he had purchased in Ethiopia.

First, they led Sasat before the feki Islam, the religious doctor. My mother was unusually animated upon their return and told us the story.

"The feki Islam is shrinking," she declared. "Since I saw him two years ago the sun must have dried him out, and now he looks like a white stick with a turbaned prune on top. A prune with glasses and a long, gray beard. But his voice is still strong and so is his mind. He consulted his religious manuals and searched the ancient, astrological charts for the cause of Sasat's disease, just like he always does, but after his deliberations he ruled that physical illness was not Sasat's trouble."

"Ha," interrupted the haboba, who knew the ritual well, "then he looks at the charts again, pronounces that, indeed, a jinn controls her body, and performs an exorcism."

"No, no," cried Zaina not to be outdone. "Before the exorcism his female assistant fastened different charms and amulets around Sasat's arms and her neck, and chanted verses from the Qur'an commanding the jinn to obey and leave her body."

"It all is no good," twittered the aunts excitedly, "everybody knows you can't exorcise a red jinn."

They led Sasat to a mattress in the large communal living room shared by the women and children. She was still covered with the colorful charms and amulets, and they propped her up with pillows and scooted the children out into the hosh. Fashioned from feathers, stones and sacred cloth, the amulets were very powerful and brightly colored. It was unusual to see such brilliance on one person, for dyes were expensive and we usually wore white or gray clothing.

I wondered if the charms had worked already. Sasat's eyes appeared a bit brighter as she sat beside her mother-in-law who stroked her hand and fed her juicy orange slices. My father's youngest brother, Halim, was Sasat's husband.

"No good, that one," murmured the aunts among themselves.

"I would not like him for my husband," they purred, and although they whispered so Sasat would not hear, they didn't take notice of me and talked loosely of his liking for strong, sweet wine and the dancing girls in Khartoum.

"All his money goes there, to the wine sellers and the sharmuta."

Of course, Muslim men are supposed to abstain from drinking wine, although the Qur'an does not outright forbid it. With Sasat possessed, everyone knew that Halim was in serious trouble upon his return, because now his preferences were in the open—even the Imam knew.

For my part, I wondered how the aunts knew about such things as dancing girls and wine shops, since they never left Hofryat, let alone left the house.

One night, back when she was still sleeping beside me in the children's room, Hamida answered this question for me. "The men's tongues are loosened when they have their wives visit them at their divans at night, and sometimes they talk about their affairs in the outside world," she confided.

"How would you know?" I asked, but she only laughed and said, "The walls have ears."

The next step in Sasat's treatment was a visit to the Western doctor. His failure to cure Sasat truly established possession as the problem in the mind of the village. The finishing touch was to consult the sheikha.

"What's a sheikha?" I asked my mother. In the past she had brushed away my questions like so many gnats in the air, but with the approach of my time to become tahir, she answered me more readily.

"If the feki Islam, the most holy man and the eminent Western doctor cannot cure an ailing woman, then the Zairan healer must use her art. Sheikhas are powerful women. They are in touch with the spirit world and commune with their own possessive Zairan." I listened closely, since this was the first I'd heard of a powerful woman among us.

"Our sheikha's Zar will whisper to her the wishes of Sasat's jinn. Then, and this is most important, the sheikha announces to the public that a Zairan possesses her. Only then will Sasat be allowed to undergo the cure." My mother explained that cures like the spirit ceremony cost money, and without pronouncement by the sheikha, Sasat would be deprived of a cure.

The next morning, although the haboob, wretched wind of the desert, blew ferociously, the same procession left the gate once more. The rest of us were waiting in the communal room for Sasat's return. She finally walked in smiling; eager to tell of her visit with the sheikha.

"The sheikha lives in a small, square house at the edge of the village. Her courtyard is edged by a circle of stones. Our small party arrived, and the sheikha, a thin, brown woman with lively bird eyes, asked us to enter through the women's back door. It's a magical door, thickly hung with charms made from feathers, a multitude of bright, woven fabrics, pierced stones strung together with sacred cloth and other spiritual items. I felt calm as I entered."

My father and the uncles, of course, did not enter the hut. They sat, hiding behind the house in the howling wind, their blankets covering their heads.

The women sat on rush mats, on the floor. The hut was as unremarkable and drab as most of our dwellings. Once settled, they answered polite questions about the family, obliquely touched upon village gossip, and, at last, Sasat told her troubles. The sheikha listened closely, her hands playing with a string of large, blue beads, powerful enough to ward off evil. She wore amulets, a small, brown leather pouch and many charms around her scrawny neck. Brightly colored feather charms adorned her wrists.

When Sasat finished speaking, the sheikha closed her eyes and after a long silence began to chant, producing a high, foreign song of amazing sweetness. She sat on the bare earthen floor with Sasat positioned across from her, flanked by the aunts. Her upper body began to rock back and forth, and suddenly she fell into a deep trance. Thereafter, her small bird eyes rolled back in her head, her eyes appeared white, empty and dead. Then she spoke to someone unseen by the women in a voice harsh and foreign. After a while she opened her eyes and addressed Sasat: "You are possessed by a Western jinn. It is a white woman who was very powerful in her former life. She resents that she can't partake of the sweetness of earth's bounty, and wants to experience once more the things she enjoyed in the past."

The women were distraught. A Western woman? Allah be merciful.

"How can I placate such a Zairan?" asked Sasat as she has been instructed, and the old, almost toothless crone, beseeched her Zairan once more: "What does the Western woman want?"

"Buy her a Western gown of red silk, and she must have henna, of course," dictated the Zairan. "You must also procure for her fine European perfume from the city they call Paris and bathe her body using Lux soap."

"All of this? This is expensive," the women groaned in unison.

"There is more," said the Zairan, hissing powerfully. "You must feed Sasat's body, now host to me, with delicious meat that comes from a tin. She must have chocolates and a soft bed, and she must do no work until she feels better."

"Avoid all anger, bother and frustration," admonished the sheikha as the women stepped out the door to leave.

Henceforth, Sasat's life became quite delightful. The pronouncement of the Zar possession legitimized her every complaint. My father journeyed to Khartoum and brought back the protesting Halim by force, and Halim, although reluctant, provided the things ordered by the sheikha.

As soon as the bounty arrived, we gathered in the day room. The floor was covered with rush mats surrounded by mattresses stuffed with cotton, upon which flocks of cushions rested. Bursting with excitement my barefoot female relatives wanted to examine Sasat's wonderful gifts. She smiled shyly and held up the shameless red Western gown.

"Ahhh...nothing on the arms," breathed the women. They clicked their tongues expressing their disapproval of the low-cut bodice and its sparse length. Hamida's mother, A'isha, clicked the loudest so that her tongue protruded into the space between her front teeth. Held before Sasat's body, the dress looked as if it would cover her only to mid-calf. Dutifully, we admired the beautiful, red-satin box filled with chocolates and the bright blue tin featuring a phalanx of pharaonic women, their red hands upturned holding mounds of henna. We were mesmerized. I, for one, had never seen anything like it because during the last Zairan ceremony, my presence was not desired.

No wonder Sasat seems happy, I thought. It seemed a good thing to be possessed. Could this ever happen to me? Possession was more fun than humdrum, everyday life.

A few of the aunts stared, silent with envy, while others who had once experienced Sasat's new reality, chanted their approval generously.

Although immersed in our joy, Sasat suddenly began to shake—the Zairan craved attention. And then, right before our eyes, my pure, shy aunt began to sing and trill. She moved, she danced—but not with the mincing pigeon steps the young women use at weddings. She danced seductively, provocatively swaying her hips, stripped off her garments to her few under things and wiggled into the new, red Western dress.

Until this moment I hadn't realized that Sasat was pretty. To me, she had always been the quiet, shadow aunt, a thin, gaunt ghost. Now it was as if I saw her for the first time. Brown, satiny skin covered long, elegant limbs and her body, although thin, was rounded in all the right places. I was startled to find that she had breasts because she had looked so flat under the layers of her tob.

The dress fit her as if the Zairan made it for her. My aunties covered their mouths in mock despair, making little bird sounds of disapproval while urging her on with laughing eyes and giggles. Encouraged, Sasat continued the sensual dance, as if entranced. Her eyes were half closed, her face sweet and serious; her arms extended gracefully as bird wings above her perfectly arched back. Her dance was not the chaste kind of dance the aunties taught us girls. I didn't know what kind of dance it was, but it mesmerized me and incited me to move in the same rhythm.

I wanted to leave my place on the couch and join Sasat, but my mother forcefully caught my arm and pulled me down beside her, motioning for me to be silent. Later, Mother revealed that a woman possessed can dance like this in front of the entire village.

"Among us lives a Zairan they call Luliya. She is a female Ethiopian prostitute spirit demanding wedding incense, the necessary jewelry and the bridal shawl, then she appears in her human host during the possession ceremony and dances a strange, sensual dance. Oh," continued Mother, looking dreamy for a moment, "a woman inhabited by Luliya is a lucky woman. When she dances the wedding dance as Luliya the wanton, pretending to be a chaste Hofryati bride, there is always much laughter in the village, and the woman dancing feels wonderful."

Meanwhile, I observed Sasat closely. She, and the spirit within, enjoyed life. She slept late, and Grandmother, who watched with black, hawk-like eyes, saw all that transpired, and allowed her to come and go as she wished. She walked about with hennaed hair, henna-stained hands and even the soles of her feet had been colored, oblivious and disregarding of custom. And, oh, she smelled delicious as if she had been to heaven.

A new gold anklet dangled about her ankle and two new, fat gold rings sat on the fingers of her left hand. The ring on her ring-finger held a large, oval, sparkling stone and the other wound as a golden cobra with two emerald eyes around her middle finger.

· · · · ·

Sasat's possession made my own worries temporarily retreat. I had quite forgotten the looming harr ceremony that I had yet to face. Perhaps I secretly hoped they'd forgotten about me and the thing would pass me by. Then, one morning, before sunup, they came. When they raised me from my bed, I was terrified and fought them, throwing myself onto the ground, but the unrelenting aunts grabbed my arms with vice-like fingers and pulled, half carrying, half dragging me out. I wanted to scream, yet my mouth stayed closed; my clenched jaws were fused by a terrible fear.

They forced me into a darkened room and pushed me onto an angareeb prepared for the ordeal with layers of cloth, and held me down with all their strength. They covered my chest with a silken, red shawl, heavy with gold thread and golden tassels. Two strange women appeared and pulled my legs apart. My head, my arms and legs were held tight, as pincers applied to the horse's hoofs by the big Nubian farrier when trimming their toes. Outside, in the hosh, the voices of habobat and village women rang out. Fear made my body rigid; sweat beaded on my brow.

The village midwife, Hadija, knelt between my legs. I felt her cold hand on the place that is not to be touched, felt the sharp prick of a needle. The needle stung again and again, and the flesh between my legs turned numb. The silence in the room was deafening. I was so afraid, I thought my heart would stop. Hot, searing, terrible pain shot through me, and for a moment I thought I couldn't bear it. But I bore the burning agony, and the hurt subsided somewhat. Time stood still while Hadija seemed to tug and tear at my flesh. A scream rose in my throat, but a hand, covered my mouth and muffled the sound.

At last Hadija finished her horrible task. The women around me as well as the habobat waiting outside trilled joyous ululations proclaiming that still another girl had reached the pure state required to become a wife and the mother of sons. They lifted me onto my feet, straightened my shift and told me that now we were having morning tea in my honor.

This honor I would have gladly foregone. My soul seemed to have vacated my body leaving behind a rigid shell of what once had been me, Amina. I found it difficult to breathe and stood dazed in the midst of their busy preparations.

Before the tea was made and poured into my cup the pain began to awaken between my legs. My mother, dressed in her best gown, a white, silken robe, stood beside me. It was for her sake that I bit my lips and swallowed the tears that flooded my eyes.

Before the tea, I had been alone with my mother for a brief moment in the common room. I asked her then, and to my own ears my voice held both accusation and grief that would never heal, "Why did you let them take me? Where were you when they did this to me? Only Grandmother was there."

"Amina," said Mother, her eyes boring deeply into mine, "I cannot watch the cutting because I hurt when I see it done. I still remember my own circumcision, done long ago in the old way without benidj [anesthetic]. In my day they cut even more flesh away and pinned the skin together with Acacia thorn. Forty days I lay to heal—forty days of agony. I have never forgotten the pain. Every move hurt, every fiber was aflame. I couldn't have this done to you when you were younger. I thought a bigger girl could withstand the pain better. Now I am proud of you because you are like all our women—tahir."

Hadija the midwife was busy on this day. Besides me, five other girls lost to her knife that with which they were born. As their ordeal ended, the excised, pure girls were ushered into the room where their mothers and tea awaited them. They had a dazed, faraway and yet surprised look on their faces as if they still did not understand what had happened to them.

I felt the same puzzled hurt upon my face. The pain showing in their eyes burned in mine. We stood, huddled together, for none of us could sit. Rejoicing chant and talk surrounded us while we stood mute, almost forgotten among the happy, celebrating women.

Elsewhere in the village, out in the open, perhaps near the school, the boys were circumcised. I heard the grandmothers sing the praises of their grandsons' new manhood; they sang of their joy and their pride. They sang about their greedy anticipation of the feast held in honor of the snippets of foreskin lost to the merciless knife—a feast awaiting all but us, the tormented, excised ones.

At last they allowed me to retreat, to return to my angareeb. Hours passed. The earlier pain was replaced by a fire that seemed to scorch my nether parts to cinders. My mother came, murmuring, forcing me to sip a special tea. I became drowsy, and the incredible pain became a phantom as I drifted to sleep.

I awakened hours later, feeling that I would surely die. Pain seared between my legs, coursing through my body, up through my chest and into my head. My body, arching, tried to raise from the ground and fly away, and could not. And again the pain came. Heat, heat, red flame, fire over my head. Black. Black. Nothingness.

I recall now that I awoke screaming, wishing I could retreat into oblivion, return to nothingness, the other world. Yet what I believed to be loud screams were only stifled moans. A cloth, fastened around my head, ran between my teeth and kept my screams muffled. Later, many days later, they said the cloth prevented my teeth from cracking and my lips from being torn when my body went rigid with pain. Finally my mother knelt beside me and removed the cloth from my mouth.

"Ah Amina. Poor little one. All better now. Now you are true, pure Hofryati woman. Smooth and clean. Now you are worthy to bear children. You are one of us."

I only half heard her words, but the wet, cold cloth she placed on my brow felt good. She dripped sweet, strange tasting tea into my mouth, which I swallowed eagerly. I felt dry and hot as the desert wind, and I whispered to my mother that the fire raging between my legs would surely kill me.

"No," she said, "no. It will not kill. It is what purifies us. You will live, my little one. You will." She was so good to me, but I wished she had always shown me such kindness. I did not want to suffer such agony merely for her to be kind. She gave me more tea, and slowly, slowly I became drowsy and I dreamed.

I dreamt that I ran away from the village out into the desert. Far, into the swirling sands, stirred by gusts of hot, fiery wind, which claimed my body, searing it and flaying the skin off me with stinging fury.

When I awoke next, Hamida sat beside me.

"Now you know," she said simply. "The pain is the secret. That's what they don't tell you. Had I known, I would have run away and died in the desert."

I didn't care that my Hamida was back, eyes moist with knowing and compassion. The heat jinn possessed me. I was too hot to speak. It felt soothing when she moistened my arms, hands and face with cool water. Then she left.

My hand reached for the pain between my legs, and I felt sticky-moist, warm cotton and more pain.

The desert dream claimed me. Again, I was running. Again, unbearable heat desiccated my flesh, and sand flogged my skin. Women came and left. They gave me tea. They gave me broth. They moistened my flesh. I went away; I came back; I dreamed the desert dream. Night changed to day, and to night again.

"Not good, this," my mother whispered. "She feels hot. Too hot. Too long."

"Not good," the aunts agreed.

People came. People left. A man entered and read from the Qur'an. He anointed me, fastened amulets to my wrist and my hair and then he, too, left.

Suddenly, I wasn't hot anymore. Within minutes I knew that a new demon had taken hold of me, freezing and shaking me. I shook with the demon's cold fury, whimpering for the warming covers they had removed when I was burning with heat. The violent shaking caused more pain and hurt. The terrible wound in my body throbbed, sending vicious waves of pain upward throughout my flesh.

"Control the shaking," I thought, but I could not. The evil force was more powerful than I. Darkness settled again, and the cold demon left me. Hot darkness with hissing snakes enveloped me. Grandmother came and sat on my right side, holding my hand in her gnarled claw. She spoke. Her words were like drops of water falling from a jar into a cup. I didn't hear words, just a strange dripping noise. I thought perhaps she was praying. Then my mother came and sat on my left. The watery dripping and murmuring of their voices, like rain on the tin roof of the cotton shed, reassured me, calmed me.

Later their voices grew louder, waking me from half-dreams in swirling desert sands. My mother left the room, and a commotion ensued throughout the house. Loud, grating voices assaulted my head; clanking, scraping sounds penetrated from the street. Once more my mother came, behind her, my father. He grumbled. For a moment my head cleared, and I heard his voice clearly and understood his words.

"You are sure that we must do this in the middle of the night?"

"Yes," my grandmother answered him firmly. "You must do this before the sun comes up. She will not survive it in daylight. So make haste. You must reach the Western doctor by sunrise."

Mother swathed me in clothes and Father bent to lift me. When he raised me from my bed I thought I would surely die from the agony; all became black once more.

I awoke, not knowing when in time, to such torture that I can hardly find words to explain. I lay on a pallet atop Father's ox-cart, which bumped along on two large wheels. Mother was quietly sitting beside me. Winking and twirling above in the black sky were stars, a dazzling array, which, at times, seemed to grow big and dangerous and threatened to fall on me. Uncountable were the times when the wheels struck rocks and holes in the road; uncountable the agonies washing over my body. I whimpered. A few times I cried out loud and begged for it to stop. Once I pleaded with my mother to stop the cart and let me lay by the road side to die in peace. But the cart kept moving, unending, forever jolting, hurting me.

When my eyes opened next, a rosy glow portended dawn. Mother shouted to my father who walked with our escort composed of uncles ahead of the cart: "How much farther to the hospital?"

"Soon," he shouted back.

Yet when the glaring sun began to beat down upon us, my mother grew anxious. "Faster," she shouted, "faster. Goad that lazy animal. Amina will not survive long in the sun, and her torment will be for nothing."

Upon her urging, the rocking and jolting of the cart increased. The pain and heat worsened, and the jinn of heat sped me to oblivion.

● ● ● ● ●

I heard the foreign doctor before I saw him. I didn't know that he was a doctor and thought the fire jinn had conjured a foreign devil to torment me. Alarmed, I looked around and saw my mother standing nearby, while my father and two of the uncles leaned against the white wall. My mother, sensing my fear, stroked my head.

"No worry, Amina. No worry," she whispered. I relaxed.

The doctor's voice was deep, booming out like the voices of the river pilots calling to their crews. "So you brought me another victim of your horrid custom," he growled. His Arabic rang with harsh inflections. It pained me to open my eyes. All around me was brightness and whiteness. Directly above me was a strange looking, white face, spotted with copper, as if dusted with nutmeg. The doctor had a big nose, but most remarkable was his hair, which was as red as a woman's hennaed hand. His penetrating blue eyes bored into my face, while one hand held my arm, lightly pressing.

"Child mutilation," he said angrily. "Now she is infected, maybe septic, like the others you bring here, if they don't die on the way."

I now noticed a woman in a white gown behind him. He turned to her and said, "The usual—penicillin and Demerol. Give me the Demerol first."

The woman gave the doctor an object with a sharp metal needle. He told Mother to turn my head to the side, which she did. I felt a sharp, small pain on my arm and looked up. His voice boomed at me: "You will feel better in a little while."

He then told the men to leave with him while the nurse gave me the second treatment. Some of my worst pain had miraculously abated, so I turned willingly when the woman in white told me to lie on my side. Again I felt the sharp, small pain into my lower back. Another woman dressed in a white, fitted garment came into the room. They asked my mother if I had urinated after the circumcision. Mother didn't know. The women in white looked at each other poignantly and called for the doctor. Another prick with the sharp needle, and the heat jinn carried me off to nothingness once more.

I awoke feeling no pain. I lay on a strange angareeb, far above the ground. It was anchored, like a bird's nest on metal branches above and below. This strange pallet sat in the corner of a large room with walls of ochre clay. Aligned with my bed were other pallets with women laying upon them.

On the wall across from me hung a large wooden cross, like an ankh, upon which the carved image of a man was nailed. Nails driven through his hands and his feet looked vicious and piercing; like the pain I had suffered. The martyred image had another large, pierced wound from which red blood dripped in a stream. How wondrous. Perhaps they had brought this man here to be healed by the foreign doctor? He had helped me. I felt so much better now.

My mother lay sleeping on a blanket beside my bed. Cautiously, I sat up and looked around. The woman next to me, a Nubian with a beautiful face black as coal, a newborn in her arms, smiled and said, "Ah. Awake now little sister? You sleep a long, long time. But you sleep a healing sleep. No demon troubled your sleep." She smiled happily and I smiled back.

"I am hungry," I said suddenly without meaning to, but I realized that I was very hungry indeed. The Nubian woman laughed, flashing two rows of perfect, pearly teeth. My mother woke up. She looked around and saw me sitting up.

The broth and the kofta made from millet and meat that Mother gave me tasted as nothing had ever tasted before. I tasted life itself and thought the food conveyed healing power and strength. At length I slept again. I ate and slept until I felt so strong that I felt the urge to use my legs.

Next day, one of the women in white, whom they call nurses or sisters, came to my bed and said to me, "Amina. Listen to me carefully because I will tell you important things about your body and your health."

I looked around for my mother, but she had gone to get food. The nurse noticed my anxious glance and said, "Don't worry. Your mother knows these things. But she will not tell you herself. So I will do it, because you should know."

The nurse looked at me with serious, large, dark eyes, which looked even larger because she had darkened the lids with kohl, like many women of Arabic descent. Her skin was beautiful, light brown, much lighter than usually seen. It is said that the prophet Muhammad was fair of skin and it's desirable to be light complexioned. Our own family is said to be of an Arabic blood line and most of us are brown, rather than dark, but I don't know much about these things. I peered into the nurse's eyes. They were velvety and kind, like those of our oxen. I trusted her.

"Amina, when they took you to your circumcision rite, they cut with a knife all the meat from the female part between your legs. Then, they took needle and thread and sewed you shut like a garment. This is called infibulation. It is a terrible thing to do to a girl, but your people still practice this. They say it's been done since Pharaoh's time, although I believe the practice should be stopped. What happened to you should not happen to anyone."

She looked at me as if I was the saddest person and asked, "Do you understand what I am saying to you?" I said I did, and began to cry. I remembered how the women had come for me and held me down. The pain. The burning. My family had done this to me. Why?

"Smooth, perfect, clean and pure," Mother had said. Was I now clean and

·pure? I was the same as before, only hurt. The nurse held my hand and continued: "When they did these things to you something went wrong. That was the hot jinn you were talking about when you came. We had to open the stitching, and put medicine in your wound. When you go back to your village you must use the medicine until you are healed. The doctor told your mother not to stitch you again until you are all healed. They will do this surely." She got up to leave, and her eyes filled with sadness.

The next morning my father came for us with the ox-cart. The red-haired doctor boomed at my mother, giving her instructions for my care. The velvet-eyed nurse pressed a small glass vial into my hand and said, "This is for the infibulation. It will help with the pain, keep it well."

For days after our return I wasn't very strong and worked only on small tasks for short periods of time. It was hard enough to simply walk about. Eventually the day came when I was healed and well again. Mother said the stitching had to be done. When they took me away again I swallowed the pill, and so I remember no pain.

It was strange. When I went to void my water it did not flow anymore in a continuous stream. Now I trickled like a stopped up jar. I complained to my mother and she said, "That's how it is. You get accustomed to it. In time you get used to everything."

CHAPTER

"Now that you are pure," said the aunts, "you can be taught to grind millet and prepare food."

It is the man's job to work the fields or trade for the food that is brought to the house. And for that reason, men, who have more ʿaqel to withstand the forces of corruption (or so it is said) were sent beyond the pure, peaceful boundaries of Hofryat. They are not sullied dealing with impure matter because they do not bear the children.

Meals in Hofryat were simple. Millet and sorghum were staples. Vegetables came from small plots along the Nile. Fruits arrived through trade, particularly nuts and dried dates. One did not eat meat often; when we did have meat, it was the flesh of goats or pigeons. Everyone kept chickens, but unlike pigeons, which will bathe when given water and so are tahir, hens never bathe. They are unclean, washkhan, and therefore are never eaten. However, their eggs, protected by smooth white shells, are tahir and so we ate them.

To this day, only the pure women carry the water and make dough for our bread by mixing ground sorghum with the water. They wash the fruits, vegetables and the clothes we wear. All work that women undertake is clean and pure. I learned to mix the sorghum flour with equal amounts of water in the gulla, a small, round clay vessel. I spread this mixture thinly over an extremely hot, seasoned griddle until the edge crisped. At the moment of crisping, the flat, moist crepe, the kisra is removed. Our bread is seen as a symbol for the union between man and woman. The aunties said a man's seed is the substance, but a woman's blood is the liquid with which the heat of the womb creates human life. According to this metaphor, only women purified by circumcision can bake bread, using the womb-like gulla and the hot griddle.

On hot summer days Hamida, the cousins and I learned to sew with small stitches, and had our education delivered to us in harsh pronouncements. One aunt would begin and the others fell in the moment she gathered her breath to continue. The women sat shaded by the veranda roof in groups revealing to the observer their friendships and power struggles. My mother, the haboba and Hamida's mother A'isha were always grouped together. Their power over all other females was immense. Aunties Zaina, Zainab and Sasat sat bent over small items of clothing. Their children were in the same age group and their worries and their joys pealed from their lips as the sound of one bell. And so the groupings were formed.

"When you marry, your husband takes your father's place," an aunt would direct to our gaggle of unmarried girls. "You will be subordinate to him, and must honor and obey him."

"You are much too inquisitive. You ask too many questions about things that do not concern girls," chimed in another when I asked questions. I regretted being forward, for they followed up by making an example of me.

"Most of all, Amina, you must learn to control your emotions. You are too quick to complain," said one. "Your temper is aroused too soon," said the haboba. "You cry too quickly," added my mother

"And by Allah and his prophet, you must learn to control your face. What kind of husband wants to see a sullen mask? Husbands like smiling, friendly faces. Neither cry nor laugh too loud, let moderate happiness show."

They assured me that my failure to heed these morsels of wisdom would result in a difficult, unhappy marriage. My feeble attempts to fathom whether the groom would play by the same rules were not heartening. Would he, for example, have to smile at me and curb his temper also? I inquired about how men's roles differed from women's, but they shushed me and told me to stop asking silly questions.

Another part of my education began when they said, "You are as pure as the pigeon now," and painted high on my cheek the small mark of a pigeon's toe for a celebration. Hamida, my cousins, Shirin, Rishana, Meme, Nazila, and I, stood awkwardly in the fig tree's shade, wrapped in clean tobs.

"You must learn to dance with the steps of the graceful, clean bird," instructed Auntie Zainab, who loved dates and laughter, as she showed us the steps.

Following her movements, we joined the ranks of nubile girls preparing to become brides. In small groups different women demonstrated the movements, postures and steps of the dances. Some of us, like Meme and Hamida, managed to imitate pigeons to an amazing degree while others pranced about like camels on hot sand ready to throw off their load. At last, I thought I'd mastered the mincing steps, the turning and gyrating, with the required purity and dignity.

"Henceforth you must dance at the weddings. You will be a pigeon going to market," explained the aunts, using an old expression which described girls trying to attract a suitable mate.

During this time of preparation we were scolded time and again for our awkwardness, inattention and childish behavior. How well I remember being taken to task by Haboba's sister, Farida, who scathingly accused my mother of being too easy on me.

"Your mother was much too lax. My girls knew. I trained them early on to become proper Hofryati women."

"Oh, and aunt herself laid smooth, tahir eggs, like the ostrich, in which her girls were hidden," quipped Hamida, making me laugh. Hamida's heart had softened toward me after she heard of my near-death experience. Once more we slept together in the quarters set aside for the very young women, once more we shared the same work. Like me, Hamida was tormented by questions pertaining to the fate of females. She pestered her mother for the truth about the painful rite of passage. What was the reason for us to undergo such torture? Her mother said, "Men believe uncircumcised women could not restrain themselves and would bring shame upon their families. That is what these men say. Women proclaim that pain ennobles us, transforming us into vessels of morality which can be entrusted with the bearing and raising of children."

"Do you feel transformed?" I asked Hamida.

"Yes," she said, "my body will never be the same and my mind lost trust."

We both understood that money and possessions were prerequisites to "nest" (aish) a wife. Of late I had begun to notice that most metaphors and symbols pertaining to women and the home were drawn from the avian realm.

Before a man owns enough property to keep a wife in chaste seclusion he must amass a fortune. Usually, many years of arduous work precede a wedding, and therefore excitement in our village rose to a fevered pitch the moment a groom announced his ability to prepare or build a house. I thought that before a wedding the village sounded like the wild bee hives near the river, humming and buzzing with activity, for no feast compared to a wedding's splendor.

In two moon cycles the wedding of Ahmed Baqr, a cousin, and Fatime, a placid girl I knew from school, was to take place. Hamida and I were told to work hard, to practice our dance, and to behave well, for we would represent our family, would be watched closely, and, of course be measured against girls from other families. At weddings all women dance, stepping forward rhythmically with mincing, tiny steps. During the dance their wraps are draped over their arms where they hang wing-like to both sides, giving a birdlike appearance.

Our training was so arduous that I tired of the wedding long before it commenced. Suddenly the feast appeared much less pleasurable. I often offered to sweep the kitchen yard to avoid the drill. There, I had a chance to escape through a side door, which allowed traders to bring wood, vegetables and staples directly to the kitchen without meeting women and defiling the house. Once out in the street, I looked up and down the thoroughfare. For a delicious moment I enjoyed the openness and the heat of the glaring sun on my face. But the moment was fleeting, dispelled by shrill voices crying, "Amina, Amina, where are you? Come here, you lazy girl."

I'd squeeze through the portal, and pretend that I had been present all the time.

For the wedding, Hamida and I received new garments. White, fresh, clean and pure. On my left arm four new bracelets dangled, tinkling seductively whenever I moved. The teaching went on relentlessly. Our mothers interpreted for us the symbolic meanings hidden in women's daily lives.

"The food women consume is needed for fertility. Enclosed foods are especially nourishing, clean. They are tahir, as the purified woman is," said my mother.

So, it followed that oranges, eggs, bananas, grapefruit, tinned fish, tinned jam, from the outside markets of Europe and Egypt, and watermelons were pure and highly potent for blood making. It is believed that a child receives the bones from his father, but flesh and blood from the mother.

Not all information came via Mother and the aunts.

Hamida's mother, A'isha, was a beautiful, but silly, garrulous woman whose husband was besotted by her. He was my father's fourth brother, Majid, a happy, likable but not overly bright man. He worked for Father who ordered all his affairs. Majid loved to talk as much as his wife did. In the privacy of their conjugal chamber he told A'isha everything he heard. She, in turn told Hamida, who then told me.

Whenever Hamida gossiped, she repeated without alteration the coarse details escaping her mother's mouth. For a moment she'd look like her mother as she pronounced her words precisely with her mother's inflection: "A Sudanese girl is like a watermelon because there is no way in."

We laughed madly at this because by now we understood the meaning of this simile. It was through Hamida's mother, whose ability to detect worthy news transcended the high walls of the neighboring compounds, that we learned of another possession; another village secret.

Zairan jinn delight in the torture of married couples. They might choose to hold a couple hostage by stealing their children through still-birth or miscarriage. A'isha, reported that the young neighbor woman miscarried some moons ago and was gravely ill. She was married to a good, young man, but his mother worked her into the ground.

"My mother said she is exhausted. That's all," said Hamida. "They never let her rest, even after she lost the child."

Not long thereafter the young woman fell victim to a Zairan.

By that time my Aunt Sasat was much recovered from her possession. Already she worked part of the day. Her husband came home frequently and faithfully provided the objects to placate the Zairan, and my mother, who knew these things before all others, pronounced that Sasat was pregnant once more.

• • • • •

At last the wedding day arrived in the middle of February, the month loved by brides for its temperate weather. For many months the families weighed and measured the dowry and bridal gifts, considered status and the position gained or lost by the marriage and mutually agreed on all aspects of the union.

The members of the husband's extended family prepared the feast, and most of the village was invited. Tents were erected outside the village to accommodate the guests not far from the house of honor. The village droned with activity, as if locusts had fallen upon it, beating their wings in unison, creating a stir.

The men slaughtered choice lambs, goats and braces of pigeons for the feast, their donkeys and camels carried in fruits, delicacies, honey and white sugar, and loads of wood for the cooks' fires. The women prepared breads, cakes, egg dishes, couscous, almond cookies and small delicacies with fruits.

I observed that during the wedding ceremony the bride had the most boring part. For three days the celebration was enjoyed by families and guests, but the bride was held with two aunts in seclusion. At the feast we ate and drank. Hamida and I sat chastely with lowered eyes beside our mothers, yet we still managed to see much. We spied the groom, a handsome man, tall and slender with a face well made and pleasing.

A'isha thought that Fatima was one of the lucky ones because low breeding shows itself in coarse features.

"He is not too dark, that is good. Her children will be light in color," whispered the irrepressible Hamida. The groom sat among the men of his family, high on piled cushions as if they were a throne.

The men of our family sat in a tight knot with others; unmarried men mingled with men of all families. They prowled; they were restless and their eyes were everywhere, although they pretended that we did not exist. Hamida whispered to me that their glances burned holes into her tob.

When the dancing began we were urged to join the throng, but we lowered our heads modestly and refused. More urging was needed, and when the proper moment arrived, we arose as we had been taught and began the dance. Uncertain and shy at first, we moved awkwardly, executing the pigeon steps. After a while we enjoyed being free to move and became braver. Indeed, we became so brave that our mothers, who had joined the circle of dancers, insisted that we stifle our exuberance.

When we sat down after our first dance, Hamida winked at me and asked, "Which of the unmarried men did you like best?"

"I can't say. I never really saw them. I worried so much about my steps and so I never noticed them."

Hamida called me a worthless she-camel. "You are here to see and be seen.

Not that it will make much difference whom you like. But I've heard that sometimes your mother might nag your father on your behalf. Then, possibly, you could get your choice of a groom."

I had heard such tales too. We were not supposed to look at men at all, but romantic notions persisted, and so we subtly observed. I tasted all the wonderful things offered us to eat, while trying to appear dainty, easy to fill.

"Don't be greedy," warned the aunts. "No man wants a wife who eats too much. The men say among themselves that if a woman is hard to fill, a man has to work all the time and never gets rest," they laughed. "You can eat all you want once you are married." Their laughter sounded forced.

Near the end of the third day the long-anticipated moment arrived. The shy bride was led from seclusion by her kinswomen to perform the wedding dance for the groom and the guests. She was led there by her hands—for she could not see—and positioned on a red mat in our midst. A murmur ran through the wedding party, then a hush fell over the crowd.

From head to the middle of her legs she was covered by the bridal shawl of red and gold silk. The shawl, the symbol of womanhood, covered her during circumcision, and would cover her when she gave birth. She stood immobile and barefoot until her husband stepped onto the mat and unveiled his bride.

We all sighed. What beauty. A vision of femininity, gentleness, and exquisiteness. She was dressed in the finest silks and bedecked by her family's gold. Her hands, elaborately hennaed, were shyly raised covering her face. Her gestures and demeanor were timid, almost abject, even though this was the greatest day of her life.

My mother and the aunts remembered their own weddings, their own finery, their shyness, their dread and anticipation, and so they rocked gently, sighing, whispering their remembrance. Once more we hushed because the groom gently released the arms of his bride. Music filled the air and she began the bridal dance.

So very exacting she stepped, the way my mother would have preferred my movements. Her young face was round and soft. Her skin was smooth, of rich golden-brown color, with a sheen as silky as her garments. Her mouth, opened slightly at times as if in a trance, revealed perfect, white teeth. Her eyes were tightly shut. Her back was arched and her arms were extended to the sides. She stepped rhythmically with mincing steps, so small that she hardly left the minute confines of the mat.

In this manner she danced for awhile, pausing for the musical breaks and changes of rhythm with her abject pose, hiding her face with her hands. So danced the bride, enchanting the guests and her groom until she decided that she would dance no more. When her movements ceased her escort of women returned and led her away to the bridal chamber.

We feasted until late and although many guests lingered, my mother rose with stately dignity signalling that we would return to our dwellings. The aunts followed Mother's lead and soon, escorted by my father and the uncles, we returned home enveloped in the balmy, blue night air, enriched by the smells of the feast.

● ● ● ● ●

In retrospect, it seemed that Hamida and I did not conduct ourselves fittingly during the wedding ceremony, appearing to be too easy of manner and too flighty to be seriously considered finished. This judgement concerned Hamida greatly because her twelfth birthday was approaching soon. Like her ambitious mother, she was consumed by the desire to marry well, some day granting her high status as haboba of a clan later in life. In our village almost all girls were married by their sixteenth year, although a few women in the village were already twenty and still unwed.

Men were fickle we learned. Deformed girls, those suffering from a limp, a clubfoot or a cleft palate needlessly underwent the pain of circumcision because few men chose them.

After a stifling summer we were enjoying cooler, sweeter air at night. Light breezes from the river, blessed by mist, enveloped us during the night. The jinn of the desert, appeased, created sand storms no more. Since becoming tahir, my importance had diminished to the point where I once again felt unnoticed like a child. As long as I performed my prescribed duties, pleasing the haboba and my mother, no one was aware of me. Around me everyone was forever busy, working hard raising children, preparing meals. Like a shadow I glided through the house, smiling politely when I encountered the aunts murmuring greetings: "Salaam. May your morning be bright."

They hardly acknowledged my salutations. There were times when I was terribly confused, times when I despaired of their scoffing and scolding. Each rebuff, the fear of failing, rendered me incapable of making the simplest decisions. Instead I froze, speechless, until set upon another task. Yet, I was not alone in my torment. I drew comfort from the fact that many young girls shared in this condition.

Oh, those times of blankness, of nothingness. For myself, I found that simple things were just as effective at lifting my mood as the more complex. A ray of sunshine creating patterns on the kitchen floor as it fell through a crack in the mud wall or a butterfly lifted over the hosh wall by a breeze, these simple things could cheer me.

School was in session once more, the source of my greatest joy. It seemed as if a door had opened and finally, after years of learning how to read and write, I had stepped across a threshold beyond which the beauty of the Qur'an's verses lay revealed. It was as if blindness was lifted from my eyes and I could see. When I read especially sweet, comforting verses, I was moved to tears, and had to hide my face behind my loose sleeve. For how could I explain this weakness of mine to the other girls?

Most of them had a miserable time deciphering the text, never mind investing more effort searching for the hidden meaning of soul-treasures, or rejoicing in the divine choice of words. I never told anyone, not even Hamida, that I lived for the reading hours. Besides the Qur'an, the teacher offered other religious texts which I devoured like kisra when starving.

For me the Qur'an was a source of tales and pictures from the world beyond the village, of romance and love. I couldn't conceive of a greater tale than the Prophet's own wedding and married life. I had no books of my own, but Grandmother, becoming more spiritual in her old age, sometimes allowed me to read her own Qur'an.

I fled into the world created by the tales of Father and the uncles, where the persecuted Prophet daringly escaped his enemies. In this realm, flights on horseback through the desert quickened my heart beat. Where rescue from certain death by thirst was facilitated by the Prophet's great steeds smelling the river's water: when, with their last strength, trembling with weakness, tongues swollen and eyes bulging, they carried the Holy One and his men to safety. When I read, I longed to see what lay far beyond the village walls. How vividly I remembered the trip to the foreign doctor, the strange new surroundings and the people who acted so different from my family.

Sometime after the wedding, my father came to stay with us for a week. On his first afternoon home Mother sent me to his divan to pour tea for him and my three brothers. He was sitting on the divan, looking across the carpeted floor through wide open doors into the walled-in yard. Holding my tray with care and making my way up the veranda steps, I studied him. Opportunities like this one were rare. Striving for comfort he'd shed his turban and instead wore a white Arab kaffiyeh. He'd arranged the square cloth with two simple folds and held it in place twisting an agal of black and green wool around the head.

Clad in a white, long-sleeved shirt reaching to his ankles, his bare, long-toed feet were visible. All my brothers were tall like Father and had inherited his long toes. I knew their toes better than their faces as my gaze was always to be directed down. Father was remarkably good-looking. His large, dark eyes overshadowed by strong black brows were kind and contemplative. His mouth was wide and generous. The kaffiyeh suited his hawk-like nose and contrasted favorably with his deep brown skin. Although desert travellers protect themselves, the merciless sun finds many opportunities to tan hands and faces.

Flanked by my handsome, sleek brothers, he dutifully inquired about their knowledge of the Holy Book. I sat my burden before them on the carpet and, kneeling, began pouring the fragrant tea when Father began his questioning. My brothers are older than I. They never paid attention to me, except for the youngest, Mahmood, who was older than I by two years. He resented my fleetness when we raced and he tormented me whenever possible. At times he had pulled my hair so hard that I thought I would lose my mind; at other times he had beaten me about the face, leaving bruises, all for the possession of a shiny rock or a piece of fruit.

"Stay out of his way," admonished the haboba. "It is your fault if you annoy him." I sobbed, asserting that I had done nothing to deserve his torment and was told that I must have been at fault somehow.

My brother, Karem, was seventeen, and almost as much admired by the women as Khalid, who, of the three, was most like my father. Even tempered, without vicious anger flare-ups, he never tormented women or children. But perhaps one could attribute that to the fact that he seldom noticed anything or anyone not connected to himself.

"Recite what is said about lailat al-qadr [Night of Determination, or Power]," Father asked my oldest brother, Khalid. Khalid was eighteen, handsome, and good with numbers, but now he stammered painfully through his recital and finally failed. I had finished serving the tea a while ago, and in total disregard for propriety, I heard myself recite.

I spoke without faltering, my heart in my voice. My brothers stared at me, wide-eyed, as if a camel had entered the room and befouled the mats. When I finished I saw that Father was astonished, moreover, that he was moved.

"Where did you learn to recite?" he asked. When I told him, he marvelled that one could learn so well in such a poor place as the village school. Had he not sent Khalid away to a much better school and what was the result? I was suddenly embarrassed and hurriedly gathered the empty, midnight-blue ceramic pot and cups, but Father stopped me.

"Do you know other passages as well?"

When I assured him that I knew many passages he allowed me to declaim my favorite passage. I chose a passage with a bit of malice, because whenever I read it I imagined my wicked brother Mahmood standing in Allah's sight. In my vision Mahmood stood, bowing, holding stones in his outstretched hands—one gray, heavy stone for each of my torments. I wondered if the women holding me down during excision would have their deeds levelled against them. Oh, there was much I wondered about while I quietly moved about, but now I recited from Surah 18, Al Kahf:

"The life of this world is ephemeral,
And its gains will not last. Good deeds
Are the best possession in Allah's sight:
All will be levelled up on the Day
Of Judgement, and a new order created
On the basis of Truth, according to the Book
Of Deed...."

"Amina, Amina where are you?" Mother's voice rang shrilly.

"Forgive me, but Mother needs me. I must hasten so I don't offend her anymore," I exclaimed and tried to flee. Yet, I was not to reach the door. At that moment, an enemy more powerful than Mahmood was revealed. Khalid, embarrassed by my fluent recital, stuck out his leg as I passed and I, encumbered by my tob could not avoid his leg and to the amusement of my brothers was flung headlong on the ground.

I hurt. But the pain flooding my soul was far greater than the hurt of the body. As I gathered my shroud and collected the broken tea things in confused, unseemly haste, a truth struck me, much as the sun's ray illuminates a room. For the first time I saw clearly that my brothers had everything. They had freedom to move where they chose and do as they pleased. They owned part of the family's wealth, commanded Father's attention and Mother's respectful devotion, while I had nothing. Mine was the pain, the work, the seclusion and the dullness of the kitchen yard. Yet, they, being so enriched by Allah, envied me this insignificant ray of Father's attention.

As I fled, I heard a sharp rebuke from my father, but I knew not what he said. Nor did I care. I only wished to disappear behind the kerosene barrel outside and to be alone. How well I knew that it was ill-fated to be disliked by your eldest brother, for next to your father and your husband, he was the most powerful person in line to rule your life. Why did fate create an enemy for me at this moment? Only heaven knew the answer. However, I was to learn the importance of this enmity much later.

The moment my mother set eyes upon me she scolded me. There was no need to tell her of the event, or of my despair, because she did not care. First, she wouldn't have heard my complaint, her ears tuned only to her inner driving voice; but second, a complaint against her first born, much-favored, Khalid, would have instantly been dismissed.

So I made myself small, as inconspicuous as the miniscule, gray lizard that lives in the mud walls of the house, and crept out to the courtyard. Even there I was not to have peace. Evening was approaching fast, and a refreshing cooling breeze from the river blew gently across the village, filling the yard with women happily free of the wall's confines.

Visiting habobat, some thin and spry, others round and therefore less wrinkled, sat with my grandmother in a corner chewing on sticks, while cleaning their teeth. Sasat knelt before the large grinding stone pounding millet inside its hollow with a large, wooden pestle, which the women jokingly called the "elephant's thing" when they knew they were alone.

Hamida and her mother, gullas in hand, baked bread on the huge iron griddle, which required that the fire in the box below be carefully stoked to provide even heat. Younger cousins and my sister came with clay jars filled with water from the village well, and left moments later, jars empty, to fetch more.

In the corner, under the fig tree, sat aunts with nursing babies, the ends of their tobs draped chastely over their breasts. Their toddlers played in the clay dust nearby, while their older, uncircumcised boys could be heard shouting and screaming outside in the street, playing stick games, mock fighting and racing.

"Amina come here," called my grandmother, and inwardly reluctant but outwardly eager to please, I joined the old women. The moment I was near, Grandmother's sharp eyes spotted yellow tea stains on my white tob. A sharp reprimand for my carelessness followed. Then she remarked to her friends that, although in some respects I was unfinished—as my spotted shroud evidenced—in other respects I was a very worthy young woman.

She said carelessness could be overcome. Meanwhile I, a strong, healthy, good-looking woman of excellent parents, would be Allah's blessing bestowed on any young man. Of course, only if he were lucky enough to induce my father to let me enter into marriage. Before the searching, evaluating looks from the old women I felt excised once more. It was as if life's vital energy drained out of me.

I thought of Khalid, my brother. He would marry upon assuming the position as overseer on one of the many dhows plying their trade along the Blue Nile. Father was trying to purchase such a position, enabling Khalid to marry after a few trips. The thought of anyone being married to Khalid was frightening.

Woe the small girl, married to one who could become so enraged by a young sister's recital. Frightened by the threat of my own marriage I had to go and void my water.

Crouching in the spot of concealment, the water trickled slowly. As if by accident, my hand strayed along the seam they'd sewn down there. It was hard and rigid. An impenetrable wall of scar tissue lay below my searching fingers, as if my body had resented the cutting and slicing and made up for the loss by generating more, unyielding growth.

Arousing an adversary is an act one should not dismiss lightly. Having forgotten last day's incident I was the perfect victim for mischief, and it must have been only heaven's providence or my qismat that saved me from harm.

I had spent most of the day with Mother remaking a ceremonial shawl for my sister. A shawl, wonderful, richly textured that came from Haboba's chest. She, in turn, had received it upon a niece's death. We did not use the garments of the dead, but shawls were too expensive to be burned, and so, purified and stored for a long time, the garment was acceptable to be worn again. Some gold threads were broken through creasing, and Mother with her clever hands taught me to mend them, invisible to the eye.

Under the old fig tree, leaning against its trunk, we worked sipping fruit juice. Once we had warmed over the newest gossip, we fell silent. Shortly before the midday meal, Khalid courteously sent our cousin, Abdul, with a note asking Mother's permission to visit. Of course, she accepted with joy. Sent to warn the women that a man was visiting, I swept through the house disturbing their ease. Tobs were tightened, heads bedecked and pushed up sleeves were pulled to wrists.

Khalid, white-kaftaned and smiling broadly, sat already on two fat cushions when I returned. Imitating Father he wore the kaffiyeh instead of the turban. He could imitate the head dress, but could not project Father's kindness.

His presence intimidated me. Facing me with a sweetness I knew to be false he said, "Salaam, little sister." Mother's glance sweeping over him could have melted stones. My heart knew better, pounding away as if in a race. As I sat down beside Mother a movement caught my eye. A rough hemp sack next to Khalid would bulge at odd moments. I lowered my eyes to my work but nevertheless watched the bag's ominous twitching. Moments later we were crowded by every female in the house. Answering patiently the boring questions of the aunts pertaining to his health, his future bride and employment, Khalid made Mother proud.

Khalid's stay was short lived. After complimenting Mother on her food and telling her a few droll jokes, he walked by my kerosene barrel. He stopped for a moment, and then suddenly left through the gate separating the men's hosh from ours. I breathed a sigh of relief, though a nagging thought stayed with me. What was his purpose for this visit? He was not affectionate as some sons who came for tidbits and fuss. No, there was a reason behind his showing, but what was it?

Perhaps my preoccupation saved me from a horrible fate. Had I not been enmeshed in solving Khalid's puzzle I would have found a way to sneak away from Mother and her odious task. By late afternoon I was still mending. I remember as simultaneous the horrible scream and the pain as I stuck myself with my needle.

"A snake! A snake bit me." We jumped, dumping garments, needles and thread, and ran. Shaking like the roof when the haboob blows, Aunt Rehana ran from the kerosene barrel. Her eyes were enormous, bulging as if ready to pop from their sockets. Her bare left arm was lifted high into the air with its fat rolls of upper arm dangling like a fringe over her head. She alternately sobbed and screamed when we reached her. Within seconds she was surrounded by a white wall of women.

"Where is the snake?" Only Haboba would have thought to ask the right question at a time like this.

"It crawled back behind the barrel," sobbed Rehana.

"Get the elephant's thing," commanded Haboba, and I flew to oblige.

Halim, Sasat's husband, in an ankle-long, flowing kaftan arrived at the scene, followed by Khalid.

"There is a snake behind the barrel. Kill it," said Grandmother handing Halim the wooden pounder. I melted into the crowd the moment I spied my brother, never taking my eyes off him. Discerning that Rehana was the victim, his face at first registered disappointment, which turned to raw anger seconds later. His eyes were hunting for me. Now it was obvious to me that the snake had been meant for me. Why would Khalid hate me so much? Poor, clueless Aunt Rehana suffered the pain meant for me. Halim found and killed the snake with many blows.

"This is a desert serpent! How did it get here unseen?" he asked. Hah, I knew the answer, but Khalid had found me and conveyed with one look such a sinister warning that I quaked. Mahmood must have told him about my special hiding place.

Now that we knew the snake was poisonous, Rehana, almost in shock, was rushed to the western doctor. I was tormented by conflicting emotions. However horrid Khalid's deed, I could not risk revealing the truth. Who would believe me? Mother? Believing such thing of the darling one? The aunts? They were just as besotted by him. Father? Father was away, but even if he were present, could he believe such a thing? No, I could not tell anyone.

I recall that the treacherous act had a happy ending. Rehana recovered, saved by the fat of her arm. The doctor mentioned that the serpent deposited the venom in the fatty layer of her arm where it dispersed slowly, or else the antivenin would have come too late. For the rest of her life, Aunt's arm was marred by a crater where the poison dissolved the tissue. Ever after she amused the small children by exposing the spot telling them how the snake had attacked her.

After worrying for many days about another treacherous attempt, I finally came to believe that I was safe, as long as I kept still. Perhaps my brother saw the folly of his action. I will never know.

CHAPTER *three*

In the middle of my twelfth year I awoke to a morning of unsurpassable beauty. The everlasting heat plaguing the village had subsided for the moment. A gentle wind rustled the rushes of the roof. Teasing sunlight eased through the openings below the roof of our narrow sleeping chamber. Our angareebs, lined up in a row with hardly a hair to squeeze between them, left barely enough room for a path to the door. I sat up and looked at the sleeping forms of Hamida, Nazila and Shirin. Shirin was named by her father who worked for many years in Iran, and developed a fondness for all things Persian. I felt great joy and goodness in my heart, a goodness extending to the sleepers, the beauty of the morning with its silent freshness, and the village which made up my whole world. Deep emotions led me to pray the introduction to Surah 87:

> *"Wonderful are the ways of Allah*
> *In creation, and the love with which*
> *He guides his creatures' destinies,*
> *Gives them the means by which to strive*
> *For maturity by ordered steps, and reach*
> *The end most fitted for their natures."*

I was lost in the beauty of these words, envisioning the love and care lavished upon us by the Creator, when I was disturbed in my reverie.

"Why are you praying?" asked Nazila, from her angareeb. "You know that women don't have to observe the morning prayer as men do." Then she laughed, "Let them pray for us when they go to the mosque."

"Don't speak like that, Nazila," I said, hurt, because Nazila, the indolent one, aimed her cobra fangs at my heart. She knew the words would cause me grief, and she knew well that the men would never pray for women in the mosque. Oh, they would pray for a son, a job, a business deal or even a camel, but never for a woman.

At fifteen, Nazila was the oldest among us, lazy and rebellious. Rebellious, because although she was pretty, strong and of good parentage, no one had claimed her as a bride. It must have been the uncertainty of her fate that made her so sharp-tongued. She quit attending school at thirteen and had chafed under the control of our sharp-eyed grandmother ever since.

Every day Allah made the aunts scheme of ways to find her a husband. It seemed the chatter surrounding her imagined husband never stopped. Secretly, I, too, was afraid that no one would want to marry me since I was going on thirteen and no one had even glanced in my direction.

The moment I left my bed that morning I knew that something extraordinary had occurred. As I walked, I felt a warm sticky wetness between my thighs. Exploring, my hand was bloodied and I knew that now I was like the other girls in the room. They rejoiced when their blood came, giving proof that now they could become mothers, but I, far from rejoicing, felt only bewildered and frightened.

Also, there was a grinding pain in my back where I had never experienced pain, and my belly felt swollen and tender. Suddenly, I wondered what had become of my glorious morning. It seemed the sun shone less brightly, and despite the breeze, I was sweating.

Anything that happens down there is connected with pain, I thought and went in search of my mother.

"Now, Amina is fully a woman," trilled my mother to let all the aunts know that I bled, and in the privacy of her bed-corner she initiated me into the women's age-old rite.

• • • • •

About the time of my first blood I recall two equally monumental events. First, I remember I was lying on my angareeb feeling drowsy when the winds suddenly began to blow from the desert. Dust permeated the air and I had to cover my face in order to draw my breath. Within minutes, the shawatin of the desert howled with deafening strength. I knew, of course, that a freak, unseasonable storm had come to punish the village once again, and yet my terror was as strong as the first time.

Sand and bits of reed sifted through the roof, the wooden supports groaned and creaked as the unrelenting storm pressed against our house. My sheet lifted and swayed as I held onto the edge. Outside, I heard flying objects crashing against the compound walls, pounding and banging. The force of the wind increased and demons and jinn added their shrill voices to the infernal howl. I burrowed into my mattress praying for Allah's help. This calmed me a little. I realized suddenly, mastering my fear, that sometimes the shrieking was not the wind or devilish in origin, but came from the mouths of my roommates. Shirin's screams were louder than anyone's.

Then the unthinkable happened. With a mighty groan, an unseen force lifted the entire roof from the walls. Instantly, invisible hands pulled and prodded my body and a howling devil above tried to suck me into the sky. I found myself clinging to Hamida while clutching my mattress at the same time. My sheet was long gone, sucked away by the devils above. Where the roof supports tore from the wall, loose chunks of hard baked clay fell to the ground, and I heard the screams of unlucky people hit by these missiles. Mercilessly, sand showered upon us, biting and stinging our skin.

When I thought I couldn't tolerate anymore, the howl increased to yet a more ferocious pitch, and Hamida and I were lifted off the ground. I thought my life would end this very moment, that we'd be dragged into the air and blown away like dry leaves in the breeze. Just then, I heard a monstrous sigh, like a giant exhaling, and we were suddenly dropped to the ground. Tumbling onto shambles and sand, we landed, still clutching each other, our mouths rimmed with sand, our hair stiff and wild. Moments later the wind completely subsided and an unearthly silence enveloped the village.

The wail of an infant broke the frightful spell, and moments later we heard shouts. I heard my father calling for Umma Reha and Mother, and then a great babble ensued. Chaos reigned. Hamida and I brushed the sand from our faces and shook our hair to rid it of dirt. We scarcely had time to dress when we heard the haboba's voice above the din demanding that we attend to her, at once.

Grandmother was the only woman who had a room to herself. It was a medium-sized room, by our standards, with a well-made, colorful carpet of Arabic design covering the floor, and a large round opening in the wall that led to the hosh for air circulation. Her angareeb was thicker than any of the women's and was shrouded in white, fluffy cotton. We found her laying motionless looking like a brown caterpillar trapped by giant twigs. Two small beams, with the roof's thatch still attached, had pinned her to her bed.

"Move, you lazy women," she snarled. "How long do I have to put up with this indignity? Lift this thatch off me before a scorpion puts his tail into me!"

"Umma Reha, are you hurt?" my mother cried.

"No! No! No! Just let me out of here."

Thank Allah, my father, Halim and Khalid rushed in and lifted the broken supports and the thatch. I was astounded. No one seemed to notice that we were not wearing the tob, that Haboba's legs were visible for a few moments, and that the men's upper bodies were bare.

The next day, the destruction caused by the storm brought about another unusual situation. At day break everyone was in the streets. Men, women and children all milled about. Propriety was forgotten for this instant in time. Like flocks of birds chirping and squawking, we staggered from home to home viewing the devastation. Three children had died, few homes were left with a roof, even the strong walls had crumbled, and many people were injured. Men and women cradled broken arms, lifted bruised faces to the rising sun, hobbled painfully, and our haboba could not walk.

● ● ● ● ●

The second monumental event in my placid life began amid the ordinary preparations for a morning meal, when Grandmother called Hamida into her presence. Everyone was banished from the women's living room where she sat in private audience with Hamida. The rest of us, full of curiosity, milled about in the kitchen yard pretending to be working. Lively, excited guesses about this conversation flitted from mouth to mouth. Hamida's mother was also absent, which gave sustenance to more gossip and suspense.

"It stands to reason," smiled Sasat, "that someone made a proposal for her. And now Grandmother, who likes form and tradition, prepares her for the talk with her father."

The rest of the day passed slowly. At last, A'isha, Hamida's mother, appeared and announced her daughter's betrothal. We sighed joyfully. A wedding! Nothing better than a wedding ever happened in a girl's life. I had begun to comprehend why this was so. It seemed to me that weddings and births were the only events in a woman's life that granted her attention. Therefore we rejoiced.

"Allah blessed my daughter," purred A'isha with unusual delicacy. "She will be married to Fahid Mahdi, and living in this honorable, prosperous family, she will never lack for anything."

Indeed, she spoke truth! Hamida was fortunate to marry into the Mahdi family. They were wealthy and belonged to a clan that preferred women from our family above others. When the aunts spoke of Fahid, they marvelled.

"Velvety, hot eyes."

"Tall and straight as the corner beam of a house."

"Sleek, like the horses of the army patrol that rides through the village twice a year."

I had noticed Fahid at a wedding, because Hamida, pinching my arm painfully beneath my sleeve, pointed him out.

"Over there," she'd hissed into my ear, "the young one behind your father."

"With the blue turban?" I asked.

"No, you silly goat. That one is much too old to fancy. The one with the small moustache. Mmmh," she murmured. Then, slyly, almost challenging, she directed her glance fully at him for a fleeting moment. She was clever doing such things undetected. She was like her mother, A'isha, in this respect—clever at deception. Hamida's deft games amused me. Because I did not have the courage to openly look into a man's face, I participated vicariously in her daring. Apparently her gamble paid off; Fahid had noticed her at that particular wedding, and she was soon to become his wife.

We scarcely ate that evening—we were too busy congratulating Hamida. Some of the aunts with marriageable daughters clearly felt twinges of jealousy at Hamida's great luck. Their good wishes sounded stilted and carefully worded so as not to reveal their own disappointments. Yet, once we sat in a circle on the floor mats and reached for the food set out on large platters in the center, everyone was truly happy for Hamida.

The weeks following the marriage proposal were long and lonely for me as Hamida trained for her new duties. The aunts claimed her early in the mornings and released her late at night, and so we never spoke about her approaching wedding. How I wanted to ask her what it felt like to be a bride. Was she afraid of her future, anxious, ambivalent? Did she wonder what kind of a husband Fahid would be?

My concerns about my own future grew. Everyone, including Mother, praised my father as a devout Muslim, a devoted husband, provider and father. He treated Mother with kindness and respect. But in every family there were men like Sasat's husband, Halim, who were painfully negligent in their familial duties. Others demeaned and struck their wives, and neglected their children. The women had a saying: "A woman never knows to whom she will be married, to ugliness or beauty, to good or to evil; it's all in Allah's hands."

• • • • •

Hamida left for the Mahdi's quarters in July. I remember it well, because it rained for the first time after the long draught. Outside, in the hosh, women and children welcomed the gentle drops with upturned faces and open, reaching hands. They rejoiced as droplets fell on their faces, but the moisture on my cheeks were from my own bitter tears. I felt as if the heavens grieved with me, for Hamida's exodus marked the end of our life together. I'd seen many friendships die upon marriage and the finality of her leaving filled me with great, unconsolable sorrow. Hamida's wedding had been a grand event at the end of June. Indeed, so splendid a celebration, that the aunts talked about its opulence for months thereafter. A herd of slaughtered goats, braces of pigeons, mountains of saffron rice with raisins and dates, the finest bread, the coolest fruit drinks and the best tea were served, laid out on carpeted floors under enormous tents. The Mahdi's guests sat circling the bounty, using their right hands to stuff their mouths. The unclean left hand was best kept hidden.

Trickles of light falling through the tent cloth caused the women's skin to glow rosy, and in their silken finery they became animated and alive. Not wearing the everyday white for the feast, opulence reigned. They were adorned in gold and precious stones and wore richly colored, expensive garments. The daring sported bright-green, blue, orange and even multi-colored tobs with long sleeves gracefully hanging, waving with the motion of the wearer, awakening thoughts of butterflies. The men, puffed with dignity, wore mostly black or white robes, but their turbans, kaffiyehs and even a few fezzes, burgundy red and black-tasseled, attracted the eye.

Upon entering the tent we had been greeted by sweet air perfumed with rosewater. Now, the tantalizing scents of cinnamon, cardamom and of saffron mingled with the heavy smell of mutton and beef. Breathing deeply, I felt sated, as if I needed no food. After a period of feasting the empty platters and trays were cleared, the white cloth covering the carpets was removed, and the dancing began. For three days the age-old sequence of feasting and dancing continued unchanged.

As required, I danced every dance, but my heart was not in my motions. I forgot myself and stared straight into the eyes of a good-looking man, nearly tripping over the edge of my tob. Feeling ashamed and clumsy, I thought Mother would be angry. Instead she asked me, somewhat preoccupied, whether I had taken good measure of this man. Did I like his looks?

"Yes, why do you ask?"

"He is a cousin of yours on his mother's side."

Mother's preoccupation piqued my curiosity. Inconspicuously, I attempted to view this cousin and, finally succeeding, I was not displeased. He was a bit older than Fahid, perhaps twenty-three or twenty-five. He was tall, straight and fairly light of color. His face, narrower than most, was dominated by a prominent nose and ended in a square lower jaw. I liked his eyes best. They were not romantic and velvety like Fahid's, but I thought that an inner goodness shone out through them. I asked Nazila if she knew him, and as I expected, she did.

"He is Yussuf, the eldest son of Zajid Nasredi, the textile merchant."

I had heard of this family's greatness. Their young men worked in Khartoum managing an export/import business with a great store and storage houses. In the village they owned a compound of elephantine proportions occupied by an ancient grandmother and village kin. South, along the Nile river, lay their farm, which they leased to be worked by fellaheen. Such prominence intimidated me. I assumed that a man of such wealth, living in the city, had lost adat. I had heard that city men forgot customs and traditions, and married city women. So, I dismissed thoughts of Yussuf Nasredi at once.

While we feasted, Hamida was in seclusion, and I wondered if she felt lonely and deprived. As I look back, I think that perhaps she felt nothing of the kind, because she knew her importance as bride and performer. Tension arose among the guests in expectation of the bride. The guests from the other tents came and sat among us. Finally joining us, Hamida was led by her escort of women to the tent's center where the precious dancing carpet awaited her bare feet.

Covered by the bridal shawl she could barely see her feet and needed guidance. Fahid arose from his pile of large, square cushions and slowly walked to Hamida. Motionless, he stood before her. Then, slowly, sensually, as if unwrapping a gift, he removed the bridal shawl.

She looked chaste and young, almost downcast. My eyes searched every inch of her figure for a sign that at least part of her impish, challenging spirit had survived the bridal preparations. Not the slightest movement hinted at her former spirit.

When she began her dance, I admired the perfection she had attained through the years of ceaseless repetition. She performed with dreamlike ease and beauty, and we all sighed and marvelled at her grace. Hamida danced for half an hour, longer than most brides, and then, before assuming the position of submission, she turned slightly, facing the women of our clan, and for a most fleeting moment her wide, wicked smile covered her face.

Hamida was led away, and our women bemoaned her fate during that first night of marriage. I had heard enough whispers to know that whatever the night might hold for the bride, pain would be a part of it, and so I prayed that she be spared any torment.

The next three months passed by in a dull fog. I lived, but my presence made no difference and left no record. I wept, but the hot air drinking my tears cared not for my sadness. I was as one dead.

• • • • •

Our family was enthralled by Sasat's new baby. They passed his brown little body from arm to arm, and appeared lost in admiration for her beautiful boy. Sasat glowed as if she had performed a miracle, and perhaps she had, because Halim was much in evidence those days strutting about, his chest thrust out like a proud pigeon.

It was then, shortly before the ninth lunar month, at the beginning of Ramadan, that A'isha found me in the yard. She spoke formal words designed to impress on me her daughter's importance.

"Amina, tomorrow I will visit with my married daughter and the ladies of the Mahdi's. Hamida invited you and I accepted. You realize that this is a great honor for you, and I expect you to attend me after the midday meal. I spoke to your mother and grandmother, and you are free to come."

I was only too happy to follow her summons. Although I had been to the Mahdi women's hosh when playing with their brood as a child, I had never been inside the house itself. Of course, I hoped to see Hamida privately and maybe she would confide in me about the secrets of married life. Most of all, I wanted to know if there was pain.

Our visit was formal and ceremonial. Leaving our sandals at the door, we were ushered into the women's living room. We were seated on plump pillows stuffed with cotton around the edge of an old, large Persian rug. Its brilliant colors had miraculously withstood time and wear. In retrospect, I marvel that even the richest homes dulled the senses with their monotony. Islam forbids representation of the real world because mere humans cannot compete with Allah's creations. Pictures, paintings, sculptured forms are abominations—our art is represented by arabesques woven into carpets and in tiled mosaics adorning the mosques.

At the end of the large room the haboba of the Mahdi's was throned on fancy silk cushions. She was flanked by Hamida, glowing with pride and importance, and A'isha, the guest of honor. The rest of us were arranged according to status. Proximity to the grandmother indicated high rank.

We were offered fragrant tea and a sumptuous assortment of pastries, fruits and sweets. By A'isha's beaming face I was able to measure the extent of honor bestowed upon us. The polite, stilted talk around the carpet was no different from any other everyday talk. After a while the tea loosened the women's tongues, and they gossiped with abandon. On my end, two older girls amused themselves by accusing each other with slyly veiled references of being the love object of a disgustingly fat older man.

"To our misfortune he is very rich and looking for a wife again," they whispered, rolling their eyes. Comparing him to a hippopotamus they cast aspersion upon every unmarried girl's fear, the proposal of a dreadful suitor; a proposal of such munificence that a father would accept, despite the man's age, physical unsuitability, or the presence of other wives. Each of us hoped fervently that we should not be the fat man's choice.

Upon our time to depart Hamida rose and came to me. Slimmer than before, her kohl-lined eyes larger, she looked older, more mature. The sweet, innocent roundness of her face was no more. She smiled, basking in my sincere praise of her home's beauty, the splendid tea and the sweetness of the women. Asked if she was happy, she said yes. When I asked if there was pain in marriage her face clouded, her eyes became as empty as the desert, and she quietly said yes, but spoke no more.

• • • • •

Later that night, and for many nights to follow, the dominating, stultifying fear of being unmarriageable stole my sleep. My cousins who were the same age as I were now all married, and I had danced at their weddings. Even Nazila, bitter and sharp-tongued, had been claimed by a man. In the still hours of the night the childish, sleeping sounds of the younger females, barely healed from their cutting, surrounded me. Their soft sighs and moans, rooted in nightmares of recent pain, awakened me often. They lay, their round, innocent faces half-exposed, their cheeks dewy with tears, their bodies curled, shrinking into mattress and cover, as if struggling to do in sleep what they could not in day's light—to hide from a most cruel world.

Already I was fourteen, yet not the slightest inquiry had been made as to my availability. Of course, my aunts wounded me with well-chosen barbs; each missile exposing my unhappy state of affairs. Usually, before an actual proposal, negotiations between families resolved the material arrangements of both sides. These discussions of intent indicated a woman's marriageability, but it seemed that no one noticed my existence, or, if one had, he found me unworthy of inquiry.

However, by no means was I looking forward to marriage. Daydreaming over my chores I allowed myself to dream of attending school forever—of writing verse and of writing fanciful tales. The pleasure I derived through the beauty of the written word could never be shared with anyone. Apart from being heretical, such pleasures would have been deemed silly affectations. Sweeping the courtyard, I entrusted my verses to the sands, erasing them instantly when footsteps approached. I wrote lines such as, "I am, yet my shadow imprints the world as much as I."

To learn, that is what I longed for. However, I knew well that an unmarried woman counted for nothing. To begin with, her share of the family's wealth never reached her fingers, but stayed in her brother's hands. To this day, depending on a male's disposition, he may allow a woman to exist somewhat independently, perhaps even with a certain amount of dignity. More often than not, she subsisted at the whim and sufferance of others, subjected to neverending service.

How I dreaded such a fate. Our house sheltered two of their kind. Yet, although our father was a just man who looked after them as the Qur'an directs, and our grandmother was kinder than most habobat, I pitied these aunts. Always, they carried other women's children, wiping their faces and bottoms, showering love and care on another's fruit, never allowed to bear and tend their own. Worse, some of these castoffs had grown older and become wild in their ways. They danced unseemly, provocatively when in a group, and were unaware or disregarding of their appearance.

Contemplating such harsh realities I instead submitted to the ordeal to be endured: marriage. Although divided against myself, I hoped that some man, neither ugly nor cruel, should find me to his liking and save me from a spinster's fate.

Sometimes, kneeling before the hot griddle, pouring batter onto its sizzling surface, I thought that perhaps girls were prepared for life and marriage in the same manner that made bread wholesome. Were they not treated much like the grain? First, they were pounded and crushed, then given over to searing heat and pain. Who, I wondered, had determined that we should be treated thus and not in kinder fashion?

Meanwhile, as usual, new sons born to lucky mothers dominated everyone's attention. Seasonal changes determined our way of life, and the religious holidays and observations commanded the attention of those responsible for the ordered ebb and flow of our family's life. Grandmother, Father and uncles handled our affairs and conducted the rituals.

More than the seasonal or religious high days, my memory holds the few times when the dullness of my shadow life was punctuated by commands to attend to my father. Whenever he returned from a journey to the quiet of his own home, Father became philosophical and reflective. He often meditated on the transience of life, contemplating his demise. In such moods he'd call for me to recite meaningful surahs, so that he could elicit the wisdom of the ancient words to better understand his existence and the afterlife.

Father, so different from his own sons, had little schooling. His father, a trader, taught him the intricacies of a small caravan's success, and eventually left him the business. From the time my father was nine he accompanied Grandfather on caravan treks. So it was that he could barely read or write, but had discovered the world of numbers in such a wondrous way that he never encountered problems he could not solve. He was well known in the village for this ability, and was often prevailed upon to solve the financial problems of others.

Those occasions, when he summoned me to his divan, became unforgettable events for both of us. He was the only person, save a child, with whom I could share in the charmed beauty of poetry. Although he never said much, I believed that he derived a deep feeling of peace and comfort from my efforts, for the mildness and calm of his face spoke of quiet joy.

By now my days in the village school had ended, leaving me only one book, the Qur'an. Not that I had much time to read. The women in our family were as fertile as pigeons. Their work, abed for forty days of childbirth and recovery, fell upon all others. Therefore I often knelt for hours in the hosh grinding sorghum in the hollow of the huge grinding stone for our bread. Other times I mended garments and tended the small children.

One little girl in particular warmed my heart. Khurshid, Sasat's eldest, came into her seventh year, and I saw myself in her when I was her age. She was agile and quick and had a smiling, oval face, dominated by deep, dark eyes. Her hair was kinkier than the family preferred, but the tight, frizzy curls seemed to belong atop her head as a sign of her spirit. Khurshid moved about, dipping and darting, as the swallows do that visit the river's shore each spring.

Best of all, she was bright. Intrigued by her intellect, I recited verses for her and was gratified that she understood the magic of poetry. Whenever I saw her, I prayed that one day I should be given a daughter just like her. My love for her was reciprocated with the greatest tenderness. Mornings, she awaited me in the hosh with the patience and alertness of the she-camel looking for her offspring. The moment she spied me she was quickly by my side, as if the wind had carried her.

"Salaam, Amina," she'd shout joyfully, "what will we do this morning?"

And then she would cheerfully accompany me to the tasks determined by our haboba, helping me as strength allowed. There were times when the haboba sent her away from the hosh. Girl children carried water because women, enclosed in voluminous tobs, could not transport the vessels.

When Khurshid was sent to the well, I fretted, for she was much too small for the task. The zirs, our water jars, were made of pottery, more long than round. Porous, they allow the water to sweat from the clay and to evaporate, thereby cooling the water inside. Some were so large they held forty liters of water or more. In the hosh, by the entry door to the house, sat a stack of zirs, from which the small girls chose the one they could carry when filled.

I watched Khurshid struggle to empty her zir into a larger one many times in one morning. After a few trips to the well she could barely lug her heavy zir, nevermind pour the water into the larger jars with a steady stream. I would help her whenever I could, but often the women forbade me to help.

"Amina, you are spoiling the girl. What's to become of her if she does not learn early enough that a woman's life is hard work? How can she bear sons when she can't even pour from a jar?"

Rebellious thoughts surfaced. I would ask myself why water carrying and hosh sweeping conferred the power to bear sons? I wondered also why water carrying was only work for small girls?

My brothers were older and stronger than I, yet they never carried anything. They were allowed to uselessly roam the village and the surrounding areas to the torments of the farmers whose grain they trampled, and the water fowl along the river, which they shot with their sling shots. While they flew about in loin cloths or short pants, their chests bare, our bodies were wrapped even during heat spells when the temperature soared past one hundred degrees.

To relieve Khurshid's drudgery, I would bake kisra for her, a food she desired above all others. I would sweeten the last hot cakes off the griddle with honey or syrup, and roll them up. These we ate with gusto, gleefully hidden behind the kerosene barrel. There, safely ensconced, we would hum songs or solve riddles.

"Halim goes to market to sell a camel. 'I want you to pay me for these two camels,' he says to the first buyer.

"'Allah, the Great, has given me two good eyes,' replies the buyer, 'and with these I see only one camel. So, why would I pay you for two?'

"Halim whispers into the buyer's ear whereupon the buyer pays for two camels. What did Halim whisper into the buyer's ear?" I would ask her.

Joyously she would shout, "The camel is pregnant."

Given time, she correctly figured out the answers to my riddles. We relished these hidden moments.

Then one morning, during the season of ayam el tahur, Khurshid was not waiting for me. Moments later I learned that she'd been taken to be circumcised.

In my mind I saw Hadija kneeling between Khurshid's tiny legs, performing her gruesome task. Suddenly, I hurt again with all the torment I thought had been forgotten. Although it was the season of ayam el tahur, I had preferred to think that they would not yet take her. Khurshid looked so tiny, so birdlike and fragile, that I erroneously believed tender Sasat would postpone the cruel ceremony until the child was older.

I never saw Khurshid again. That night she bled to death in her sleep. In the morning Sasat's wails filled the air, tearing our souls as hands rend cloth. My little swallow was no more, a sacrifice to the ideal of female purity. But, then, I did not yet entertain such heretical thoughts. Like the other women, I wailed and bemoaned her fate, but dared not blame the barbaric custom and the women who kept it alive. Blaming custom and an unchanging culture came later in my life when education tore the veil of deception from my eyes.

Khurshid, dead, became more precious to Sasat than she had been in life, for Sasat had truly loved Khurshid. More than any of the other women, Mother included, Sasat possessed a rare appreciation for fine things, including the different and unusual, such as her daughter. Her loss was deep and real, and she grieved for a long time.

Yet my grief was greater because I knew her child better. I'd seen Sasat lavish more time and care on her son than on both daughters, and I wondered whether she had wholly understood the depth of her daughter's quick mind, her joyousness, goodness and her power to brighten life.

How I missed Khurshid's small hand in mine, her careful way of capturing every last crumb of kisra. My day began with tears because I missed her joyous Salaam. For the longest time a breeze stirring a leaf could startle me into looking for her, as the sound was fleeting, like her movements.

I grieved and I brooded. Why had they taken her so early? Why at all? I knew all their reasons, but that didn't alter my pain. It was done in the name of controlling passions. So, in the end, a woman was left without any passion at all. It was as if she were dead.

After many months my emotional turmoil subsided, yet deep inside me I nurtured cold hatred against our haboba, Sasat, my mother and Hadija, the cruel circumciser. It was women who killed Khurshid. It was women who pinned her down, and women who had mutilated her, and it was women who sang joyously outside all the while.

CHAPTER *Four*

Before Ramadan I turned fifteen, and my brother Khalid married a woman of the Mahdi tribe. Father's efforts and generosity had secured him the desired position on a river boat, and he had accumulated enough money to marry. I heard that the bride was beautiful, sweet and gentle, properly trained and was considered an asset to our family.

Since our compound was already painfully crowded, a substantial part of the property next to ours was purchased. Indeed, Allah granted us good fortune, or perhaps it was Father's foresight, enabling us to buy, when the family next to us was forced to sell part of their land and buildings.

A portion of the new place became Khalid's, the rest was to be shared with our brothers and their future wives. Meanwhile, the family spilled into the new realm after removing a few rear walls. Especially nice was the enlarged hosh for the women and children. In the spirit of renewal I begged Father's permission for me to raise flowers and herbs in some large, old zirs that leaked and were useless for water storage. Persuading the haboba was his specialty and, granted permission by all powers, I began planting my small garden.

Before Khalid's wedding, which promised to become a great event, A'isha purposefully sought me out. Since Hamida's wedding A'isha had grown fat, her face transformed into a brown moon in which her lively eyes were compressed like raisins in sweet dough. Her small nose, always too small for her face, now looked like an almond sliver. Her hands, plump and round like water skins filled for a desert crossing, seemed to have lost the ability to bend.

Although A'isha's sharp, loose tongue often caused pain, she was not deliberately cruel. To the contrary, she was rather helpful to those she liked even if her efforts did not always have the desired effect. This time she wanted to alleviate my fretfulness over my unmarried state and assure me of a good future.

"I know you are distressed, worried that no one has asked for you. But things are not what they seem. I know that your father rejected five men of good family, before the families could even discuss the desirability of a match."

At first, I misunderstood. I asked cautiously if, indeed, someone had demonstrated an interest in me.

"But of course, silly girl, didn't I say just that? You must listen more attentively when your elders speak. I haven't all day to explain." A'isha was out-of-sorts because her stream of information was interrupted.

My heart stopped beating, and my breath came faster. So, there was hope for me after all. But why would Father reject all five? Wasn't at least one man acceptable to the family? I was about to ask A'isha these questions when she continued.

"This is highly unusual," she mused. "In all my life, I have never heard of such a thing—rejecting good men without cause. Your mother was alarmed, for such fickle rejections may ruin whatever chances you have for marriage. The haboba was furious with your father, severely admonishing him for recklessly diminishing your chances.

"'What is the reason for such fickleness?' she asked him, and do you know what he answered?

"'Allah blessed Amina with a special gift, and therefore she must marry a special man. A man who will value the gift lest the gift be wasted, and the One, All Powerful angered.'

"I swear that's what he said. The haboba glanced at him with such venom. You know the look, reserved for us, when she thinks us to be lazy. Then she growled at him like an angry cat. Even her age and position did not permit such breach of conduct.

"'Special gift. Amina special? Like the others, she sweeps, bakes bread and mends clothes. She is lazy, shirks her duties and tries to hide behind the kerosene barrel. Hah! As if I didn't know. Nothing special about her. She is too old already. Marry her off while you can and leave the rest in Allah's keeping,' that is what she said.

"Your father was obviously annoyed. Yet, he bowed his head as if in prayer. He told her to trust him, and walked away. I don't know what this is about, but I have been thinking that you should know. The women decided to keep the matter silent, but I feel that perhaps you can use this knowledge to your advantage at your brother's wedding."

Her look was penetrating. Her raisin eyes seemed to be bits of flint for a moment. "I wish you well, niece," she said, leaving me lost in thought.

"Amina, come here," cried my grandmother sharply. Forgetting everything I rushed to her side. Who would dare delay when she beckoned?

"What did gossipy A'isha fill your ears with?" she asked.

"Nothing," I lied smoothly, certain in the knowledge that my life would become never-ending misery if I tattled on A'isha.

I slunk away under her distrustful glance and busied myself on the grindstone. There is never enough flour ground for a family as large as ours. Throughout the day every woman takes her turn at the stone. Momentarily the work suited me. Although hard and demanding it ensured privacy, time to think. One never talked while grinding flour because one could hardly be heard above the pounding of the pestle. At best, one could sing or chant rhythmically, drowning out the din. Considering A'isha's facts for a long time I found no reason for Father's behavior, save one.

I decided that the emotions conveyed in my recitals were the reason for him to think that I was special. Yet this quality would bring me neither a husband, nor status among the women. To the contrary, the women would mock me were they to know my secret, for they value neither reading nor writing. In fact, they looked upon these things as useless for their daily survival. Only marriage, sons and age bring honor, respect and power, all else is useless baggage. These other strange desires plagued me, weighed on me and filled me with dejection. How I wished I could be more like Hamida, living life narrowed to the barest essentials of female existence.

• • • • •

After our conversation, I decided to influence my fate in such manner that A'isha could only approve. Breaching an unstated rule by telling me the secrets of the older women I now had to prove that I was worthy of her confidence.

Khalid's wedding provided me with the staging ground. I talked Mother into a richer garment than she would have bought for me otherwise. Feeling sorry for me she purchased the white raw silk I favored, although my gown now rivaled her own.

My father gave me a gift of three fat golden armlets dotted with rubies. They were pretty things clanking weightily with my every movement. From Sasat I begged a few drops of heavenly perfume. She gave them with a glad heart, pouring the precious scent, drop by drop, through a funnel made from a waxed papyrus leaf into a tiny, blue glass bottle. This bottle, ancient and fragile, was in itself a treasure.

Those were my requisites to tempt fate at Khalid's wedding. I wadetermined to be noticed by a man in need of a wife. My father's choosiness in selecting my groom had eased my mind, for now I knew I would be spared a cruel, misshapen or lowly bred husband. I nightly thanked Allah repeating Surah 17:

> *"Thy lord hath decreed*
> *That ye worship none but Him,*
> *And that ye be kind*
> *To parents. Whether one*
> *Or both of them attain*
> *Old age in thy life,*
> *Say not to them a word*
> *Of contempt, nor repel them,*
> *But address them*
> *In terms of honor."*

When my father bowed his head in front of Haboba, defending his rejection of my suitors, he must have repeated these words in his mind, as I often had when reading this verse to him. I realized that my father was dearer to my heart than Mother, for he knew my spirit, while to her I was only another female body.

To describe the splendor of Khalid's and Zaynab Mahdi's wedding requires divine inspiration. The Mahdi's were delighted with the match and spared no expense. The entire village was invited to the feast. Therefore the feast was prepared outside the village, where emptied cotton sheds provided shade for the cooks. The guests sat on carpets and mats woven from rushes in the shade of white tents.

Never before had I prepared my body with such attention to detail. I groomed myself lavishly. Among our women I am considered tall, yet I wished I had my mother's fine bones, her small wrists and dainty feet. But my frame is sturdier. My face is rounder than is admired by our people. But I have large eyes with long lashes. I believed, that with proper care, I might look well enough.

I scrubbed my skin, warm-brown as a desert date, until it glowed like the copper urn in the kitchen. I scented my skin, hennaed the soles of my feet and the palms of my hands and brushed my hair, straight and shoulder-long like my mother's, until it shone like polished ebony. Next, I wound my hair and fastened it to the nape of my neck with two carved, wooden pins. Cunningly, I lined and darkened my eyelids with kohl, and then chastely covered myself with the yards of silk that made up my tob. Lastly, I hung my arms and legs with bracelets and anklets. Finally, I felt ready to challenge fate.

When the time came I danced chastely, mincingly, as required. Yet, for the first time at such a dance, I scanned the audience for a suitor using A'isha's coy deception.

My brother, splendidly attired, sat on the cushion throne. Shyly glancing at him I saw that he was exceedingly pleased. However, none of the anticipation and the joy I had seen on other groom's faces showed upon his. No, only smugness was written there. He was as filled with himself, I thought, as if this spectacle was due him alone, not performed to honor two families.

My thoughts turned to the poor bride. Did he consider her at all? After all, it was her most important day too. I did not know Zaynab well. She was thirteen years old, too young for me to have met her at play or in school. According to custom, she was in seclusion and would not make her entrance for almost two more days.

The men of our family and the Mahdi's men, sat on either side of Khalid. The women of both families sat across from the groom, between them a sea of carpets and rugs. Toward midday a slight commotion arose. All at once the men arose to greet a group of new arrivals. I was surprised that even my father stood. A'isha, always quick to see and understand a reason to gossip, informed Mother in a whisper that the Nasredis had arrived from Khartoum.

Had A'isha been mute, I still would have known who had come. For while spying Yussuf Nasredi beside his father, Zajid, a strange pleasure took hold of me, saturating me with a feeling akin to weakness. I resolved not to glance in his direction again, for I believed that my attraction to him was like possession, an unwanted takeover of my feelings. However, it soon proved a useless vow that I broke not long thereafter.

After the wedding, the aunts remembered a thousand details of the event, mulling them over for months, yet I could remember little. It seemed to me that after Yussuf's arrival a haze spread over the crowd. Except for his face, everything was blurred and diffused. I knew that my brother must have unveiled the bride, yet I did not see. She must have danced, yet I never noticed. I must have eaten and danced myself, yet cannot remember doing so. I wondered whether a jinn had entered my body and lived my life during the wedding while I was somehow pushed aside. Had I been more like the others I should have spoken to someone about this unusual phenomenon, but I could not confide this strangeness to anyone.

Ten days after the wedding my mother rushed into the hosh where I was sewing under an awning. I hated this task. My stitches were never fine enough for Haboba's inspection, but I enjoyed the shade and solitude.

"Put your work away, Amina, and come with me. Your grandmother asks to see you. Hurry, she is bursting with something important," Mother trilled. I detected a touch of madness in her voice, and that worried me as she is the most rational of women. She helped me gather my cloth and thread because I didn't act quick enough to suit her. The moment I stood, she clutched my hand and pulled me into the deserted women's common room where the haboba sat with great dignity upon a pile of pillows.

My grandmother was a small woman who had learned early in life that people are led by appearances, and therefore employed a regal demeanor and upright posture. No one thought of her as small or unimportant. Her dark skin was deeply creased. White, bunched hair, like cotton wisps blowing in the wind, sprouted from her scalp. Her eyes were small and piercing, and her mouth was a blue-black slash across her face. I always knew, even when I was very young, that she was the brightest woman in our family, and possessed a burning will.

She ruled her son's wives, grandchildren, nieces, nephews and, to a degree, even the males in the family through my father with great detachment which enabled everyone, particularly the women, to follow her orders without resentment.

As I stood before her, somewhat puzzled, she studied me, running me through with piercing glances. Then she commanded, "Sit. Here, beside me." She patted a round, beige pillow of unbleached, rough-combed cotton with her brown, wrinkled hand. I sat. With another wave of her hand she invited Mother to sit opposite us. My heart beat with such force that the blood roared in my ears. My mother's hands fluttered nervously, so that her bracelets tinkled like the bells on a camel's bridle.

Of course, the haboba sensed our overwhelming curiosity but savored her triumphant moment by observing silence. When she finally spoke it was as the reading of the Qur'an, "At last, the day is here. A man has asked to marry you. Finally, your father, who has rejected a number of good men, found one worthy enough."

She expressed enough sarcasm in her voice to amply convey how unwarranted his selectiveness had been for one so inferior of such consideration. Despite her sarcasm I almost burst out to ask about the man in question. Yet strict training forbade it. She obviously enjoyed the suspense, and said nothing to lift my uncertainty, but instead instructed me to go see Father and behave myself.

Thankfully, Father cut through all ritual. He allowed me to sit and said, "You are a good daughter, Amina. Many times you filled my heart with peace and quiet joy, for you speak well. Over the last years I observed that you were also a good daughter to your mother and grandmother, and gave trouble to no one. For such a one as you, a good man should be found, and it is a good man who asked for you."

Oh, what a moment, so poignant my heart stopped beating, and my breath fled my body in a deep sigh. Father began to speak again, but of all his words I heard only, "Yussuf Nasredi." Was I content with the match? he asked me. He had to repeat the question, for I was struck dumb with wonder. Finally, I murmured yes, and he allowed me to leave.

Why could the name of this stranger, whom I had seen only fleetingly, and of whom I knew nothing, shake me to my core? What had happened to me? I couldn't remember ever having wished for such feelings. Oh, I had hoped for marriage because marry I must, but why did I feel such tumult in my breast? Perhaps Mother would be able to explain this confusion.

My legs hardly carried me back into Haboba's and Mother's presence. Their looks, searching, filled with curiosity, told me that they didn't know the man's name. They were burning to know about the proposal, and were piqued because Father had chosen to tell me first. I sank onto a cushion and was not yet nestled when Mother asked, "So tell us. Tell us! Who is the suitor?"

"Yussuf Nasredi."

"Ahhh," breathed my mother.

"Allah is Great. Great good luck," intoned my grandmother, and then they were both speaking at once.

"He must have noticed her at Khalid's wedding," said Mother.

"Why *her*?" asked Grandmother disagreeably, but then she softened and added, "You do have good looks Amina, and you are a sweet girl. Stubborn sometimes, and given to hiding, but not quarrelsome or mean."

They pondered the question why this Khartoum-bred man would want to marry into the village, and surmised, that it was because of Amna, his mother.

"Although she has lived in Khartoum since her marriage she has not forgotten her roots. She carries our blood and was brought up properly," warbled Grandmother, happy in the knowledge that she had done her part to keep all of us tahir.

"What honor to our family," said my mother, nearly swooning. I could clearly see that they were both pleased beyond sensibility with this new development. I noticed, particularly in my grandmother, a profound change in their attitude toward me. Where before I had been a shadow person, a worker bee not to be considered or fussed over, I had now reached a new stage.

I had value. It dawned on me, during the next few weeks, that my ability to bear children was a highly valued commodity. Especially if I were to bear sons. That's all they talked about—the valuable, never-to-be-broken connection my children would create to one of the wealthiest, most powerful families in the region, perhaps in all of Sudan.

I began to see the upward change of my position in the treatment accorded me.

"Sleep a little more," said the haboba, smiling benevolently, "don't get up too early. You mustn't look tired, ever, before your wedding. Wear only fresh, spotless clothes. The Nasredi ladies will visit unexpectedly, and you must always look your best."

"Assuredly, they will come to see our house, and note your manners before the marriage deal is finalized," cried Mother excitedly. And she was right.

Three of their women did, indeed, come to tea one day after sending notice of their arrival. The Nasredi grandmother, an ancient, wrinkled crone of ninety, wound into a cocoon of a tob ten times too voluminous for her small frame, was almost carried to our house. Behind her and her two servants, walked Yussuf's mother, Amna, born to our family and married at twelve to Yussuf's father, and a woman named Meriame.

As a young bride, Amna was considered to be a priceless beauty, dazzling the beholder with almond skin, large eyes and eyelashes as long as a camel's. Even now, walking into our midst, she was stately and beautiful. She must have been forty-five then.

From her immaculate, uncalloused hands, her fine-boned face, rarely exposed to sunlight, and her heavy gold jewelry, evidently much worn yet unblemished, I deduced that she had never knelt in a hosh pounding grain or baked kisra on the hot griddle, the age-old culprit of burned and scarred female hands.

Her demeanor was calm and observant, and I felt that she studied my every move. Therefore, I believed her to be intelligent. Later, I discovered that her mind was even less agile than the minds of our women who, although shut away and confined, had never-ending work requiring planning and decision-making, while Yussuf's mother was deprived even of those simple processes. Instead her world was one of leisure, ensured by the hard work of indulgent servants.

The young woman, Meriame, married to one of Yussuf's younger brothers, was docile, unassuming and had pleasing looks. To my annoyance she habitually, almost slavishly, deferred to the old Nasredi haboba and Amna. I'd rather she had not spoken at all.

Our common room was transformed into a dwelling worthy to receive a sheikh by a grand, old silk carpet blazing with every shade of colored silk thread its inspired creator could obtain. On this masterpiece we assumed the required positions, with our haboba perched on her throne of pillows. Beside her, on equal seat, rested the diminutive Nasredi haboba, and on either side of the grandmothers Yussuf's mother and my own were positioned. The moment Meriame and I were seated on low pillows across from the powerful habobat, polite questioning began.

Amna led the talk because the Nasredi grandmother suffered from loss of breath rendering her barely capable of speech. Amna courteously referred to her happy childhood in our house, thanking the haboba for her kindness as aunt to the motherless child of her youngest brother. I remembered, then, that her mother had died in childbirth, when Amna was only three, while giving birth to a still-born brother.

Amna then lavishly praised the cleanliness of our dwelling and praised the lovely fragrance permeating our rooms. To dispel cooking odors, the haboba instructed us to grind cloves and burn them in small clay vessels together with orange peel. Bunches of fresh mint were crushed and hung in corners to be touched by the breeze. Favorably elaborating on the quality of our tea, the sweets and pastries, Amna was a very agreeable guest.

She looked at me directly for the first time and mentioned how pleased she was that her future daughter-in-law should come from her own family.

"Peace of mind arises knowing that you were raised pure and are properly prepared."

For my part I sat erect, smiling when required, and answered politely the few questions directed at me. On the whole, I felt as if I was not needed at all. Our mothers extensively expressed their wishes concerning our wedding and future lives as if discussing their own.

At last, after a rather lengthy, tiring visit, the ladies left amid a whir of final pleasantries. Residual contentment mixed with subdued excitement of good things to come wafted through our house.

Henceforth, a whirlwind of activities blew around my person. Not that I was actively involved in the process. No, it was more a matter of watching the progress of my wedding preparations. Both families set the wedding date for the end of September—a well-appointed time, for late in August or early in September the Nile reaches its highest floods, setting the stage for the greening of the fields. So that by the end of September we are blessed with fresh food.

Father ordered citrus fruits from Kassala's irrigated gardens that stretched along the Nile, sesame to press into fine oil for baked delicacies and rice and wheat from the farms of the south. He arranged for cattle and goats to be slaughtered in time for the feast.

My mother and Haboba planned the dishes to be served. Far ahead of the event, they ordered all the green, leafy vegetables and treasured herbs like coriander. Besides the food, they ordered mats, cotton sheets and fabric for new tobs.

Depending on their disposition, the women in our household either hailed my good luck in finding such a distinguished groom, or fretted over the announcement. At first, some aunts were filled with jealousy.

"Why *her*?" was every woman's burning question. "Why should she be so special to catch a Nasredi?"

How well I understood their agitated musings. I had asked myself that very question when my cousins married and I remained unclaimed. In reality we knew that we caught no one. Our marriages were but an elaborate game played with social obligations and positions—a game in which we were simply pawns, not players. Their petty jealousies receded into the background once they remembered these facts.

So after their initial barbs, they made peace following up with rivers of advice. To my surprise every day another relevant detail of marital relations was revealed to me. Some information was frighteningly vivid, as was a lesson on intercourse. I was kneeling in the dirt before the hollow grinding stone, dreaming of Yussuf, when Sasat joined me. A curious look in her eyes caught my attention. She stopped me from pounding the grain by raising up my arm, whereby the wooden pestle aloft in my hand, the "elephant's thing," became an ominous metaphor.

"See this wooden club," she asked mysteriously, "pounding the stone before you? That's what your wedding night will be like. Sewn up and scarred as you are, his thing will be pounding against your door, but he won't be able to get in. I have known couples who have tried for a year or two before that happened. Imagine the agonies! The women couldn't become pregnant and meanwhile their men groaned with frustration."

Sasat then swore me to secrecy and confided that shortly after their wedding Halim had bribed Hadija with a goodly sum of money to open Sasat up a little. I swore to keep this secret or incur the wrath of Sasat's red jinn.

"What a remarkable cut this was," whispered Sasat. "It wonderfully shortened my travail and pain, although, in itself, it was not painless."

It was during the pre-wedding days that they told me of the processes which accompany childbirth—of cuttings and re-sewings. The details made me cringe. I felt cleaved apart. At night I curled into a tight ball because now the prospects of marriage and childbirth terrified me. Yet when dawn sweetly colored the world rosy, I'd awaken to Yussuf's face in my mind's eye erasing all thoughts of pain and travail.

"You can't have marriage without pain," said Mother.

"Wait till you have a child," said the other women, "then you can send him to a prostitute and sleep in peace."

Such thoughts were unthinkable. The Qur'an speaks of the good woman's love for her husband. Muhammad praised his incomparable wife as the perfect helpmate. Khadijah, the one who understood, encouraged and supported him when persecution, insult and torture threatened.

I wanted to be such a woman. How I wanted Yussuf to see me as Muhammad saw Khadijah. But when I mentioned such romantic notions the women laughed, teasing me tenderly. They called me daft, besotted by Yussuf, and declared my head addled by idealized notions unconnected to real life.

"It happens to all of us before our wedding," they smiled, "but it vanishes like a bad fever."

"It's like a meal of bad meat," Zainab laughed, "you suffer terribly, but it ends quickly after a good purge."

"You will bless the nights your husband sleeps alone. Precious nights uninterrupted by a summons to join him in his chamber."

In such manner they spoke to me, one after the other, endlessly, like the flow of the River Nile. They laughed, deriding my fanciful notion of being a husband's friend.

"Do you think he wants talk when you are summoned to comfort his body?" asked Rehana.

"Oh, sometimes, when he is satisfied, when miraculously all has gone well, he might speak of more than daily drudge out of a sense of gratitude. He might confide some business hopes, perhaps speak of a journey to undertake. He might mention marvels encountered during travel, but more often he inquires: 'How are the children?...Is my mother as well as she pretends?...Are you pregnant again?'

"That is what men will say. But, if you ask about the exciting things in the world outside, what he does during his day, whether he goes to see these movies of which we have heard, whether he visits coffeehouses and the tempting shops stocked with Western commodities, then he remains silent. Perhaps he will venture that such things are of no consequence to a good Muslim, for they often tempt the senses in ways contrary to the teachings of the Qur'an. But mostly he'll ignore such questions as if you never asked them."

"So you see, little sister," Sasat smiled pityingly, "do not expect to become your husband's friend. We have our world, and the men have their own, into which they will not allow us entry."

Some of the women thought we were better off for not knowing the outside world—better for not knowing the temptations and dangers of such a place.

"Security and peace of mind is here," proclaimed Mother. And shy, little Zaina, gesturing to the stark confines of our quarters astonished us by proclaiming, "Here is cleanliness, health and order, but on the outside reside powerful spirits and demons. No, it is better to live inside the walls."

They believed that poverty and harm awaited women outside the walls. Yet, I had noticed women among us aching to explore the shops of a city. Even the arduous journey to the Western doctor was a memorable event as it had been for my mother when she tried to save my life. For the longest time Mother recalled even the smallest detail of this journey, remembering the vast emptiness of the road and the deep blackness of the night, which she vividly described for the other women. She also described the fears that assailed her—fears of wild animals, robbers and jinn. "If not for my sick child I would have turned back and fled to our house."

She recalled the comfort she felt when the stars bathed the countryside in mild light, and how she'd heard the frightening sounds of hunting creatures. She remembered the cut of the nurses' gowns and their smart, leather sandals. But she was most intrigued by the red-haired doctor with his huge nose and speckled skin, which she described most comically to the enjoyment of the women who laughed until their eyes teared. Oh, I remember well how stimulated she was by this journey.

Listening to her lively description I remembered my early yearnings to escape into the desert, to see, to feel and to explore. I knew that given a chance, I would venture out into the world. But now, as my wedding drew near, Mother did her best to dispel any such notions.

• • • • •

My wedding day approached rapidly. Like every bride before me I was fussed over, as the women of our tribe tried to shape me into a desirable bride. I was forced to practice the wedding dance until my neck and legs ached from repetition. Everything was meticulously rehearsed. My clothes and jewelry were chosen, and tried. From the depth of a chest containing Mother's treasures my ceremonial shawl, given to me at birth, joined the rest of my costume. Holding its resplendent folds, woven in red, blue, green and burnt-sienna silk with threads of real, spun gold and pure gold tassels, I saw that it was a beautiful work of art.

A bride's last tasks are designed to create the illusion of other-worldly pureness, a look of shimmering whiteness for her wedding day. Hofryati people measure their chance of attaining a seat in heaven not only by one's good deeds, but also by skin color. To be white was considered a blessing because Muhammad's gabeela were white, and therefore we thought whites were favored to enter jannat.

While our village people come in all shades of brown, desired shades range from light (asfar), to medium red (ahmar), to dark (asrag). Happily I was born asfar, and my skin looks like light, golden honey. Yet, apparently even my light skin was not pale enough for the ceremony, and so I had to endure an elaborate cosmetic regimen. Several days before the wedding feast my preparations began.

This time heat and pain were to be spread over my entire body. Under Haboba's watchful eyes, I knelt before a cauldron in the kitchen hosh, for once empty of children. A thick, sticky brew of sugar, lime juice and water, which I stirred with a wooden club, bubbled in the cauldron. While I worked, I listened to the women's defense of the hot ordeal. My lively Aunt Sasat, my mother and the quiet Zora had helped me squeeze the mountain of limes needed for the syrup. They talked while they worked.

"All evil thoughts and body impurities are removed from us through heat and pain. It beautifies soul and body, rendering us white and smooth for the children we are to receive."

"So why don't men suffer the same rigors?" I asked. "Are they not to become the fathers of the precious boys? What ritual do they endure to cleanse bodies and souls?"

I believed, and rightly so, that since we all are Allah's creations, beautiful in his gaze, we should share the same burdens. How the women fell upon me, shocked by my question! Had I reviled the Prophet himself, they could not have been more severe.

"You speak as if possessed by jinn," they scolded, while defending men's rituals. But I could not comprehend how their circumcision and ritual bathing compared to the extremes we were forced to undergo. Although rebuffed and silenced, the troubling thoughts remained.

How could the pain rooted in excision, or the pain of the heat ritual make my future child better?

I had observed pregnant women closely, and I saw that children born to mothers enjoying occasional leisure and good food were well formed and happy, while babies born to harried, hungry mothers fared badly, fostering thoughts that our pain and cleansing rituals had no influence on the bearing of children, but were important to grandmothers and aunts who had undergone these ordeals.

Bitterly, I kept my thoughts to myself and stirred the foaming syrup. When the mixture reached the right consistency, the sugary lime brew was left to cool slightly. Clenching my teeth, I shed my shift and stood naked under the sparse sun rays that seeped through the thatch roof, feeling vulnerable and anxious.

I was told to spread the hot, toffee-like syrup over my body beginning with the pubic area, for every bit of hair had to be removed. A groan escaped my lips as the hot goo touched my skin. Sasat left her needle work and kindly came to help me with the hard-to-reach places. Her deft hands and murmured encouragements comforted me—especially later, when she had to pull the hardened substance with quick motions off my skin, thereby removing every last hair. When the last patch of sticky depilatory had been torn off, I felt as if I were on fire. The urge to submerge myself in clear, cold water was overwhelming, but Sasat offered only a moistened rag for relief. At last, I was allowed to leave. I dressed and went in search of water.

Sometimes, performing dull chores I pondered our world of mono-chromes, a world composed of rough-textured surfaces and somber shadings. Every waking moment the grayish-brown walls of house and hosh confronted the eyes with gentle boredom. The stamped mud floors differed little in color from the dull walls. Our everyday garments were white or of undefined dark hues. The rushes on the roofs, bleached by the sun, offered shades of brown and gray.

Apart from all other spaces, more textures and shades were evident in our kitchen. Since wooden bowls age differently, we owned them ranging from almost white to deep ebony. Their simple carved designs added subtly textured shadings attracting the eye. Large bins, constructed from leather and wood, held colored grains, rust-red, golden and pearl-white. A large bowl seated in a tripod was filled with white goat's milk left to curdle. Black iron utensils and a few pretty glass bottles and ceramic pots sitting in wall niches added refreshing touches of art and color.

For those reasons I had always liked the kitchen. Compared to the rest of the house it was excitingly alive. Yet, the very next day my enjoyment was marred. Entering the kitchen early in the gray gloom of morning, I found every opening to the hosh covered by blankets for the next part of the ritual.

Long ago, off to one side, a hole had been dug into the earthen floor. On this day, the pit had been filled with fresh, fragrant wood, which Mother lit the moment I arrived. The smoky fire gave off a pleasant, aromatic scent. Ordering me to remove my shift, Mother covered me with a shamla, a special camel hair blanket, and told me to crouch over the rising smoke. Only part of my face was visible through a slit in the blanket, while my body bathed in the smoke collecting under the blanket.

"Take care to envelop the smoke and keep the blanket edge tightly on the ground," admonished my mother. Then she left me, curing over the fire like meat drying in the sun.

Hamida, Shirin and Nazila together, with other young married women in remembrance of their own curing, had come to our home to keep me company. Excited by the promise of my grand wedding they came to relieve my boredom and amuse themselves by noisily detailing my discomfort. Wearing loose-fitting, dark cotton shifts they sat on the kitchen floor, their legs comfortably outstretched, their fingers husking peanuts with great dexterity while they entertained me with gossip. From time to time someone reminded me to throw a few sticks of wood onto the fire in order to create more smoke.

Although I was uncomfortable, I had to suppress the irresistible urge to scratch the skin off my flesh. Thank Allah, the cousins made my ordeal bearable by recalling droll bridal-preparation tales and the comical turns they can take. Apparently, not everyone survives the cleansing rituals intact—as the bride with delicate skin can testify, who bled from numerous places after her depilatory treatment. Then, there was the bride who lost her balance and toppled onto the burning sticks scorching her thighs and bottom.

"I wonder how she explained the blisters to her new husband?" smirked the heartless Nazila.

"Imagine having to do 'it' with a bottom all blistered," giggled sweet Shirin, who was already the mother of two.

I shuddered so hard my blanket shook and the smoke escaped making the cousins scream with excitement.

"Keep still! Keep still! You will never be done."

In this vein they entertained me, and I laughed with them despite my misery. The cousins mentioned the easy way the groom prepares for the wedding. He, too, must shed body hair, but he can do it the cool way by using a razor.

"No pain for the groom," smiled Hamida. Yet, secretly my cousins were extremely proud that women's rituals were fraught with pain because our suffering conveyed an unspoken superiority—a superiority that we surely didn't enjoy in our daily lives where men ruled. But I was learning that our women resisted subtly. Watching our docile draft-oxen I noted they can be goaded only so long before they resist the drover. As with oxen, so it was with our women—they learned to avoid the goad. Look at the clever ways they developed to avoid their painful marital duties—deflecting their husband's attention with dropped hints of sick children in need of attention during the night, or that their "moon period" rendered them unclean. Some even administered sleeping droughts to their amorous husbands.

While they openly chattered of useful ploys in the never-ending scuffle with men, my cousins ate most of the shelled peanuts. I barely listened to their prattle, drowsing uncomfortably in the smoke. At least two hours passed before I was allowed to leave the stifling confines of the curing tent. I threw off the blanket and stretched gratefully. They passed me an earthen jar filled with the smoked dough we call dilka. Made from millet flour and powdered aromatic wood, dilka has the ability to slough off skin loosened by the smoke treatment. I massaged my body with dilka and heard my cousins cry out in amazement.

"You are white! By the Prophet, you are white."

"Amina, oh, Amina. Even your own mother won't recognize you," cried Hamida.

"If you die now, you shall go straight to heaven," sighed Shirin.

The treatment result astonished me too, yet there was no time to linger and admire my white skin because it itched remorselessly. I hastened to complete the ritual by oiling my body and lavishly dousing myself with Sasat's perfume. This task completed, I hennaed the soles of my feet and the palms of my hands, deeply appreciating the soothing, cooling balm on my abraded skin. As I handed the henna jar to Hamida, Mother, with Sasat in tow, entered the kitchen. Both inspected me with critical eyes.

"How very attractive you have become," remarked Sasat.

"You are as white and smooth as an ostrich egg," offered Mother, her rare tenderness touching my heart.

I felt honored. What more could I ask for but to be as perfect as the prized ostrich egg? Sasat assured me that this stringent regimen would render me totally dry for the wedding. (Our people greatly dislike sweat with its accompanying odors. It would be unthinkable if the bride performing the wedding dance were to perspire.)

That night, I lay on my angareeb deep in thought. With the sounds of the village stilled, the inevitability of what was to befall me came to my restless mind. Despite the hard work and the ceaseless tasks, my life had been an easy one compared to many others. I had been secure. My days had been, with few exceptions, repetitions of sameness. So that at times I thought I'd die of boredom. However, now that I would be leaving these safe walls never to return—unless my husband divorced me—I wished I could remain there forever.

"Turn me into dust," I prayed, "and let me remain here." Yet, in the next breath I begged Allah, "If I must leave this place, show me kindness."

In my heart of hearts I knew that I must leave; it was the only path open.

CHAPTER

I awoke in total darkness. The night's stillness carried all of the familiar sounds of my desert home; still, I knew instantly that I was not in my own bed. The heavy, musky smells surrounding me were different than at home. The mat I lay on was thicker than my own, and the breathing beside me was the deep, long breaths of a man, not the accustomed soft sighs of slumbering women.

Carefully, my hand felt across the mat, and as expected, I touched the warm skin of a sleeper beside me. It wasn't a dream—it was real. My wedding had taken place. My part of the ceremony, a precious few moments, had passed like a rain cloud, leaving me oddly entranced. It was as if my body had performed the wedding dance while I—Amina—had watched from afar.

I hadn't actually seen the guests at the feast, neither my father nor my mother, but viewed while blurry eyed an amorphous mass of faces. I saw Yussuf only for the brief moment as he removed my ceremonial shawl. As he walked back to his seat he again became a shadow in the crowd. Rather than his looks, I remembered his scent lingering long after he'd gone back to his seat—sweet oil and mint.

My trance, sustaining me throughout the dance, ended when my attendants, two elderly aunts, led me to the bridal chamber. They didn't mind missing the feast because they had attended many weddings. The moment I entered the chamber I was flooded with uncertainties. My bridal gown and the shawl seemed heavy, as if soaked in water, and horror upon horror, the unthinkable happened—I felt perspiration on my brow. Dabbing daintily, so my aunts would remain unaware of my predicament, I breathed deeply. A part of me wanted to be in this room body and soul, while another wanted to save myself and flee into the desert. But I knew I would only be running to my death. At that moment I understood the truth—that my fate had already been decided at the moment of birth.

Panicked, I looked around for something familiar, something friendly to ease my heart. I found no comfort. Two oil lamps of ruby-red glass hung above, suspended by copper chains from chased holders, casting an oddly stirring disturbing glow over the room. Little did I know that the light was intended to create erotic feelings.

Unreality overcame me. This strangeness was increased by the effect the red light produced on my aunts. Years seemed to have melted from them. Their skin appeared smooth, unwrinkled, and their gray hair was not gray anymore, but orange-red. Transformed, they didn't look like my old familiar aunts, but instead resembled wanton creatures sent to do mischief.

Although subdued in the red light, it was still obvious that the wedding chamber, although austere, contained more luxury than I had ever seen before. The bridal bed was a low, but well-cushioned divan covered with a fine, brocade quilt. In the corners of the room white smooth ostrich eggs, symbols of purity and fertility, hung in grape-like clusters. Every inch of the floor was covered by exquisite Persian rugs of the finest designs, and beside the divan sat a tray with fruits and a pitcher of juice.

"Recline on the bed. Rest your legs. You danced a long time and your performance isn't over yet," advised my aunt Rehana.

"Sip a little juice and refresh yourself," said Zora, while Rehana quipped, "That's all you will get out of your wedding feast, so you might as well have some fruit."

Following their advice I sat, but was too nervous to eat or drink. Yet they pressed me, and I drank the juice. It was an ambrosial blend of fruits, cool and refreshing, and I became less anxious. To pass the time, Zora and Rehana told stories of strange wedding nights, and hinted that there were ways to ingratiate myself with the groom. However what they said fell on deaf ears because I remembered nothing of their homilies.

A strong knock on the door announced that my groom had arrived. The aunts rose at once. Smiling mysteriously, they salaamed and left. A moment later Yussuf entered. His look turned me to stone. I could not move or glance away.

He pulled the door shut behind him, never taking his eyes off me. The chamber's lighting made him appear younger, glowing with passion. For a moment I was terribly afraid. This surely wasn't the man I had married, the one of my fantasies. That man had calm, warm eyes, and a face I could trust. This man's face radiated with lust.

He sensed my fear and confusion and said, "Come here, Amina." I rose as if pulled up by invisible hands. Step by slow, halting step, I moved toward him. When I stood before him he took my hands into his and said, "You mustn't be afraid. I don't want you to fear me." He pulled the shawl from my head, placed there by the aunts, and negligently let it drop to the floor. For a long time he just held me at arms length and looked at me. He pulled me close, embracing me tenderly.

I could have died right then—swooning dead away would have been perfect. Yet this tender moment led to the inevitable event.

No woman could have wished for a kinder or more thoughtful husband. Yet even he knew not how to overcome the barrier created through excision and suture. Oh, how we tried to overcome this artificial horror. Gentle and searching at first—wilder, more ardent—heedless of pain and consequences as the night went on. I feared that to push through the barricade created by Hadija he would need a member of steel. Many hours later, after tears and frustration, we clung to each other defeated.

Had Yussuf been a villager, my initiation to marital relations could have had a bitter ending. Frustrated village husbands, so I have been told, sometimes walked away from their wives in anger, leaving them as if they were a dirty robe. Or, worse yet, struck out at them in frustration. There circulated among the village women the hideous tale of an impatient man who cut his wife open with his sword.

Fortunately for me, Yussuf was kind, urbane and enlightened. He said to me, "I am sorry to cause you pain. It doesn't have to be like this and I won't have my wife suffer unnecessarily."

A flash of hope lit my being. I remembered Sasat's whispered confidence. Excitedly, I was about to interrupt him, yet he continued.

"In a week I must go to Khartoum. You will go with me. Everyone will understand that I want you along because we were just married. In Khartoum I know a Western doctor, a woman, who works for a foreign company. She will help us and you shall never suffer again."

I forgot my shyness, anxieties and fears, and without thought wrapped my arms around Yussuf and put my head on his chest. I couldn't speak, but he knew what I felt since my tears wet his skin and my body shook with relief.

Moments later I realized that I had been shamelessly forward, and hastily drew away from him, but he pulled me back and told me not to be shy.

"I like you to be yourself. Nevermind convention."

When, at last, exhausted, he fell asleep, I said prayers of thanks to Allah for bestowing a blessing upon me in the form of such a man.

• • • • •

At first glance the Nasredi compound was much like my family's. Stamped, earthen floors, earthen walls, verandas, the hosh, the kitchen—all seemed immediately familiar to me as I walked about, wrapped in the cocoon of newly awakened love.

Only after a few days did I notice subtle differences. First to penetrate my awareness was the pervasive quietness of the place. It was too quiet, almost life-less, for few children were about. Indeed, this house, deserted by its young, was inhabited mostly by ancient men and women. Besides Meriame, the young, shy wife of Yussuf's younger brother living here with a three-year-old and a new baby, only her cousin, Bashira, with two toddlers resided in the compound. All others lived with their husbands in Khartoum. The inclination of many Nasredi men to marry city women drained the compound of the next generation.

The work load in this household was greater than at my home. For the ancient ones were needy, and the feeble, old women were more hindrance than help. To be sure, there were servants, but soon it became obvious that hired hands work at a different speed than your own. Beneath the rich furnishings and trimmings the neglect showed. The room's center was swept, but one dared not look closely into corners because there spider webs hung, the desiccated bodies of their victims still trussed in their silken wraps.

The copper pots in the kitchen were tarnished and the spreads on the beds smelled musty, for no one washed and aired regularly. The griddle on which the servant girl baked kisra was dirty, the gulla for mixing the batter was crusty. In short, this house was dying, deserted by the young as quickly as they could. Meriame would have fled also had she been able, for here she enjoyed none of the female companionship to which she was accustomed. For no discernible reason she disliked Bashira, a dislike returned by her cousin with equal measure. Bashira had tried to live in Khartoum with her husband, but unable to overcome her terror of the city, she had chosen to endure the compound's loneliness in hopes of becoming the matriarch someday. Perhaps because Meriame acted hostile, Bashira saw her as a rival to her ambition. Whatever fed their feud I never knew.

Unable to flee the gloom and mustiness, Meriame clung to me as if, like water in the desert, I was precious. Together we would have gladly supervised the servants, but the old haboba was not yet relinquishing her power. Wrapped, many-layered like an onion under camel hair wraps, the grizzled, frail shell of a woman sat upon a cushioned chair. Two listless servant girls moved her, chair and all, from room to room whenever she commanded them in her screechy, breathless voice. That way she felt she was the center of activity although her weakened eyes never saw the sloth.

"Don't tell her that the servants cut corners," advised Meriame, early in my stay. "Say nothing of the dirt and the cobwebs, for she will fly into your face should you even hint that things are not right. I have learned to go about my business and do the things she tells me to do, and to never mind the rest."

Wealth has its own inherent problems, I observed. Elsewhere, in a poorer home, Meriame and Bashira would have learned to tolerate each other by necessity. But here, where empty rooms beckoned, Meriame chose to sleep with her children in a room of their own, while her cousin and I had separate rooms also. Intrigued, I thought about women's interactions at home, surmising that they must have been sometimes very distressed without the simple choice of avoidance.

Our own rooms were kept spotless, although I ran afoul of the haboba, whose shrill voice followed me always, after I removed my bed covers to be cleaned and aired. When crossing the powerful, punishment follows. My punishment, administered by the spiteful old woman, was deprivation of food. I wondered if she knew me by her nose, sniffing for my scent as I was still using Sasat's precious perfume, for surely her bad eyes could not spy me. I had to humiliate myself and beg for every morsel. Too embarrassed to tell Yussuf,

I finally confided in Meriame who covered my needs.

Despite our physical problems Yussuf came to me every night. No one told me to crush mint to sweeten the air, nor reminded me to offer him refreshments. I provided such because I loved him. I dared to ask a thousand questions about the world beyond the village, which he answered with the utmost patience. Then one night he said, "Your father spoke to me of your gift with verse. Show me this gift and read from The Book."

Handing me the Qur'an, he reached for the choicest pillows and reclined luxuriously on my angareeb. My hands trembled. At this moment I knew that my wish had come true. I would live with this wondrous man like Khadijah had lived with Muhammad.

What simple creatures are we women to think that our romantic fantasies will come true. But then, I believed my own fairy tale and, as I had for my father, I read for Yussuf from the Holy Book. Like the feki Islam working miracles with spiritual power, I poured my heart-magic into verse, chastely proclaiming my love with my voice.

I succeeded. For when I stopped, he was as still as the night at its deepest and his eyes were liquid, deep and dark. At length he motioned me to join him, and when I complied he kissed my forehead saying my father had spoken the truth. This loving touch endeared him to me even more, and he reciprocated by drawing even closer to me.

The following days were spent in preparation for our journey to Khartoum. Mother came to visit me before I left. She wondered if the journey to Khartoum was necessary and made direct inquiries pertaining to our marital relations.

Strangely, the look of concern in her eyes raised thoughts that she was questioning on behalf of my father because Mother, on her own would have never asked such questions. I assured her that Yussuf was a good husband but kept silent about the real reason for our leaving. Deep in my soul I knew I could not trust my mother. She could not sanction what we were about to do and, told that we were about to break tradition, she would have raised an alarm.

My needs were simple, therefore I spent little time preparing for the journey. All my earthly goods were stored in a chest of Lebanese cedar. At the bottom were wrapped sandals and slippers, followed by folded tobs, upon which rested a cushioned tin with my armlets, rings and amulets. My ceremonial shawl, folded and wrapped within cotton cloth, completed the simple content of the trunk. However, there was much more to pack for Yussuf. His men-servants prepared numerous trunks and crates for him.

Preparing for bed that last night in the village, Yussuf pulled a book from the recesses of his loose-fitting shirt.

"I would like to give you a gift. If you like the verses, I hope you will read them for me."

Tears moistened my cheeks. On one hand I could count the presents received during my lifetime. Each had so filled me with exultation that they were burned into my memory. Being given a book of my own was a sensual experience.

As eagerly as I anticipated our journey, dread of the unknown allowed me hardly any sleep. On one hand I was wracked by fears and uncertainties, on the other hand I had hope. That, and a thirst for change, prevailed and kept me looking forward. Yussuf's free and easy ways promised an interesting life.

The pivotal day approached, and I was certain that no future day would hold the same poignancy and excitement, or most of all the unknown impact of change. Long before sunrise I lay awake awake, silent not daring to disturb Yussuf's sleep. Fantasies about the wonders I was about to see titillated my mind until I felt a pleasant tingling in my fingertips and toes. Finally, Yussuf stirred.

From the moment Yussuf's eyes opened, things progressed rather quickly. After a simple breakfast of tea, bread and fruit, the servants came for my chest and carried it into the quiet road along with Yussuf's cases. Out front, a high-wheeled, dented, rusty truck and a fairly new Jeep were waiting blocking most of the road. Darkness still enveloped the village when the men swiftly loaded our possessions onto the rickety-looking truck.

How frightened I was when told to enter the Jeep. Yet, it was unthinkable to show fear; which would embarrass my husband in front of the servants. Muttering an incantation under my breath to ward off evil spirits, I cautiously stepped into the Jeep. I sat leaning back for support, a most unusual and awkward position for me. It felt as if my legs were useless. After a while, I hardly noticed the strangeness in my limbs. Yussuf entered quickly and moments later the Jeep roared as if it were alive, moving onward, away from the compound, the village, my youth.

Leaving the confining village walls we saw the first rosy glow of the rising sun illuminating the horizon. I was enthralled. Rarely had I seen this phenomenon as we were always enclosed by walls. A few large birds flew lazily towards the Nile. From far away an eerie sound, unlike anything I had ever heard, penetrated the motor's steady purr. From the south a camel caravan ambled toward the village, its silhouette outlined black against the rosy sky. The camels' neck-bells tinkled, their drovers shouted to each other. I thought of my father who travelled with a caravan most days of his life.

In those early days I was like a short book, consisting of a cover and a few pages. Beginning with this journey, faster than I ever thought possible, life began to inscribe important text upon my previously blank pages. The more I saw and learned, the more delightful and profound my life-text became. There were times I was fearful of new things. Too long had I been village-bound, and anything could frighten me. My saving grace was my insatiable curiosity, which overpowered my fears. Before long, I became transfixed by the scenery, while Yussuf quietly watched me with thinly veiled amusement. My fascination renewed his interest in the barren land around us.

The road mostly followed the contour of the river but we drove through the endless desert when the topography demanded change. When driving alongside the Nile I saw fishing dhows, their tiny red or striped triangular sails seeking the breezes. Their crews strained, lifting heavy nets teeming with fish. Some men proudly held up giant Nile perch using both arms to display the heavy fish. Large birds, soaring high, seemed intent on meeting the sun.

During rare moments, animals drank on the river's edge but I knew not their names. We flew by so quickly that questions were of no use.

Wherever the banks dipped low toward the river, fields seamed the edge. Where the gardens ended, green fields of reeds stretched along the shore well into the river. The farmers lived in clusters of small huts, square, unattractive buildings blending into the sands of the desert. How lonely these villages looked at the desert's edge. But, all this was new to me, fresh and exciting, and my eyes never tired.

Watching me indulgently, Yussuf pointed out objects of interest. Gazelles spooked by the motors, vultures soaring far above. On my own I never would have raised my eyes so high as to spot these birds. I had been taught to look to the earth, not the firmament.

The road, once an old caravan track, paved over a while back, had yielded to the dictates of time and wear. At times we bounced over its pockmarked surface while at other times we fairly flew over ground smoothed by thousands of camel pads. Deep ruts provoked Yussuf from time to time to mutter under his breath. No one in his right mind would have attempted this journey with only one vehicle. Petrol, spare-tires, water and food were essentials one could not do without in this unforgiving landscape.

Finally, Yussuf declared that we should eat. Sated with new impressions I had felt no hunger. He stopped the Jeep and ordered food to be brought from our provision boxes. How happy we were eating cold pigeon breasts and bread, and sipping lukewarm tea in the shade of an awning erected by his men.

After lunch we travelled at good speed until suddenly the truck driving ahead of the Jeep swerved violently and came to rest by the roadside. Yussuf expelled a few harsh sounding words, and explained for my benefit, "The truck just blew a tire."

The sun beat down unmercifully so that the men had to work in the shade of the awning. Their labors, causing drenching rivulets of sweat, intrigued me as I sat in doubtful comfort in a corner of the sweltering shelter. By the time the men had replaced the tire the shadows had lengthened ominously. The sun set fiery red on the horizon and dusky rosiness settled over the plain. However, Yussuf decided to press on.

Night fell. Intrepidly we followed the lights of the truck illuminating the road. Throughout the day I had braved the relentless sun sweltering in my multi-layered tob, breathed the dusty air of the road, which burned my lungs, lived in an ecstasy of new impressions, and now, tired and worn, I fell soundly asleep rocked by the vehicle's motion.

I have no memory of our entry into the city of Khartoum, an event I had so eagerly anticipated. Drowsily I followed my husband when he awakened me; I vaguely remember falling onto a bed.

● ● ● ● ●

Whenever I think of Khartoum I remember that first day and the view of the city below from the window of our apartment. I awoke early in the darkened, unfamiliar room. A wondrous strangeness impressed itself upon me, a strangeness more delightful than frightening. I was particularly attracted to a pretty, ornamented fabric draping the wall. Light penetrated from behind this cover above and below illuminating the wall with a halo effect. Intrigued, I went to find its source.

My searching fingers parted the cloth, and instantly bright light burst on me with such force that my eyes closed. Moments later my outstretched fingers touched the hot window glass, which was fortunate, for had I gone another step, I would have surely broken through the glass and fallen to my death.

All my life was spent close to the ground. In fact, I was accustomed to an elevation of only a few feet, and now, without warning, I peered into a chasm of unimaginable depth. For a moment I felt my head spinning, much as when we whirled about as children making ourselves dizzy. I kept my eyes shut until the whirling stopped. Soon, my curiosity got the better of me.

I shivered and shook looking from this new unaccustomed height onto chaos. Below me, three major thoroughfares crossed in a giant, six-point star pattern. Today, I have a name for the fear I experienced that morning—culture shock. The scene below was as terrifying to me as a horrific battle is to a new recruit who, totally unprepared, finds himself thrust into the middle of the fray.

My hands clutched the drapes, while my eyes were riveted on the tumult in the streets below. Deafening noises penetrating walls and windows vibrated in my ears. The motors of a hundred vehicles, trucks, cars, motorbikes, three-wheelers and jitneys roared, while their sirens honked, squealed and screeched as they hurtled with extraordinary speed down the streets toward the star's middle. There, the vehicles entered a circle joining the motorized throng and then dispersed onto other roads.

This performance commenced at such speed that I was dazed just watching their progress. Adding to the commotion were caravans of laden donkeys, horses and noisy camels entering the fray, thereby splendidly interfering with the progress of the motorized columns. Although the caravans proceeded with the greatest possible speed, after entering the circle they became instant impediments to the general flow. I watched as the frustrated caravan drivers beat their animals, mercilessly exhorting them for speed, while the creatures galloped and hopped as fast as possible. Behind them the motorcade honked, beeped and clanked. Oh, what great rage was unleashed in an unceasing, obsessive fight to gain a few feet of advantage. Carelessly weaving in and out of the throng were turbaned men on bicycles.

Besides the ceaseless, violent movement, vibrant colors dazzled my eyes and dizzied my head. Buses overflowing with people screamed pride of ownership with their gaudy, multicolored designs and garish illumination. Vehicles, large and small, were painted in as many colors as can be mixed from primary base. A few dust-covered trees beside the road were, thankfully, soothing, restful islands amid the melee.

Alongside the roads, on barely visible paths, white-clad traders carried backpacks stacked with goods high above their heads. Passersby in multiform garb walked among them. I feared for their lives, for any misstep might pitch them into the chaos. At that moment I decided that nothing could persuade me to ever leave the safety of this house. Surely, I would be swallowed up by the maelstrom below, and perish miserably if I were to set foot into the road, long before reaching the other side.

I clutched my poor spinning head and lay back on the bed, confused and distressed by the angry tumult below. Moments later I heard a knock at the door. Little did I know that the knocking was meant for me, and that I was expected to answer. Cautiously and silently the door opened and a woman, perhaps as old as my mother, enfolded in a long cotton shift entered the room. She salaamed and said, "So you are awake then. Mr. Yussuf wondered when you would wake up. He wanted to see you before leaving, but said not to disturb you."

I noticed that the woman spoke of my husband formally and therefore I assumed she was a servant. Since I was not raised with servants I knew not how to behave. I asked for her name.

"It's Aziza," she answered. "I have been with the Nasredis for many years. I looked after Mr. Yussuf since he was a boy. He told me to look after you and ensure your comfort."

Aziza led me into a wondrous room clad in marble, where taps sprang from the walls dispensing water. This alone was surely a miracle. How could clean, clear water spring forth from a wall otherwise? However, I was to witness more magic, for the water flowed warm as well as cold. Another marvel was a white, shining floor basin that swirled waste away with the flick of one's hand.

I stood open-mouthed as Aziza explained these tricks, then clapped my hands delightedly. To Aziza, city born and bred, I must have seemed an ignorant fool. Yet, she was so kind. Perceiving my unease, she mentioned that Yussuf's mother, Amna, needed a long time before comprehending the marvels of civilization.

After tending to my personal needs, Aziza prepared my breakfast in the kitchen as I looked on with fascination. Her head was crowned by an elongated, white, cleverly folded turban, quite different from the round, roped-looking nests atop men's heads. Her turban contrasted sharply with her deep brown skin and her black, busy eyes that bespoke a bright mind and lively, open personality.

Preparing the fruit and bread I am partial to she companionably began my education by explaining the fundamental structure of the city. In contrast to village homes, almost every house in Khartoum was constructed of many layers because ground is precious in the Nile triangle. This house, and others, belonged to Yussuf's family. The bottom floor, fronting the street, was occupied by offices and a large shop. Every successive layer was divided into flats for the Nasredi family members. On the fifth floor of our house, which began as a humble warehouse, were our apartments. It seemed that families of lower status lived on the lower floors, while the fourth and fifth floors were reserved for the families of the important men. Amna and Yussuf's father resided next to us.

"You can visit Amna walking down a corridor and never set foot outside," said Aziza. "And above our flat is a roof-top garden with potted trees, flowers and a cistern."

Her words were beyond my comprehension. Yet in time, bit by bit, I came to know my new world with every sense Allah bestowed upon me. I learned that water flowed through pipes, that plumbing removed sewage, and that electricity is created by the flow of electrons through wires thereby lighting our homes. Ah, but before I learned, I walked through the flat and believed that I lived in a wonderland.

Suddenly, Yussuf came into the kitchen since all business ceased in the heat of the day. His arrival flooded me with guilt and remorse. I'd barely taken care of my personal needs, never mind performed respectable work as proscribed for women of my clan. Abject, I apologized for my worthlessness, assuring him that I would do better in the future. Unlike other men, he gave no credence to self-abasement. In the privacy of my bedroom he petted my cheek and said, "Don't worry about these things. Here, in the city, things are different. You don't cook and clean. Use your time to make yourself pretty. Read your book. Do a little sewing, and look after my clothes, which must be immaculate. You must check them for flaws and instruct the servants how to clean and mend them. Visit my mother or the other women in the house, or you might go out with them. The driver of the family car will take you to the souks where you can purchase what we need for the household."

He saw my confusion and obvious dismay, for I had never bought anything, and smilingly reassured me, "Don't be afraid. Shopping is an art instantly embraced by women, and speedier yet do they learn the value of money. They can buy things before they learn how to walk in city shoes."

His eyes glanced at my bare feet, which, unshod for the first time in days, felt comfortable and cool. "Where are your slippers? You must not dirty your feet this way. Here in the city you must wear shoes."

There was so much to learn about city ways, I thought, and went for my slippers. Late in the afternoon Yussuf changed his clothes and went back to work. He would dine with his father and their business associates, while I would eat alone.

That night Yussuf came to my bed and said, "I spoke to the doctor. She will see you two days from today. I shall pretend to take you for a ride through the city, and it shall be done."

How ominous those last words sounded. But there was no other way. Intercourse was now a torment, and it was imperative for me to make Yussuf happy and become accepted in the family. For that, I needed to bear a son, the sooner the better.

I awoke to adventure. Amna had given orders for me to dress presentably, for I was ready to go out into the world. I could hardly eat and was shaking with fright and agitation. How could I endure setting foot into the street's chaos? The view from my window preyed on my mind. I told Aziza, "It will be the death of me to go into the street." But she only laughed, "Every camel learns to cross this intersection, and so will you. Why do you worry? You will be far from harm, enclosed in a car with your mother-in-law and a driver. Nothing could be safer except for Allah's heaven."

Her words soothed me. Nevertheless, another worry arose instantly in its place. What was I to wear in this city? Fortunately, Aziza was patient as well as curious while we searched through my trunk for proper clothes. She admired my ceremonial shawl, and then picked from my meager belongings a tob of fine muslin and my best slippers.

I washed in the marble tub, brushed my hair, dressed and was long ready before my summons came. Waiting, I peered into the chaos below, hoping to accustom myself, but my fear only increased. Finally, with my agitation palpable, a servant came to fetch me. A long, dark hallway yawned before us, as if it could swallow us. But the servant girl walked unafraid into the gloom. Perspiration moistened my skin, my breath came shallow, noise filled my ears, but I kept walking. A door opened, and light streamed through the hall. I hastened toward the glow as if it were salvation, stepping into Amna's flat, a flat identical to ours.

My mother-in-law interrupted her morning tea with another woman to introduce her as Sophia, her sister-in-law. Sophia accorded me a great honor by rising to greet me. I was awed by her presence. Tall and standing erect, this Circassian woman, with her green, clear, searching eyes and creamy complexion, commanded attention. Long, wheat-colored hair intermingled with silver strands denoting her age, framed a most attractive face. Amna was a beautiful woman, but Sophia was stunning even late in life. She was a Christian when she met her husband, but Abdullah, overwhelmed by her looks, pursued her until she converted to Islam and married him.

Both ladies were exquisitely dressed and groomed. Silently I admired their nails, filed, rounded gently and painted so that they shone like pearls. I marvelled that someone could look so fine on an ordinary day. At home such personal care was lavished only for weddings, religious holidays, and visits to your husband's bed-chamber. Otherwise, we were unconcerned with appearance beyond the daily cleansing and combing of hair.

Amna motioned me to a pillow. Her serving girl, a sleek, self-assured city creature, provided me with tea and a sweet.

"I welcome you," intoned Amna politely. "I remember that the change from the village to the city can be most upsetting, therefore Sophia and I decided to take you into the city. You mustn't become too comfortable in the flat and house-bound by fear. It behooves you to remember Bashira in the Nasredi compound. She never overcame her fear and now must live alone in the village. Her husband visits seldom."

Such information inspired me. Surely I could step into a teeming street, if cowardice was punished with exile. Courageously I followed the ladies into the dark hall. Midway Amna pressed her hand against the wall, and magically a door opened, revealing a tiny cubicle into which she motioned us. The moment she joined us the the door closed, and the room began to move. As we descended, my stomach filled with sickness and I fought the desire to scream.

Somehow I remained silent, gathering strength from the calm demeanor of the older women. The cubicle came to rest, the door opened and released us into a large hall filled with people scurrying about like ants.

Although I had acted with courage, the real test was still to come. Following the lead of my escorts, I adjusted the folds of my tob to conceal my hair and the lower half of my face, leaving just my eyes exposed.

A man approached. He salaamed and bowing slightly, invited us to follow him. We stepped outside through the door he held open for us, right into the inferno I had witnessed from above. I froze.

"Amina. Amina, get into the car," hissed Amna.

"Don't be afraid, Madam, it's a very fine car," assured the chauffeur and opened the door even wider; still I could not move. My eyes fastened on the never-ending flow of vehicles, and I was completely mesmerized. At last, Amna clambered from the confines of the vehicle, and with obvious, angry impatience, grabbed me forcefully by the arm.

"Move," she commanded, "or it's back to the village. You want to be with Yussuf, don't you child?" she asked.

Her effort broke the hypnotic fear. I stumbled into the car, and moments later we sped away.

I was totally numb. My soul retreated into the deepest recesses of self. I became a mechanical thing, an automaton recording sights and sounds. It seemed as if buildings, fruit stalls, lorries heaped with sacks, goods and materials, people, trees and shops flew by, as if we were the ones standing still. This illusion was shattered when the car halted abruptly, only to proceed through an intersection as dreadfully jumbled as the one I had observed from our flat.

Flying thus through this marvelous city, I knew nothing of its beginnings or any of its history. All that came later—many lessons later.

"Khartoum" means elephant's trunk in Arabic. Although I searched for an explanation, I never found any reason for this term, save perhaps one. It was applied to an Egyptian army camp in 1821, pitched at the Nile's Mogren (confluence). This camp became a garrisoned market town when traders supplying the camp began to build around the source of their income. Perhaps in those days it resembled an elephant's trunk. To entertain us Sophia told us the story of Khartoum. "Our city is built upon the triangle of land created by the juncture of the Blue and White Nile, and so, surrounded by water it proved to be an easily defensible location. Unless," she corrected herself, "the enemy patiently waits until the rivers run low with the change in season."

Whereupon she told us the story of the Mahdi who vanquished Khartoum the moment the rivers ran low, killing Gordon, the Khedive's (prince, lord, title of the Pasha of Egypt) Egyptian legions, and their Sudanese allies in the process. Later, under Earl Kitchner, Khartoum grew around the governmental and market buildings with tree-lined squares and streets. Along the Blue Nile bank one finds the buildings of government, stone and brick structures of great importance. The British also planted a shady avenue along the bank of the Blue Nile which is a pleasure to behold.

In this, the green quarter, I was awed by the many churches—Catholics, Anglicans, Maronites and the Copts. Sophia explained that these religious communities had their own schools, and even a zoo, in this district of botanical gardens. Here, our car made better progress, and I, child of adobe brick and dust, fell totally, abysmally in love with the living green.

Sophia, noticing my entrancement, promised, that she'd take me to see the garden suburbs in the southeast of the city, the place where her friend Madam Thibodeau resided. There, she said, in an oasis, the profusion of trees, bushes and flowers would overwhelm my senses.

"You will find the rest of Khartoum rather dull," said Sophia. And she was right. For rounded corners and the minaret's crannied loftiness which softened straight, harsh lines were only to be found on mosques, which abounded. Limestone, plastered brick, adobe and mostly cement were the materials shaped to satisfy both function and small budgets, making Khartoum horribly drab in many of its parts. Gray and brown were dominant. If green entered your field of vision it almost always announced an Islamic institution or a mosque. Paint was expensive and faded quickly, and as most buildings were made of concrete or unclad cement blocks, paint was rarely applied. Most vexing to my eyes were the unfinished buildings in the city, which made up the majority of the structures. This curious aspect is found in many Islamic cities where, by Islamic law, no tax can be collected on an unfinished house, never mind that people live and work in these buildings bereft of roofs and windows in the upper floors.

Variations of courtyards and roof gardens, wrought iron shutters and smithied gates, curved and elevated staircases leading to elegant front doors marked a few homes in the green quarter. By comparison our part of town was sober and bland because Sudanese merchants with large families made few concessions to beauty. A roof garden, a fountain, perhaps a pattern in the overlay of the facade—simple ornamentation—for Islam favors purity of expression.

It seemed that the entire morning had gone by since I stepped into the car. Finally we arrived, and the car stopped. Ahead lay what looked to me like the gaping mouth of a snake seething with internal activity. Incredulous I was witnessing another marvel—Omdurman, the Grand Souk—the largest souk in all of Sudan. Hundreds of streets crossed and crisscrossed each other. Low houses on each side contained small shops which, unable to contain their wares, overflowed into the road.

Every shop offered variances of only one particular item. One was filled with a profusion of the most beautiful carpets, another stuffed with copper items spilling into the street. Still another was swelling with fabrics of every color and texture, while others were filled with glass items, and things I had no knowledge of nor could I imagine a use for.

In all my life I had never seen such bounty amassed in one place, and I stood riveted and gaped. Once again Amna grabbed my arm officiously and propelled me forcefully down the street. But how could I not be intimidated by the the bounty of wares and the seemingly endless throng of humanity? Never had I seen so many people—such simultaneous motion. And wonder of wonders, many in the throng were women. They did not observe village courtesy, and gave each other no space to move; they never looked into another's eyes but moved quickly even violently, bumping one another.

When I whimpered plaintively after having my foot trod upon Amna turned to me with gravity, "The faster you move, the faster you get accustomed. Standing there gawking won't make it better. So follow me. Look at all the lovely things one can buy here instead of staring at people."

"What is buying?" I asked.

"Hasn't Yussuf explained anything to you?" she cried. Obviously she was dismayed by my dullness, herself obsessed to examine the merchandise. Sophia, who had remained silent through most of Amna's harangue, finally intervened, "Come Amina. You seem to learn fast. I will explain."

We left Amna stationed by a table stocked with perfumes. A young man with an attractive face dabbed scents from small, exquisite glass bottles onto cloth strips, which he handed to Amna who lifted them to her nose. In a section where the carpets were displayed we found a quiet spot. There, Sophia taught me the uses and value of money.

My father, a trader, used money, yet I had never seen currency. So when Sophia showed me coins and printed paper nothing made sense, since I lacked a frame of reference. Yet she was patient and went through each denomination, patiently explaining the value.

"It is only a matter of time before Yussuf gives you spending money. I am sure he would have done so this very morning had he known of our excursion.

Yet, this is easily remedied. Here," she said handing me a large bill.

"This is my gift to welcome you into the family. I think we shall be friends."

Embarrassed, I thanked her profusely. It was out of the question to refuse such a generous gift without offending the giver. We must accept gifts graciously, for the giver gains favor in Allah's eyes, therefore, such favor must not be interfered with by rejection.

On this unforgettable morning I learned what children of other cultures know early on. I forgot Amna, the milling crowd and my fears, and discovered that buying was a most exciting game. So I bought perfume. Ever since Sasat's possession, the aroma of her intoxicating, foreign perfume lingered in my senses. Later Amna gave me a soft, white leather purse, and again I felt as if I were in a dream.

"It is time to refresh ourselves," suggested Sophia. Our destination was a small house with a front room where coffee and tea was sold to passersby. But upon our arrival, a small, brown woman in a printed cotton tob, ushered us through the shop into a courtyard.

A gnarled, giant tree shaded the hosh, and cushions beckoned us to sit. Only women were present. We'd left the driver in the tea shop. Small groups of women sat together drinking tea and nibbling sweets.

"Can you see the bareheaded ladies over there?" I nodded.

"They are from the French Embassy. They often come here to shop and have tea. They are very free and always remove their head covering. In the far corner, the blond and dark headed one, they are the wives of German doctors. The unruly group of women behind us, so very casual and happy, are the employees of a large American company."

I was astonished. Now that my senses were functioning properly once more, I could concentrate on single figures—their dress, behavior and looks—and I remarked that in our village a woman in such immodest apparel would be stoned to death for indecency.

"You will get used to things being different in the city. Here, people from all over the world congregate, and must be accommodated. They are not Muslims and therefore cannot be held to the same standard," said Sophia. Then she added, "Here, only women are allowed, so the foreigners are easier in their manner than in the street. Here, we can be ourselves and soon you will be at ease too."

When the sun stood low in the western sky we left for home. Consumed by worry I fretted, "Trouble will surely be awaiting me. I should have been home hours ago. My husband will come home expecting food, and there is nothing."

"Don't worry. Yussuf won't expect a meal from you," Amna assured me. "He will either eat out or with other family men in the communal divan. We women often eat the meals prepared by the servants together. Sometimes, we prepare our husbands' favorite dishes, yet those are rare occurrences."

I was amazed. In my village, we prepared meals for the entire family, sending the largest, best portions through the portal into the men's quarter, while we ate in our common room feeding the small children. In the weeks to come I observed that this custom held true for the less affluent family members in the apartments below.

As if on cue, Amna invited us to her flat for a festive dinner to introduce me to all the family's women. Briefly, I went home to refresh myself and found Aziza in the kitchen. She informed me that Yussuf would be out late, and that she was leaving to tend to her own family, provided I had no more need of her. I thanked her for her good services and dismissed her. It felt strange giving an older woman permission to leave; until now, I had received the orders.

One of Sophia's remarks played in my mind: "Money is very important to a woman, for it has enormous impact on her; it controls destiny. Those with access to riches have power over others, even power over men poorer than they." I was already convinced that she was right.

Aziza left and I prowled through the flat. This was the first time I was free to discover the entire apartment. Earlier, I felt constrained and stayed in the rooms Aziza had shown me. The entry was separated from a large room by a splendid, moving curtain of perfect, multi-colored porcelain beads strung on sturdy cords. Furnished with fine, old carpets, cushions, hassocks and low divans, the room beckoned one to recline. Almost one whole wall was covered by drapery hiding a large window and door, giving way to a plain balcony over-looking part of the city. Two silk carpets of exquisite quality decorated the walls, and bowls of polished stone and bronze were displayed on low tables.

Chairs, tables and couches were things I had just discovered. As of yet, I had not made up my mind whether I liked them. I found sitting on a chair all afternoon very uncomfortable and therefore doubted that I would like European furnishings.

My bedroom was in the rear. I liked its smooth, pearl-gray tile floor which felt cool all day under my bare feet. The window, from which I first espied the city's bedlam, covered back much of one wall, while to the left, abutting the kitchen, was the elegant bathroom.

These rooms Aziza opened to me. Yet, there were two doors she left closed. The old Amina of only three days ago might have been too timid to think of opening a door which could conceivably lead to a male sanctum. But, I had been so shaken and had become emboldened by all sorts of magical, miraculous sights and experiences, that I opened a door before giving the matter further thought.

It was a strange sort of room. Almost as large as my bedroom, its walls were filled with books neatly ordered on wooden shelves. On the uppermost shelves parchment scrolls were displayed. Hundreds of rolls, singly and in piles, fat and thin, with tassels and without, some old and worn looking, some newer, whiter, intrigued the visitor to this library. A finely woven silk carpet, in shades of golden brown, rust, pale blue, beige and black, covering almost all of the room vividly reminded me of the Tabriz rug I had seen earlier in a store. I knelt to admire it, touching the silky texture. It glowed. Its fine, intricate pattern, a joyous mosaic praising life, was caressed by the twilight falling into the room.

In the back, I noticed a Western desk and chair and filing cabinets, which at that time were an enigma to me. This was truly my husband's domain. It dawned on me that he might not like my being here. But I was bold and forward, and so I crossed the carpet until I stood before the final door. I tested its handle cautiously, secretly hoping the door might be locked. A sickening, choking feeling, which I had come to associate with forbidden excitement, overcame me and then the door yielded. I entered his bedroom.

At first glance, the room was much like mine. A bit smaller perhaps, but with its own bathroom. His bed was a large, wooden, carved European affair with a flock of oversized, stuffed, silken pillows. Two matching night-stands flanked the bed, and a wardrobe, imposing and overpowering, claimed the wall across from the bed, while a dressing table stood below the window. It was an innocuous, almost boring room, influenced by the years he'd spent in England. He'd gone to Eton College and later to Cambridge to forge connections for the family in Europe, but then I knew nothing of such things.

I turned to leave when my eye caught on a bright, strange photograph lying on the nightstand. It was a magazine. I had never seen a magazine before, never mind one of this type.

Surprised, I turned the pages. Each page displayed glossy, full-color, nude women. Some wore interesting cup-like strips of material over their breasts, others draped shawls over their very personal parts, some were totally without shame and lay about in poses I never dreamed a woman could assume. These women came in all shapes and colors. There were women with white skin and pale hair, as if the sun had bleached it the way our yellow clay was bleached to ashy whiteness. There were women with brown hair and creamy skin, black hair and black skin. They were slender, rounded, tall and short, but they were all obscenely naked, and yet, somehow arousing.

It came to me. These must be prostitutes. Sharmuta, those women much maligned and discussed by the women of my village. Were they thus on display for men to seek them out? I shuddered. I was confused, and I was hurt and didn't know why. Had I not always been told that men sought such shameful amusement? One could not change their ways, the aunties had told me. Nay, one had to be thankful that such women would take it upon themselves to cater to men's lusts.

I dropped the magazine as if it burned my hand and fled, but something made me turn back and restore the magazine as it had been. I closed both doors carefully and walked as if in a trance. I sat on my bed, for my legs would carry me no longer. My hands shook as if I was a palsied old woman. I hurt and felt befouled at the same time. A terrible ache expanded throughout my breast crushing my heart and lungs. I couldn't know then that the horrid thing gnawing on my soul was the uniquely refined realization that perverted fantasy leads on to greater perversion.

Many years later I was to learn that fantasy is to the soul as food is to the body—that humans need constructive fantasy to realize goals, to envision success, to realize dreams, to inspire and heighten love. Yet, like too much food leads to grossness and ill health, gross fantasies lead to unending quests of excess and the fatness of the soul. Innocent of the ways of the world, I sensed and feared the potential embodied in those lewd pictures.

I sat thus, it seemed to be forever, not knowing why I felt so disturbed. It was totally dark when I heard Sophia calling from the hall. I barely managed to answer. She turned on the lights and found me.

"What has happened?" she cried out. "Where is the happy girl I left this afternoon? What is wrong?"

Although I had not known Sophia before this day she had been kinder than any other woman, and so I let my terrible secret slip out. She laughed.

"Darling you are jealous of these awful picture-women because your husband, whom you love, is looking at their naked bodies. Sometimes I think that women should never love anyone but themselves because we suffer such torments when our dreams and expectations are not met. But we can't help ourselves, can we?"

Sophia sat beside me and petted my hand. She told me not to mind his voyeurism because it would not make him love me any less.

"These things mean nothing to men," she counseled, "for they are naught but pacifiers for their sex."

Smiling, coaxing, she drew me out of my room and through the long, dark hall into Amna's brightly lit, happy flat, into the great room where a sumptuous supper was set out.

Automatically, I performed my duties as the new wife. I greeted the other wives with the respect due them, and noted, that although I was the most recent bride, being Zajid's and Amna's daughter-in-law raised me to a higher level than most. Still, it was impossible for me to clearly define my ranking in the women's hierarchy.

Somehow I managed to eat and drink, although my throat felt tight as if bound with a cord. I complimented Amna on her food, which was delicious and new to me. That night she served palau with raisins, nuts and tender morsels of meat, a dish of spicy greens and lamb, and rice-flour pudding with ground pistachios. Pickled fruit and vegetables, herbed onion slices in vinaigrette, chopped fruit—fresh and candied—in delicate porcelain bowls accompanied each dish, enhancing its flavor to perfection.

After the meal we drank tea and talked. As in the village, most talk revolved around husbands and children. Some women, disgruntled, spoke frankly about their husband's shortcomings, oddities and quirks, while others would have nothing but praise for their husbands because they would never admit being bound to trying, terrible men.

"Don't believe a word this one says about her husband," whispered Sophia, "he beats her, and seldom comes home. She is so ashamed that she will never speak the truth."

It seemed, that here, as in the village, wives lived in a state of uncertainty. Most men neither informed their wives of their schedules nor their plans. They came and went as they pleased leaving the women forever in a state of anxious uncertainty. The reverse was true in the case of the men—their expectations were very high. Wives were to be ready and available when husbands desired their presence. Although Yussuf left a message that he would be coming home, it was not a guarantee, nor would he dream of stating his time of arrival.

The women commented with pleasure on their shopping trips, although some were kept short of funds and could buy almost nothing. Soon I felt drowsy. My head, cluttered by a myriad of new impressions was filled to the bursting point, and ached. Sophia noted my struggles to stay awake.

"I had a long day," she said, "I think I will retire."

The moment she gave the cue I thanked Amna for her kindness and hospitality and retired.

I crept down the dimly lit hallway, touching the rough concrete walls as I went. In my bedroom I let the tob slip from my body as I slid between the sheets. For a moment thoughts of this most overwhelming day crept into my mind only to be extinguished instantly by sleep.

• • • • •

I knew not when Yussuf came home that night. I slept soundly for a long time. So long in fact, that Aziza had to awaken me.

"Your husband will attend you shortly in the kitchen. You are going somewhere with him this morning, and he wants you to be ready," she warned.

I was instantly awake, remembering that today was the most important of days. The outcome of this day would determine my sexual life and fertility for years to come. Hurriedly I performed my daily ablutions, brushed my hair and dressed. Not for one moment did I want to delay what must be, nor did I want to offend my husband by foolish tardiness.

Yussuf, eating his breakfast, was reading what I soon learned was the morning newspaper. I ate in the kitchen and then, when he called, joined him in the living room. He was kind, asking about my first day in the city and whether I enjoyed living here. I responded enthusiastically. I told him of my purchase and the women's gifts, and displayed, full of pride, my newfound knowledge of money and its buying power.

My enthusiasm amused him. He smiled and said that I should go out more often with Amna and Sophia if it gave me such pleasure. Suddenly, it was time to leave. The chauffeur was waiting. Without trepidation I stepped onto the sidewalk and into the car. Yussuf, noting my excitement, took my hand, concealed by the sleeve of my tob for just a moment, saturating me with a feeling of great tenderness and peace. It is unusual for men of our culture to show affection outside the bedroom, and so I felt blessed.

The car moved in spurts and stops until it eventually came to a halt before a large, tumultuous market. Every kind of food was offered here, including a great variety of live animals caged, bound and penned. From my seat I saw only a small area, but even this segment intimidated me with its offerings and its bustling throng of buyers. Shrill calls, hypnotic sing-song and harsh, throaty commands emanated from the mouths of vendors, fishermen and traders in praise of their food stuffs. They exhorted and beguiled in Arabic, Swahili, the *lingua franca* of East Africa and a mishmash of Arabic and tribal dialects.

Yussuf told the chauffeur to shop for a few hours. He instructed him to purchase fruits, vegetables, lamb and goat meat.

"I will drive myself for an hour," he said, and moved into the driver's seat.

"I had to get rid of him," he explained, "if he were to see the clinic, there could be talk. No one must know, especially not my mother. She is grounded in tradition."

I understood. My shrewish haboba and most of the village women would have been outraged by our mission. Without hesitation they would have cast me out, or stoned me.

Yussuf pulled up behind a tall concrete building. Huge blue letters over its entrance proclaimed this to be the location of the EWAG corporation.

"Our doctor works for this company. EWAG has a clinic on the fourth floor for their employees. Their doctors are so renowned for their skill, that even the members of foreign embassies seek treatment here."

Quickly we stepped into the building. Without slowing his steps, Yussuf guided me into an old, clanky elevator. On the fourth floor we walked into a white, sterile waiting area reminding me of the desert's emptiness. There was to be no wait. The moment we entered a white-skinned, blue-eyed woman in a white cap and gown bustled forward.

"Is this Amina?" she asked. I nodded. "Come along," she said.

As I walked away from my husband, her hand on my arm gently pulling, I turned and looked at him a last time, I felt my eyes grow vast with sudden fright.

"I will pick you up soon," he said, comforting me. Then he was gone.

For three days following the operation I lay in my own bed recuperating. Before I left the clinic, Marie Latourelle, my doctor, said, "I restored you as best as I could. Yet, I had to remove a lot of scar tissue, so that for a few days you will experience pain and discomfort. You must rest to heal properly, and follow my nurse's instructions."

She was a gray-eyed woman of medium height who wore her dark blond short hair in a feminine, curly fashion. Tough, yet pleasant she exuded competence and self-assurance. I was wholly in awe of her.

I thanked her with all my heart, for her work was remarkably painless compared to the procedures I endured in the village. Asleep during the operation, I hadn't felt anything.

At home, Yussuf prevaricated skillfully about my condition. Simply implying that I was suffering from food poisoning, he rushed me straight to my bed.

My days in bed were rather pleasant. Finally, I was undisturbed for hours on end, giving me a chance to read the book Yussuf had given me shortly after the wedding. Since leaving the village my life had become magical. I was living the magnificent myth that circulated in the village—that pampered women lived easy lives—with flowing water, cars and electricity and most of all, shops. Wholly satisfied, I had seen, touched and tasted the very things women speculated about in the confinement of the hosh. For they had heard enticing tales, yet never knew exaggeration from truth.

Entitled *Beautiful Poetry*, the book in my hand was just one more wonder, a treasury of the best poems in Arabic. Containing the finest fruits of Islamic poets it sang of kings doing battle for the glory of Islam, of the sacrifice of one's life for a place in heaven. There were poems by the great Rumi, whom the Persians and Afghanis call Jelalludin Balkhi. Born in Afghanistan, he was revered in Konya, Turkey, a place to which his family fled before the armies of the Mongols. To understand fully what I read, I had to spend weeks learning about Persians and Afghanis, about Mongols, Turks and the places in the world where they resided. Sophia was all-knowing. Never could I ask a question that she couldn't answer.

After my first reading of these beautiful words, evening drew near, and a great desire arose in me for Yussuf to return. I desperately needed to speak to someone of the poems which so moved me, lest I should be drowned in joy. Aziza brought me soup and bread, believing me poisoned, but I required nothing more. Excitement stilled all hunger.

Thankfully, Yussuf came home early. How glad I was that he was affectionate, hugging me to his breast and asking about my progress. I satisfied his concerns for my health and then divulged my joy, my ecstasy.

Pleased with the effect of his gift, he asked me to read for awhile. At last, overcome by drowsiness, he fell asleep at my side, leaving me to contemplate my good fortune and the certainty that I was very much in love with him.

Confined to bed I soon grew restless. I thought to break the boredom by finding a new book in Yussuf's library, but to my surprise and utter dismay I found the door locked. Never, in my entire marriage, was it open again.

At first I was inclined to reveal my knowledge of this library, but a warning inner voice bade me not to. So, whenever I wanted to read I asked for books. Apparently choosing carefully, deliberating sometimes for days, he chose books for me, but he never allowed me to select, nor did he ever invite me into his private chambers.

During my days abed I saw little of Amna. My mother-in-law was not a cold woman. Eventually I realized she was intellectually starved, doubly restricted by culture and her own complacency. Whereas women of the same background and circumstance, whom I met later in my life, overcame cultural starvation and social isolation through their intellectual powers, Amna remained incapable of lifting herself out of mental poverty. Although she must have experienced, many years before me, the same transitions I endured now, she showed little kinship or sympathy for me. Perfunctorily she came to my bedside the second day I was laid up. She dutifully asked after my state of health and, having satisfied her obligation, she left, after drinking a single cup of tea.

But her friend, Sophia, was cut from a different cloth. She was an extraordinary woman. I formed this opinion of her early on, during my days of healing. When she entered my room it brightened. Her eyes were filled with warmth, her hands were filled with gifts. She brought small, thoughtful things, endearing morsels, a cloisonne pen, a small diary, a sweet perhaps.

No one had ever cared for me thus, and so I opened my heart to Sophia. Perhaps she saw something worthwhile in my nature, perhaps she herself was in need of a friend. Whatever the reason, suffice it to say, that she embraced me with a warmth usually reserved for daughters. Only later in life, did I fully understand the rarity of our relationship.

I rejoiced when she came to see me. She came every day, sometimes twice, and always stayed a good while. Like all truly beautiful women, she loved beauty for itself, and never allowed herself to be seen in a state of neglect. When she sat by my bedside in the comfortable chair Aziza positioned for her, she was a picture of graceful femininity.

Yet it would be an injustice to describe only her beauty. What truly raised her far above the crowd was her unique, intrepid spirit. It was present in her lively, warm eyes, her quick, quirky smile and the darting movements of her hands whenever she spoke of something that excited her. Soon, I realized that she had the brightest, quickest mind and could out-think us all. She intrigued me, and so one day I risked her rebuff by asking about her past.

"I would not like for you think that I am prying," I began. "But if it were agreeable to you, I would like to hear about your life. How did Abdullah find and marry you?"

"I will gladly tell you my story," she said kindly, "but it's a time-consuming tale, and it should wait for now. Rather, you should ask me about things concerning your new life in the city, so you can make the most of your days. Remember, and I warn you because I like you, that husbands have the power to ban their wives to live alone in the village."

I knew this to be true. Though some of my city fears remained, I savored already too many sweet moments here to ever want to live in the village again. By comparison, all my years in the village didn't amount to half the excitement and fun as one day in the city.

"How is it possible that village women lead such restricted, hidden lives, while the women in the city, although bound by the same laws have so much more freedom?" I asked.

"That's a good observation and a sad truth. But village women, in every corner of the world, are the most deprived of all creatures. They are kept ignorant of their rights and their freedoms, kept from the good things the world has to offer." Her green eyes, startling to this child of the dark-eyed village, gazed sadly at me. "Instead of being imbued with knowledge, they are indoctrinated with myths and folk tales, threatened and frightened with taboos, ostracism, violence and abandonment."

"*Ah, wy. Ah, wy,*" I moaned. "The people in my village might stone you for your opinion."

"I know that well," said Sophia cheerfully, "and I guard my tongue carefully, most times, but I trust you." She looked thoughtfully at me for a moment and added, "Although, I know not why I should have such trust so soon. Were you ever to betray me I should deny my words. And be assured my husband believes all I say explicitly and will back me."

"I could never betray you. I don't think I could betray anyone, but you, especially you—not ever," I cried fervently, and quickly continued, "How do you know so many things about women's lives? How did you come to form such heretical opinions?"

I felt uncomfortable, faithless and traitorous to religion and family. But at the same time, I listened, fascinated with the woman espousing such dangerous ideas.

"I need to go far back to give you an answer. As you know, I never lived the village way. I grew up in Cairo. My family travelled, often months-on-end, into many parts of the world. So I saw women's lives in India, Bangladesh, Thailand, Indonesia, Japan and the European countries.

"When living in Cairo, I, as a Christian, never wore a veil or Muslim garb. I dressed decently, according to local custom, but my dress was European. My introduction to the village occurred after my marriage, when Abdullah brought me to see the Nasredi haboba."

She smiled and gently pushed an errant strand of hair into place. "Oh, my dear," she went on, "that was thirty years ago. Then, she was in her prime. The now deserted compound brimmed with people and her power was awesome.

"During our meeting she loomed on her cushions like a poisonous spider in a web, ready to devour me had she but had a mouth large enough. Since she could not, she tried to destroy me. The woman who you know now as a shrunken, inconsequential mummy, was then large, fat and threatening. She began our meeting by asking if I were circumcised.

"'No,' I answered.

"'Then we shall have to prepare for the ceremony immediately,' said she.

"'No,' I told her, 'I won't have it. I am a married woman. My husband married me the way I am, and that is the way I am going to stay. No one is going to mutilate my body'"

Disbelief must have dispelled the look of fascination on my countenance, for a wide smile flickered over Sophia's face and she laughed, "You should have seen her reaction. It was as if someone were strangling her. Her eyes protruded and she roared that I, a foreign infidel, was not worthy to bear children if not properly purified. I rose from my seat and said, 'I came here to meet my husband's mother and pay her my respect. But you shall not insult me, for you know not who I am, neither do you do justice to your son who chose to marry me.' Having said this I walked away."

I held my breath in awe of such bravery. Sophia's smile became rueful at the memory of the exchange, but determined to complete the story she continued, "Now I was in a quandary. Wherever I turned, I was in her power. It was impossible to enter the men's quarters and enlist Abdullah's aid. My need to flee became so urgent that, wrapped in my new tob, I walked out into the scorching midday heat, and kept on walking. Heaven knows what could have become of me. I was so upset and angry that I would have walked into the desert until my feet gave out."

Assistance arrived for Sophia at the edge of the village, in the form of a small, kind woman. Laying her hand on Sophia's arm she said with authority, "You must seek shade or you shall perish, it is much too hot for living things to be out." When Sophia demurred that she had no place to go, the woman offered, "My house is small and poor, but it will shade you, and I have good water to drink."

Sophia found this tiny, brown woman, with skin so deeply creased that it resembled dried beef, irresistible, and followed her. Luck had led her to the village sheikha. Besides the exciser, she was the only woman in the village who earned and spent money. Sophia sat with her for a long time talking, learning much about the convoluted ways of the village. The sheikha was a bright woman with unusual intuition. Perhaps that's why she was a sheikha, performing the curative ceremonies and dances for those women who were possessed.

Sophia sipped her tea reminiscing, "Her thinking was as heretical as mine. Once I told her my troubles she chuckled, 'Sometimes I think that the troubles of women possessed by Zairan jinn begin at the moment of their circumcision. I hear their plaints of ill health and pain, their never-ending discomfort. They suffer much pain in their breasts as well, and their hearts hurt.'

"This extraordinary, little woman totally understood her world and the role she played therein.

"'Look at me,' she gestured, 'I have more freedom than any woman in the village. Consorting with spirits empowers me—nay more—it gives me license to act where other women can't. I see and hear things others do not. I have learned that the world is not arranged to favor women. Through my work I can help them a little, which makes me glad.'

"This sheikha was married to a fellah who rented the fields he planted, and she was amused that she earned more than her husband.

"'He was fearful I'd leave him when first I mastered my Zairan jinn and began to hold the healing dance. Along with Hadija, the exciser, we are the only women in control of their own destiny.'

"Time passed quite pleasantly for the two of us, and eventually Abdullah found me. Hundreds of eyes spy on the stranger in a village, particularly a woman, so his search was brief. Rewarding the sheikha with a handsome cash present ensured that the villagers would only hear of a pleasant visit. No more, no less. The moment I had Abdullah to myself I told him there would be no slicing up my body.

"'If you are to side with your mother you'd better take your sword and kill me now, for I will not submit to torture.'

"I said this hotly and added, that furthermore, I wanted to leave the village that instant. To his credit, he didn't hesitate. He knew I meant what I said, and broke with tradition. He calmed me down and installed me with Amna, who was then still living in the village, until we left next morning. Thus, Amna and I became friends."

"Were you not afraid of Abdullah and the family? How could one lonely, strange woman resist a village?" I wanted to know.

"It wasn't much of a gamble," smiled Sophia. "Abdullah and I have a rich and exceedingly pleasing marital relationship. I believe he understood from the beginning that our pleasure in each other rested in the very fact that I was different. He was madly in love with me, and knew me well enough to trust that I'd kill myself, or him, if I were forced in this way."

"I would like to know more about the Nasredis and this house. Why did they, village folk, come here?" I wondered.

"When we first came to live in this house, Abdullah explained to me how the family's lifestyle evolved in the previous century. Originally the family earned their living by farming their land along the Nile. Yet farming is uncertain business. Add to that growing families, multiplying faster than the crops, and you have problems.

"One of the great-great-grandfathers, Ahmed Abdul Rahman, became a merchant. Hofryat was ideally positioned. Two hundred miles away from Khartoum it was a stop-over place for caravans trading along the Nile and those trading with the nomadic peoples of the plateau."

Sophia stretched gracefully and laughingly said, "Fortunately for us, the Nasredi men are intelligent and industrious. Through their ambition our family prospered, buying property in the commercial part of Khartoum, and building a warehouse close to the docks. At this juncture most men lived year round in Khartoum while their wives and children remained in the village, but then, rich men, with strong family ties brought their families to town. At their insistence this building was purchased with shops at street level, and room for families above."

Sophia's eyes, dark and vast, locked onto mine, "Can you imagine what it must have been like for the first village women arriving here? Before the flats were laid out, before the servants were hired and communal rules were established? I am told that at first the women tried to live according to custom, yet that was burdensome. What worked in the village was not suited to the cramped, crowded spaces of the city. In time, our family learned from other city families."

We must have talked for hours. Sophia warned me to remain smiling and pleasant at all times to make my residence permanent. "Remember, crying eyes and bitter faces get women sent to the village."

I think she was lonely among our family, and sorely missed her own two daughters, whom she sent to be raised by her sister, the wife of an Air France executive in Paris, when they were nine and ten years old. No longer willing to wait, the family had fanatically insisted on their circumcision, but Sophia defied them. Before anyone became aware of her intentions she served Abdullah an ultimatum.

"Let me take our daughters to my sister. With your blessing all will be well. But if you force mutilation on my daughters I shall divorce you and go back to my family. You will never see me again."

And Abdullah, who loved her with a fierce, obsessive love, a passion that despite constricting laws had allowed her to retain her identity, permitted the girls to go.

"If he was on your side why did you not prevent the excision keeping the girls with you in Sudan?" I asked.

"One can never be certain and safe where children are concerned. Anyone in the family could have used my temporary absence and forced the girls. Countless times I have heard how aunts and grandmothers gleefully kidnapped small girls and did the deed. No judge and no law protects the child or the unwilling parents. Once the act is completed the girl's life is ruined."

When Sophia finally left I felt as if a sandstorm passed over me. Her vibrancy resonated within me. My head ached from hundreds of new words showered upon me, words whose meaning I tried to discern. Closing my eyes I just lay there while her treacherous thoughts swirled through my mind. Surely she would have been stoned if anyone had heard her.

Vaguely, thoughts began to form that it was my duty to report her revolutionary ideas. Didn't my connection to family and custom demand that I speak? However, such nebulous considerations vanished instantly when I remembered my own treasonous shortcut to motherhood.

CHAPTER  *Six*

The moment I was healed my married life truly began. There was no more pain when Yussuf joined me in bed. Yussuf came home almost every night. Often he did not eat with the other men, but chose to share tidbits with me. He was well read and seemed to enjoy talking about my discoveries, about books, about algebra—my new passion kindled by a book Sophia had loaned me, and about his sometimes difficult work as an exporter.

Willingly, and at length, he explained that the gum-Arabic supply of the world is mainly derived from sources in Sudan, and that the Nasredi company was doing a brisk business in this commodity as well as in cotton and cotton seed. He purchased these stocks from local sources and then sold them all over the world. No wonder that I was terribly proud of my husband. He was a paragon among Sudanese men. For, besides being kind, bright and good-looking, he was also considerate, an uncommon attribute. Indeed, I deemed myself so blessed that each day I praised Allah.

Three months after the restoration I missed my monthly blood. Elated, I asked Sophia what to do. She advised me to keep my sweet secret for another moon to see what would develop. "Strange cravings could be an indication of your condition," she acknowledged. "But wait awhile. It is a miserable office to tell a man that he will not be a father after raising his hopes."

So I waited patiently for two moons to complete their passage. Then I was certain. One night, with Yussuf safely installed in my bed, relaxed and happy, I told him. "Yussuf, I think you are going to be father."

At first he did not seem to understand, his eyes showing confusion, but when I repeated the message he sat bold upright and said with comical surprise, "Already? After only five months?"

He jumped from the warm bed in his baggy night clothes and ran off without slippers. Soon he returned to tell that he'd informed his father and Amna. Overflowing with joy he hugged and kissed me, as if I had performed a miracle.

"The operation! See, it paid off already. Other fellows who live by the book have to wait years, and here I am going to be a father." He looked at me expectantly. "What does it feel like? Will it be a boy?"

"Who can tell?" I laughed. "You must wait and praise Allah's kindness."

Time flew. Yussuf treated me like queen, granting my every wish. One morning he handed me a roll of money and said, "Go out with my mother and Sophia and buy all the things you will need for our child. Buy the best, and buy what pleases you."

Following Sophia's advice I bought the crib she recommended, and positioned it in the brightest corner of my room. Next to it sat the wide, many-pillowed English pram, because Sophia said it was versatile.

Pregnancy became me. Never had I felt so well, and although my figure was gradually enlarging, I would never again look as vibrant, glowing and healthy as I did then. Yussuf gloried in my plush beauty and spent every available moment with me. Every wish I uttered was fulfilled momentarily, and every night he fell asleep, his hand on my extended belly. As my pregnancy progressed it was cumbersome to have him close, yet I never had the heart to complain how burdensome his heavy arm was. As my delivery drew near Yussuf's family exerted great pressure to control the event.

Yussuf, to share our joy, sparing no expense, invited the inner circle of the family to a splendid banquet. The great room was filled with flowers in tall vases, attar of roses perfumed the apartment, and servants carrying large platters and huge trays walked from the elevator to the kitchen. Wearing my most elegant gown, long-sleeved, richly embroidered and falling straight to the ground, I felt beautiful and special. A diaphanous, midnight-blue and silver shawl covered my hair, silver slippers my feet.

Our guests arrived in a festive mood, but their spirits truly exalted during the banquet. The aroma of cardamom, cinnamon, cumin and mace mingled with the scent of fresh cilantro, of nutmeg, coriander and clove. Shorba, or puree of lamb Khartoum, a most delicious soup with peanut butter and lemon, was served to be consumed with rice. Beside it was a bowl of Salatet Zabady Bil Ajur, a cucumber and yoghurt salad that my family loved. Rice, plain, sweet or spicy, with chicken and beef followed. Roast lamb and fowl competed with Molokhia, a green leaf vegetable dish. Eggplant with tomato meat sauce and yoghurt vied for attention with Mullaah Bamyah, an okra dish, and Mashi, our beef-stuffed tomatoes. There were Kofta, the ground meatballs, and a fish pyramid with green sauce, and Tamayya (Falafel) the green hamburgers, and Sudanese Custard and fruits and nuts, and tidbits too numerous to count. And, of course, no meal would be served without mountains of kisra and Fool Medemmas, fava beans.

Ending the hours of slow feasting, came servants bearing the tea sets laden with sweets and baked desserts of Egypt, greeted by the sighs of our guests. Slowly sipping our tea and sampling morsels of sweets, we listened to family stories told by the elders. Among the cluster of men jokes were told, vibrating the room with ensuing laughter. I sat flanked by Amna and Sophia in the seat of honor. My wedding had afforded me less attention than was showered upon me that night. Of course, some only came to me indirectly through praise heaped upon Yussuf, but I was well satisfied. I gloried, uplifted, in the moment.

However, the exceedingly pleasing mood of our gathering was rudely destroyed by Zajid proclaiming, "No doubt that Amina will return to the village for the birth. The local midwife will deliver the child in the presence of my mother. All of our children were born thus, and so it shall be with Yussuf's."

My face fell, all joy drained from my heart. Yussuf forestalled the ensuing debate, ending the night calm and festive. Yet, the very next day, drawn together in family council, were Zajid's brothers and their wives, highest ranking in the family. Over time it had become apparent that Yussuf was an important, integral partner in the family business. Therefore, his firstborn, if male, would be of interest to all, as he would be heir to Yussuf's position.

Like a heavy boulder between trees, my middle swollen grotesquely, I sat between Sophia and Amna. Zajid's pronouncements made my blood run cold. A chill shook my heavy body, for in the village, frightful Hadija would deliver my baby. I never wanted her to touch me again. No doubt, the discovery of my restoration would have horrendous consequences.

"Of course," said Amna, "the child must be born in the house of the haboba, so she can inspect it, as is the custom."

Everyone, excepting Abdullah and Sophia, joined to form a bleating chorus praising birthing in the home compound. Silently I prayed, repeating the same words, "Allah, who art great, permit me delivery at home."

The Highest must have heard my prayer. In the face of such formidable pressure Yussuf exhibited amazing courage and strength. "I am the child's father, " Yussuf began, looking around the room with a challenging frown. "I live in a modern world. We are wealthy. We can afford to have our children born where the children of royalty and ambassadors are delivered. In a hospital. My son shall be born there."

As might be expected, his speech caused an outburst of anger and hostility. Although citified, our family's roots were deeply embedded in the village. Defying their vociferous opposition, Yussuf remained firm, and I remained in Khartoum for the delivery.

When my birthing time drew near, Yussuf contacted the doctor who had enabled the conception. My son was born easily with hardly a pain, although he was a big, strong, healthy baby. Black-downed was the crown of his head and creamy his skin, strong the grip of his tiny fingers which clung to mine from the first. I would have fallen in love instantly, even had I been inclined to resist. I loved him from the first with passion encompassing tenderness and devotion, with a love stronger and deeper than any other in my life. The nurses and Marie Latourelle, the doctor, shared my happiness, rejoicing in my good fortune.

As is often the case, no joy is without a bitter drop of sadness. In my highest happiness, when holding my babe to my breast, I realized that my gladness of bearing a son was sweetened by the knowledge that he couldn't be snatched from me by the midwife. I remembered with horror constricting my throat, how Khurshid had been snatched away, mutilated and killed.

"Not for you the mutilation," I murmured to my son, who lay cradled in my arm, "for you just the smallest sacrifice of a snippet of foreskin."

Beaming in the manner of new fathers, Yussuf took us home the next day. Indeed, he was a man favored by Allah over others, prospering in every business venture, enjoying excellent health, and a family begun with the prayed-for son. Thus, beaming and happy, we entered our home and presented our son to the family.

Henceforth my status rose to new heights. Forgiven was the breach with tradition. I became Zajid's favorite daughter-in-law since I had borne the only male grandchild thus far. In fact, Zajid sat at family gatherings, my son resting in his sheltering arm, and discussed at length my son's inherited attributes. He delighted in the strength of his tiny fingers, the determined way in which he tried to raise his head, and the force exerted by his sturdy legs when he pushed his feet against Zajid's hands.

It was touching to hear him claim that he could see already in the babe's miniscule nose the hawk-beak of the great Abdul Rahman. Given the power of his wishful eye, he also recognized his father's forehead, his own eyes and Amna's mouth. Of course, Amna saw other family features in the child's face as well. We named him Abdul, after his famous grandfather, and Hassan Majid, in honor of important uncles, but we would call him Hassan.

I was content. My searching eyes discerned nothing in Hassan's face, except his own sweet features. So we were happy. I read and learned and cared for my son. Besides these most delightful tasks I kept Yussuf happy and satisfied. When Hassan was six months old we made the arduous trek to the village to satisfy my parents and the haboba's desire to view the child.

In Hofryat everyone was well pleased. They praised the child, passing him from hand to hand, savoring his softness and clean smell. However, even though everyone was kind, exuberant even, in their praise, I felt ill at ease. Something fundamental must have changed in me. The cord which had bound me to my family and the village had been irreparably cut. Seeing my sweet babe handed about, being touched by hands less than clean, I fought an urge to tear him away and hide him safely inside my tob.

Yet, there was nothing I could do but watch over him and suffer. Strangely, I had begun to think of my family as *them*, as separate from me. Moreover, I felt alone, disconnected, as there was little to say to them. For they still talked about the same things women had brooded over like hens sitting on eggs, since the Pharaoh's time: birth, death, weddings, marriage, kisra preparation and hosh sweeping. Listening to their placid murmurings, I wanted to scream, "Wake up. There is a world not far from here where women go to school. Where they go to markets and handle the family's money. A world filled with hustle and bustle so exciting it would strike you dumb with astonishment."

Yet, to what purpose would I have made such a speech? They wouldn't have understood, nor would they have wanted to. They were sublimely content in their prison. I counted the moments when we'd leave again, my eyes seeing the village as a stranger. I noticed the infernal dust, the dirt that clung to everything, the bare, calloused, dirty feet, the black lines under fingernails, flies, children afflicted with sores around their eyes, and the open wounds that would not heal of their own accord.

How I wished I could be my old self again for the duration of our stay, but I had become another woman—a woman who did not belong anymore—who would never return if given a choice. Even my parents were strangers, speaking slower and more awkwardly than I remembered, often about nothing. It was amazing that so profound a change had occurred within me in such a short time. Exposed to witty, scintillating and stimulating people, like Sophia, I thought the village folk dull by comparison.

How fervently I had inhaled Sophia's teachings about hygiene, admired Aziza's rigorous cleaning regime, and come to appreciate the luxuries of modern baths. Although the villagers were extremely concerned with cleanliness, and I knew this well, they simply lacked the means to achieve it. Beholding the village now I felt great sadness, noticing flaws where before there were none, and it was precisely my new discerning, critical mind that soured my taste of homecoming. No wonder that tremendous relief filled me the moment we were tucked into our car for the return home.

"I am so glad that we are going home, I am weak with relief," I admitted to Yussuf. "I worried that Hassan could contract an illness. I am so changed already that I can't see myself living in the village ever again."

"It is true. You are fundamentally changed—changed for the better. I like that you smile more, that you have a sense of humor, and I am impressed with the sheer volume of knowledge you have acquired. Over and above the promise of your father, you are special. He told me, 'She is different, not like the others,' and he spoke the truth."

●   ●   ●   ●   ●

Ensconced in my happy life as in a cocoon, I came to believe that contentment was more desirable than ecstasy. Sophia proceeded with my education, bringing me books (foreign authors translated into Arabic), which I devoured.

"Don't tell Yussuf about this one," she'd warn handing me a particular book. At first I demurred. *Was he not my husband whom I had to obey? Was it not my duty to tell him everything? After all, the Qur'an said I must do so.*

Why should you? asked the temptress of my mind.

"The Qur'an also says that you should be treated justly, and with honor. Is it just and honorable that Yussuf locks the doors to his private quarters, denying you access? Is it just that he parcels his books out like a miser? Where does the Qur'an state that a woman must be deprived of knowledge, and be kept in semi-ignorance?" Sophia, eyes splendidly flashing like lightening, gestured, the Holy Book in her hand. "As it stands, men do not trust us to read with critical judgement. They believe only books deemed mild and innocuous are good for us as if we had no brains to sift the intellectual chaff from the grain. The Qur'an gives men no right of censorship; that is a privilege men have taken for themselves. Men have their secrets and we have ours."

"Do you keep secrets from Abdullah?" I asked her.

"Of course, I do," she said rolling her eyes. "If he knew that I read the books by Daphne du Maurier, Balzac, Tolstoy, or the poems of Byron, Shelly and Keats, or worse, T. S. Eliot, to name but a few, he'd have spasms. Oh, I might get him to relent, if I blackmailed him again, but why stir up trouble?"

To me, her last statements were problematic for a variety of reasons. First, there was the matter of forbidden books. Few of the authors she mentioned so casually were available to me. Admittedly, my passion for more books was quickly becoming an obsession. I was driven to read these forbidden books—even if it meant losing my life.

Then, there was the matter of Sophia's position in the family, and the matter of her marital relations with Abdullah, which interested me for some time. To elucidate my situation I had been observing their private life carefully.

Abdullah, besotted by Sophia, wished only to hold onto her. He loved her with such depth and passion that he could not bear to be without her. Subsequently, such passion bestowed extraordinary power upon her. Of all the marriages I knew, theirs was the most unusual arrangement. Somehow they had worked out a partnership, touching to behold, in which both seemed equal. Each ceded whatever ground they could, yet retrenching, stood doubly firm on the remainder of their beliefs.

Zajid and Abdullah were the most powerful men in the family with Zajid, being the elder by two years, outranking Abdullah. Therefore Sophia's standing in the family should have been equal to, or maybe slightly lower, than Amna's. Yet I had observed, that whenever the family gathered for a celebration or a women's dinner, that Sophia, although treated with great respect and formality, could hope for little warmth or inclusion into the women's circle. Instead she was barred from intimacy, excluded from true friendship. Amna was her only friend, a circumstance I believe was a result of Amna's imperturbable placidity; once Sophia became her friend, family politics could not disturb her loyalty.

"Forgive me if I ask the forbidden, but I must know. Why do our women treat you with the cold respect reserved for strangers? You are the kindest of women and should be cherished, and yet, they exclude you."

Sophia's silver green eyes danced with mirth, and she burst out laughing. Her long hair which she always wore loose when among women tossed about as if joining in the hilarity. Without hesitating she blurted out, "But, Precious, haven't you figured it out yet? I am the unclean one. The only one among them unharmed, left intact. The only one who can truly enjoy her husband. Furthermore, despite my supposed unfitness, I was chosen in marriage. More so, I was openly pursued, courted and asked to consent. Something they could never dream of."

Her slender hands open and upturned as in praise, seemed to delineate her words.

"It aggravates the proper wives that we are happy and doting on one another. Never have they seen me unhappy. For my Abdullah is a kind man while their husbands often have cruel ways, which they must endure without choice. Perhaps I aggravated things proclaiming that sex need not hurt, and that one can bear lovely children without being cut and sewn shut beforehand."

My face has always been an open book, and now Sophia read incredulity there. I marveled at her courage—to speak thus was inconceivable to me—but she went on to strengthen her point.

"So you see, every day's dawning paints rosy their uncomfortable reminder—me—living proof that their torture is useless. Forevermore, looking into my face they must contemplate the distressing fact that I lead a most pleasant life, proving their own existence to be a malignant lie and hoax."

Instantly, I understood that her power was stupendous—equal to Abdullah's even—because she could deny him; she owned her own fortune. Were he to divorce her she could walk away with her head held high. He adored her, and she was invincible. Impregnable to all appearances, yes, but what if she crossed him, or tried to leave? I had heard of husbands killing their wives rather than let them walk away.

Admittedly, I identified more with Sophia than the other women in the family. Had I not been restored by a doctor? I felt no pain while having relations and I enjoyed the peace of mind that I would never be infibulated again. Like my inspiring mentor I read, daily expanding my mind. I mulled over the probability of achieving the same sort of balanced relationship with my husband that Sophia enjoyed—a state of equality.

Although I was happy in my marriage, my conviction grew daily that being an equal like Sophia was much more desirable than my traditional, protected state. Already my understanding of the world had grown quickly, as if a stone flung into a quiet pond had caused a wave to spread in ever lager circles. Beyond every new discovery I found another and yet another. Observing Sophia fostered my belief that greater independence lay grounded in education. So, I, too, wanted to be well educated. I presented my problem to Sophia.

"How can I get more books? Would you let me read those forbidden books you talked about? I promise to keep their knowledge to myself."

"Amina, dear, we have a problem." Sophia's lovely face expressed regret. "I have never seen Arabic translations of these books, perhaps they don't exist. I don't know."

"But you read them, indeed, you said, you own them," I countered.

"Certainly I own them, but they are written in French and English."

I was crushed. How could I learn without the books? Sophia saw my dismay and to console me she told me the story of her life.

Long ago, her ancestors lived in Circassia, a region in the northwest Caucasus of Russia. According to Sophia, Circassia was Paradise. A land of fruitful orchards and fields, mountains, streams and verdant valleys. Circassian men, she said, were noted for tall stature, the women were celebrated for their beauty. Poets lauded their creamy complexions, their heavy tresses of blond and honey. Yet the greatest praise reserved in their poems lauded the "celestial" eyes of the "fairy women."

Her clan dispersed from the region in the mid-sixteenth century, during the persistent, fearsome Persian invasions continuing well into the seventeenth century.

"I believe my ancestors fled because most Circassians converted to Islam and became Sunni Muslims, thereby pleasing the conquerors and gaining protection, while our clan retained their Christian faith."

Such resistance was heresy to the conquerors. Sophia's clan, viciously persecuted, fled, settling in Lebanon where peoples of many faiths lived peacefully together because tolerance was good for business and trade. Yet, in the mid-nineteenth century, the Druse Muslims began to slaughter their Christian Maronite neighbors. During the ensuing bloodbath many of her relatives were murdered.

"My family was fortunate and managed to escape to Alexandria where I grew up. Already at age three I was taught French, English and Arabic, a regimen adhered to throughout my youth. So you see, Dear, I have no problem reading whatever I like in world literature."

I said nothing. Her words fell like crushing blows. Suddenly I felt defeated. I turned inward, as is the village's way when hurt comes from beyond. Outwardly, I remained in careful balance, a feat achieved with utmost willpower, leaving me consumed inside with the wish to penetrate the marvelous world of ideas.

Days passed. Then, a few days before Ramadan, Sophia hosted a fabulous dinner for the Nasredi women. Her efforts, combined with her unique touch produced a tempting banquet of Lebanese dishes. Meats cooked in yoghurt, pigeon breasts in savory sauces, kabobs, vegetables with dressings of mint, honey and yoghurt, various breads, sweets and fruits. Our hearts sang the moment we savored the aromas of the many spices while feasting our eyes on the colorful, many-textured bounty of the spread. Usually women ate sparingly. Every day we prepared small, well-seasoned dishes that satisfied our children's needs and appetites, but on grand occasions women ate with gusto, tasting everything offered.

Honeyed praise poured into the ears of our hostess; however, while Sophia mingled with her guests, they maligned her unmercifully behind her back.

"See how willful and arrogant she is? She acts as if she is royalty."

So spoke the most envious. I knew enough by now to recognize the jealousy contained in their slander. Harsh criticisms came easily because

Sophia stood up for herself, defending her rights vigorously. Sometimes, I admit, she did so in a most free, direct manner, which is abhorrent to our culture, and seemed tactless on occasion.

Yet, in my heart I always knew she was right, that her seemingly confrontational style offered the quickest path to the truth. Too often I observed that the very same women chiding her, loved and praised the meeker, defenseless women. They manipulated the faint of heart to their advantage, while despising and maligning the strong.

After the long feast, Sophia sat beside me while sipping her tea and said in a conspiratorial fashion, "How would you like to learn French? I will teach you. You are bright and learn quickly. I think you will speak and read the language in no time."

The prospect of such an opportunity took me aback; words failed me. How does one give thanks when the gift is overwhelmingly beautiful? I silently hugged Sophia, and the passion of my embrace must have been most expressive, for she said, "We shall begin tomorrow."

"Sophia," I confided, "not only am I ignorant of languages, but when you speak of foreign countries I am puzzled beyond belief, for I know nothing of such places."

"You shall have the best geography book in my library, and we shall peruse the maps of the world. Soon, you will know all there is to know about the globe," promised Sophia. Meanwhile, surrounded by women conversing about the enticements of the souk, I waited impatiently for tomorrow to come.

Whenever I compared Sophia and Amna, their differences struck me as unbridgeably vast—so vast, that I marvelled at their friendship. How could two people of such opposite character and disposition be so close? While Sophia brimmed with ideas and kept alive a vital curiosity, Amna's mind was still, as untroubled by thoughts and questions as a deep, protected pond. I wondered if perhaps long ago as a child, Amna had been bright and curious. Perhaps she had been, but was now broken by years of intellectual deprivation?

Married to wealthy Zajid at thirteen, Amna lived a protected life with little toil or hardship. She might have found many interesting pursuits after moving to the city, but her complacency and mental torpor allowed her to wallow in a comfortable mud of sameness every day of her life.

In the mornings she rose, proceeding by cleaning, preening and beautifying her body. She ate, shopped or met with the other ladies and talked about nothing for hours. In the afternoon she lunched, napped, visited some more, ate and eventually slipped into bed at night, only to begin the same cycle the following morning. Long ago, when her children were young, there must have been long periods of time devoted to them. But even then, she most often turned the children over to the servants' care.

By comparison, Sophia lived life as the bee, utilizing every precious moment of the day. Yet, she allowed herself relaxation between the work hours and study time.

It was exceedingly impolite to ask direct personal questions in our culture, but finally I gathered my courage and asked her, "Explain what bonds you to Amna. To my thinking you are an ill-matched pair, and yet you seem to be genuinely fond of each other."

She explained that Amna's very complacency calmed the family storm during Sophia's first visit, that they were almost the same age, married to brothers of the same social stratum, and lived in the same house. Those were powerful inducements to live harmoniously. Sophia, ever determined, manipulated the tone and content of their meetings, filling them with humor and fun, thus ensuring the survival of the relationship.

Since Sophia was independently wealthy, and as part of her marriage agreement had retained full power of her fortune, she spent large portions of her days managing her funds. She invested, divested, bought property and traded in goods.

Fate had bestowed upon me an amazing fortune in this remarkable friend. Who better to teach me algebra, geography and French? Who else to invest me with the intangible insights stemming from childhood experiences, a different religion and world travel. In the village learning was viewed as men's prerogative—the concept of the learned woman did not exist. So, when Sophia instructed me to teach my children all that I knew, I was at first taken aback. I had never thought of myself as a teacher.

Nevertheless, heeding her advice, I tended to Hassan. I always spoke to my beautiful boy as if he were able to understand everything I said. His dark eyes sparkled with interest and the desire to please as he tried faithfully to replicate my messages.

Four times weekly I left the sleeping Hassan in Aziza's care and joined Sophia for my French lesson in her exquisitely furnished apartment. Arriving in those first days, I was overwhelmed by the foreign flavor of the flat. I became claustrophobic by the jumble of objects crowding the room, as I was accustomed to bare walls and a minimum of furnishings.

Besides tables, lamps, chairs and couches, which I had accepted reluctantly, her flat startled and confused my untrained eye with paintings by Van Dyck, Rembrandt, Degas and, most befuddling of all, Gauguin, whose island maidens appeared to be deformed, out of proportion. Later, when I felt free to comment on such things, Sophia confirmed my feelings. Gauguin's period of primitivism, she assured me, made bodies appear flat and distorted.

Islam allows no depictions of real life, of figurative art, and so all paintings and tapestries were hidden in her private sanctum, a treasure-filled room entered only by Sophia, Zajid and privileged me.

Her priceless art, possessed long before her marriage, was a considerable family investment, and astutely she reasoned it was not wrong to live among the items she had known all her life until they could be sold for the best price. For as long as I knew Sophia her art objects were never sold.

Furthermore, Sophia owned machines that made what passed for music, but sounded to me like cacophony. My ears were used to the pleasant blend of flutes, drums and simple stringed instruments in sweet, wailing, monotonously repetitive songs. However, over time and with Sophia's help, I came to like much of the music I heard in her flat.

Within a year I spoke, wrote and read French well enough to please Sophia. By that time I had also absorbed enough knowledge of the globe to place my finger with confidence on any country and know its name and capital. Moreover, for the more prominent countries, I had bits of information of the inhabitants, their way of life, their culture.

Finally, after months of tutoring, Sophia decided the time had come for my ultimate test.

"You are my Pygmalion, my creation. Now you shall perform for the world," she cried gayly. Of course, this remark led me to read about Pygmalion and compare myself to the romantic myth, the marble form made flesh through love.

"You too were like a diamond in the rough. Now you sparkle, scintillate and dazzle." Her happiness was infectious and I believed her when she promised me that my coming out into European society would be memorable.

"It shall be a light event with well-connected people," she mused. "There should be no pressure on you, yet there should be a challenge of some sort."

Her words stirred my imagination. In my mind I rehearsed the French phrases polite society used. My mind was awhirl with questions one might ask of me, as well as my clever responses. Yet, as most things in life, events often turn out other than what we envision. The occasion of my "coming out" was case in point for the old adage.

Well-connected as she was, it was fairly easy for Sophia to have us invited to a luncheon given by the French Ambassador's wife. Bedecked in carefully selected outfits and jewels, we arrived at the home of Madam Thibodeau. I could hardly breathe during the long drive into the green part of Khartoum. Sophia chatted lightly in French trying to put me at ease, yet nothing relieved my tension. At last, we arrived at the stately home.

I was to discover, in years to come, places more grand than this home, but at that time it was to me what fairy tales are to children, a dream. An ornate, hand-wrought gate opened for our car and we proceeded through white marble portals down a palm-shaded drive which ended in front of a large, white, pillared house. Sophia informed me that originally the house was built in the Moorish style, but had by its many different residents been altered over the years and added to with classic Greek design.

"The columns are Ionic, as you can see by the acanthus leaves on the top, but we will learn this tomorrow."

Forever my teacher, she never let slip an opportunity. Surrounding the house were the most well-designed, charming gardens, drawing the eye before concentrating on the house. Shaded bowers, fountains and walkways of crushed, white rock wound through beds of flowering plants; all were carefully chosen and interwoven to please the eye with color, texture and aroma, and so to enchant guests taking their leisure in their midst.

Inside the house pleasant coolness refreshed the visitor. Ushered across the marble floor of a large hall by a native butler, turbaned, and wearing a long, flowing, white robe, we reached the dining room which held a table so grand it could seat at least thirty people. Excepting a monumental sideboard, two huge flower arrangements and a magnificent, over-sized carpet, the room was bare in deference to Muslim guests who came to dine.

Dismissing the butler, Madam Thibodeau came to greet us, kissing Sophia's cheek, and warmly welcoming me to her house. I responded that I was enchanted to be in her charming home and remarked on her wonderful gardens.

Madam thanked me and looked well pleased. Sophia, in passing, pressed my hand signifying that I had performed well.

"We shall not dine in this formal room," announced Madam, leading us to an adjacent, much smaller chamber. The walls of this room were covered by elongated panels of rose colored damask, framed by ivory painted wood. The oval table with chairs for ten were designed in the style of Louis XIV, as Sophia edified me in an aside. Here, as in the larger dining room, gigantic Chinese vases held artful arrangements of diverse, fragrant flowers that I had never seen before.

Lavish settings of fine china, crystal and sterling silver, and a low arrangement of creamy flowers atop fine Brussels lace linen made the table a creation I would never forget. Mentally I compared our tables to this splendid array and found them dismally lacking in style, where, by tradition, everyone ate with their "clean" hand—even the palows, chalows and puddings—scooping from a communal platter with bits of bread. It was with foresight that Sophia had taught me the uses of the different utensils on a European table so I would not disgrace her.

Madam Thibodeau bade me sit to Sophia's right, while she sat to her left at the head of the table. Seated beside me, by design I am sure, was Marie Latourelle, the doctor who had played such an important part in my life. When I addressed her in her mother tongue, thanking her, a vastly pleased smile lit up her face. She congratulated me profusely on the fluency and proficiency of my French, and asked how my son and husband were faring. We spoke for a long time until the neighbor on her right claimed her attention. In deference to us, besides me there was another Sudany lady present—no men had been invited to lunch. The other guests departed soon after coffee and dessert, but we were asked to stay.

After lunch, Madam walked us through her shady gardens. For awhile she walked beside me and kindly asked many questions about my mother, the village, my husband and my baby. Sophia had told me that she was a brave, intelligent and kind-hearted woman with a dictatorial bent, which was a bonus to her husband when she had to arrange difficult affairs in foreign lands.

"If she takes a liking to a person, she would defend this person's rights and liberties, even though her own life might be endangered. That's the kind of woman she is—upstanding, unyielding. I have seen how she helped, and saved lives, on numerous occasions."

Late in the afternoon, shortly before leaving, we were served ices and lady fingers in one of the shady bowers where we sat leisurely in cushioned lounges. Taking our leave, Madam Thibodeau asked us to visit again, while Sophia hoped that Madam would join us one evening for a ladies' supper, an invitation which Madam graciously accepted.

I could hardly wait for Yussuf to come home that night. Excitedly, I spilled my tale of this unusual, exhilarating afternoon. But his closed, stern face dampened my happiness.

"I wish Sophia would be making her visits by herself instead of involving my wife," he grumbled. Now I saw that he was visibly displeased.

"What do you want with European company, anyway? Our ways were good enough for our women for centuries. There is nothing for you to gain by such visits. To the contrary, your head might be filled with stupid notions and fancies. I don't mind Sophia teaching you geography and algebra, it adds to your usefulness, but her European company is too light and careless in behavior and thought. I forbid you to ever go again."

He scowled, his handsome face suddenly a frightening mask. His last words were spoken with such great anger that I was shocked. I would have never believed that my otherwise progressive husband would make such a scene over a simple women's luncheon.

"I thought you would be glad, nay, overjoyed that I could make such a powerful acquaintance," I protested. His anger had reminded me how quickly I had abandoned the village way. For I had not even thought of asking his permission. I was puzzled. Had I truly forgotten to ask, or had I, fearing that he wouldn't consent, deliberately kept quiet about the affair? Did I, deep down, know that he was not quite as liberal as I thought him to be? It was frightening to contemplate that I truly did not know my husband all that well.

"It is for me to make such connections; not my wife. This is an intolerable state of affairs, and you will not participate in any such outings. Go shopping with Amna. Fine. But these excursions with Sophia have to stop. I shall presently talk to Abdullah."

He stomped from the room slamming the door so hard it shattered part of the frame. I don't know why, but I began to cry. I wept not knowing why, for it was his right to deny me. Did I not lead a life a thousand times better than most women in Sudan? Did he not give me more freedom than I ever had before? More freedom than most women? So why was I crying? Perhaps my tears came with the realization that when one begins to savor freedom and thought, the craving for more becomes overpowering. Perhaps when a person drinks this strong, intoxicating brew of knowledge and freedom one cannot stop but must drink more.

Deep in thought, my tears finally dried. I held my son and rocked myself to calming peace. I found abiding comfort in the notion that while he could deny me exit from the house, he could not control my thoughts, nor could he keep me from learning. Thus, my inner calm was restored and late in the night I fell asleep. I did not hear Yussuf return home.

Next day I poured my heart out to Sophia.

"I suspected that Yussuf is not half as modern as he pretends," smiled Sophia. "He is not as far removed from the village as he would like to be. Well, Darling, there are many ways to irrigate a garden. In this case, we must do as he allows us to do. We will go shopping often, give dinners and invite interesting people. Never shall you tell him the whole of your experience again, for what men don't know won't hurt them. He doesn't tell you most things he does either, and you might be unpleasantly surprised if you knew of all his doings."

This very thought had occurred to me also. Many a night I never heard my husband enter the flat, leading me to wonder what weighty business would keep him so long. Of course, it had occurred to me that he was out visiting what the village people call sharmuta, a word that also means dried, shredded meat, a comical synonym for prostitutes. But it was not for me to comment on his life.

At this very moment began my life of conscious deceit, although I did not outright lie to Yussuf—I couldn't have done that—but I modified the truth, never quite telling everything I encountered, learned and thought, skillfully switching the content of my experiences. Instead, I carefully changed myself in his presence into the kind of woman I imagined he wanted.

Heeding Sophia's advice, I was always cheerful and bright-eyed. I avoided unpleasant topics, dealing with distasteful domestic matters myself. I carefully read the innocuous books that Yussuf chose for me, and hid the delightfully interesting books given to me by Sophia.

With silent sorrow, I noticed that Yussuf never brought me books of poetry anymore. It had been ages since he, the lover of the Prophet's verses, had asked me to recite for him. I wondered at this change. Could the love of poetry die overnight, like a plant deprived of water, or were there other reasons which had poisoned what had once united our souls?

When depression threw its bony arms around me I drew comfort from the poems of Jalaluddin Rumi—poems Yussuf had once read to me. One part of Mathnawi particularly calmed my soul and soothed my injured spirit:

> *"...but creation usually unfolds,*
> *like calm breakers.*
> *Constant, slow movement teaches us to keep working*
> *like a small creek that stays clear,*
> *that doesn't stagnate, but finds a way*
> *through numerous details, deliberately."*

I felt like a small creek deliberately moving to keep from stagnating.

I had never told Yussuf how far I had progressed with my French. When he asked, I told him that the lessons were discontinued because I found it too difficult. Instead, I said that I was learning geography because I could use it to teach our son when he entered school. To that, he gave his blessing. Anything connected to furthering our son was acceptable and exceedingly preferable to all other activities.

CHAPTER *Seven*

So our lives continued, seemingly content and mutually agreeable. A month after Hassan's second birthday I announced my second pregnancy, which my doctor, the wonderful Marie Latourelle, confirmed. My delivery was expected around the time of my eighteenth birthday. Yussuf once again was delighted by the prospect of fatherhood. Once more I became the treasured family darling. Amna, who had neglected me somewhat, which was understandable since Sophia and I must have bored her to death with lengthy conversations far beyond her ken and liking, favored me again with her attention.

"You will need a bedroom for your children," mentioned Sophia one day as she looked around my bedroom, crowded by Hassan's bed. "This looks like a cramped attic. Soon you won't be able to move about in here anymore."

"But isn't that what a mother's room looks like?" I laughed and added, "The more children crowded around her the more revered is she."

"By all the camels in the desert, Amina, you are not living in the village anymore. I suggest you ask Yussuf where he wants to spend his nights with you. Hassan is becoming too old to sleep beside a marriage bed. Maybe Yussuf will have you visit him in his sanctum."

She laughed gleefully, her eyes crinkled and her silver-blond hair shook and danced. The idea of having more space was something to consider. I looked around the room. Near the window stood my pride and joy, a small, carved, rosewood desk, bought with Yussuf's permission. Adding the crib, no matter where I placed it, blocked another piece of furniture.

"How did you manage when you had your second and third child?" I asked Amna one day. I guessed if I presented my case properly she might make it her problem and broach the subject with Yussuf or Zajid.

"What do you mean?" she asked, and so I explained that things had become so crowded they interfered with married life, since Yussuf chose to visit me. My gamble paid off. After she looked around my room she decided to take matters into her own hands.

As a result of her efforts walls were knocked out, creating openings into Amna's own spacious apartment. Two rooms, once chambers of her son's, were added to our flat as a new nursery and children's play room.

Halfway through my pregnancy an upsetting incident illuminated the precarious position we women find ourselves in. Of all the sisters-in-law who lived here in the house with us, only one suffered from Zairan possession. I had been amazed how few women in the building suffered from this affliction that plagued almost half of the village women. Nahid was the least sturdy among us, no wonder she succumbed to a jinn.

Problems like Nahid's often began shortly after a husband wronged a woman. In this case, Yussuf's youngest brother, Ibn Majid, had beaten her for informing Amna that he had infected her with a venereal disease. Amna never mentioned her youngest son's conduct, but her actions spoke loud and clear. She accompanied Nahid to the doctor, and after Nahid's disease was cured, she procured a sheikha to cure "the jinn of shame," as Sophia phrased it.

Often, sometimes twice a week, Nahid attended dances that moved the participants to ecstasy. They were led by the sheikha and were meant to relieve the pain caused by red jinn, but Ibn Majid was furious that he had to obey the sheikha's commands, doubly furious to endure the disapproval of the family.

The foreign jinn wanted Nahid to wear well-cut suits and silk shirts. He demanded perfume, chocolates and sometimes flowers. To aggravate matters, the jinn demanded finer garments than Majid was wearing.

"I don't believe in jinn," he told everyone who wanted to hear. "I believe my wife is malingering. She has invented this foreign devil to torture me. It's a figment of her usually dull imagination which she uses to revenge herself on me."

"But the Qur'an says that there are jinn, and the Qur'an is the law."

With such reasoning his wife defied him time and again, and everyone, even his father, Zajid, warned that he must obey.

In this conflict, obvious to all, Nahid was blameless. Family opinion went against Ibn Majid's drinking and whoring, severely censoring him. Yet he was a man, and little could be done to constrain him. Finally, an angry Zajid curtailed his monthly share in the family's enterprise, hoping thereby to restrict his appetites.

When Nahid wanted to see her sheikha, or go to the dances, Ibn Majid had to arrange for the family car or send for a taxi. It was impossible for her to leave the house without a chaperone—a family member or servant had to go along.

"This is our chance to learn about the Zairan and observe the dances," proclaimed Sophia one day. We were sitting in my bedroom after a French lesson. To this day I have no clue how she suddenly came up with this idea. I looked stupidly into her eyes, searching for the antecedents of this remark. Finding none, I patiently waited until with thoughtfully up-turned eyes, she explained. "Nahid needs support in her endeavor to get well, but she has a hard time finding family members to take her to the dances. Everyone is busy, and besides, many are afraid to offend Ibn Majid by being kind to his wife. We should offer to chaperone her a few times and discover what the healing dances are all about."

Once Sophia decided upon a course one might as well have tried to divert the Nile before changing her mind. I arranged that Amna, who showed no curiosity about the dances, would look after Hassan, and we would accompany Nahid in the chauffeured car.

There is a section of town along the water, the Blue Nile, where the green promenade ends, well away from the usual business activities, where local fishing boats are docked to sell their catch. The heavy stench of decaying fish pervades the area, making it unpalatable to more refined tenants. There are the houses of the poor of Khartoum, and at the very edge of the smelly blight live the porters—day laborers who hire themselves out for small wages with their wives and children to clean cotton, sew and mend sacking, and to weave netting.

It was into the better part of this section that our driver headed. I had never been in the squalid parts of the city before, and so I was revolted by the roughness, the dirt and the pervading stench. Yet I held my tongue because Sophia had promised this to be entertaining. She did not believe in jinn, and hoped to prove that the disenfranchised, downtrodden women simply used the ecstatic dances to have a good time.

The streets were narrow, lined by drab cement-finished or mud-daubed houses four- and five stories high. Their windows were miniscule squares and slits, their paints and washes were stained and dirtied. The doors of most houses were small, dwarfed by the expanse of the fronts, reminding me of holes into which animals scurried.

We arrived at twilight. No street lights were discernible, leading me to comment that in a few hours the streets would be frighteningly dark. How would the driver be able to find us again?

"Don't worry," smiled Nahid. "He has come here quite a few times before. It's not a bad place. The people here are just poor, not bad."

The house which was our destination differed little from the others. Perhaps it was a bit cleaner, but it had a much larger than usual double front door.

Nahid knocked on the right side of that door and momentarily it was opened. A woman's large face, like a round, shining, black moon appeared, in which the whites of the eyes and teeth shone unnaturally bright. Nahid gave her a password and we were allowed to enter.

Through an empty, long, narrow hall the huge, fat woman swathed in acres of white, led us to a small back room in which a thin, upright woman held court. Her coffee-colored skin shone like buttered parchment, giving the appearance of youth and hiding the lines of age. She had deep-set eyes that shone and sparkled alternately with great warmth and wit. She sat in a soft, large chair covered with a vibrantly colorful cotton throw, radiating energy.

Each of her female patients, seated on cushions, standing or leaning against the walls of the chamber, was called, one by one, into her presence, and greeted with a mixture of genuine warmth and attention. Even from our vantage, we felt the glow of her personality.

In turn, she asked the possessed women about the most intimate details of their lives, probed their relationships, their secrets, pains and fears. She encouraged, pressed hands, petted shoulders, handed them amulets and beswore their jinn to be kind by ending their torment and pain. She gave advice: How to deal with a cruel haboba, an intractable husband, jealous sisters-in-law and, to those who handled money, how to manage it.

"You can't befriend a miser if you are generous," she counseled a middle-aged, comfortably heavy woman with soft features and an agreeable demeanor. "Before long such a friend will embarrass you, take your largess and revile you behind your back as a wastrel and a dunce without proper regard for money."

To another young woman she said, "Whenever you want to speak, catch your tongue between your teeth, else you won't fare well in your marriage." When the young woman asked her to explain this riddle, she told her, "Your husband is a quiet, stolid man, who shows nothing of himself to you; meanwhile in your light-hearted way, you have given him the key to your heart and soul and this is how he torments you. Ask your jinn to come to your aid in time of need and lock your lips."

"Did the doctor treat the gonorrhea?" she asked Nahid unabashed. "Are you clean now?" To our amazement Nahid, who was quiet and subdued at home, gave her answers firmly.

"Thank you. I am much better, but my husband thinks I am malingering. He says he doesn't believe in jinn. He has threatened to keep the children from me if I don't get rid of the jinn."

"Did you inform him that a jinn is with us forever? And did you tell him that as a good Muslim he must follow the word of the Qur'an?"

What followed in their exchange we never heard, for suddenly the music started drowning their voices.

We watched as at the end of each emotionally charged audience the women bowed before the sheikha and discretely deposited money into a polished copper urn, and thereafter joined the other women in a hosh behind the house. To me the hosh looked strange, surrounded by high walls, but just as in the village the walls and floor were made of stamped earth and swept clean.

Oil lamps hanging from wall sconces and mounted atop ornate metal poles provided enough light for us to see the proceedings. In the left far corner of the hosh three musicians sat on a carpet. Crouching on their heels, knees bent outward, they created hypnotic cadences with drums and flutes. Although the evening was young, already a few women were dancing. They did not follow the dictates of our national dances, but instead improvised as their spirits moved them.

I remarked to Sophia that the variety among the sheikha's customers was astonishing. From the quality of their tobs and the way they conducted themselves, one could sort the women into classes. From the very poorest, across the middle spectrum, to the very rich—all classes were amply represented.

"It's a clear indication that illness, bad fortune and controlling families are not restricted to the poor," said Sophia, whereupon we joined the spectators, all family members, who were here to chaperone, enforcing propriety. They stood along the walls or sat on those hard, flimsy folding chairs the Europeans love so much. Needless to say, Sophia opted for the chairs, whereas I would have much preferred to stand.

We didn't have to wait long before Nahid entered the hosh. Nahid was a slight, olive-brown woman. Although her coloring and her fine features pointed to her Arab ancestry, her hair was hard and heavily curled. In the flickering light of the oil lamps she looked like a lost young girl. For this dance she wore a tob of black, fine cotton imprinted with swirling white leaves.

"Somehow her tob seems appropriate—" whispered Sophia, "witches' black, with white for hope and redemption."

When I asked her to explain, she pushed my question aside, explaining that her thoughts were a relic from her Christian upbringing.

Nahid wasted no time stepping on the floor. The lost look left her face the moment she joined the sparse throng of dancers and began to move. It was obvious that she belonged here. Carefully at first, almost thoughtfully, then looser and quicker she stepped and dipped as in the pigeon dance, yet soon she threw off her head covering and began a masculine sort of dance. Her legs were slightly spread in a fighter's stance, her head was held high, eyes challenging, unafraid, unbecoming a woman of my culture.

The musicians were now playing ever faster, their rhythms insistent, the flutes wailing. Nahid's hands and arms became swords slicing the air as she turned and swirled. It was as if she would attack the dancers around her. Yet like her, they saw nothing but their own visions while in their deep trance. It appeared to me that their eyes seemed focused on an inner vision, and although none of the women seemed aware of their fellow dancers, they never collided. Sometimes they brushed against each other in passing, as casually as a breeze playfully stirs a garment.

As we watched, more and more women entered the hosh and stepped into the circle. At first, each dancer followed the dictates of her own vision. Some danced slowly, contorting their bodies, some moved as if imitating Western dance, while others twirled like dervishes, or "fought" like Nahid. They bent, rose to the night sky with arms held high, they leaped, stepped and floated. As the dance progressed their movements became wilder, faster and yet, somehow, looked coordinated, as if someone outside their circle choreographed this dance of the macabre.

Finally, the music stopped. The dancers perspiring and worn, stopped in their tracks. Some, exhausted, dropped to the ground. After awhile, they gathered themselves, seemingly awakened from a nap, startled and unfocused. Many of their relatives, especially those rising early in the morning, claimed their dancers and departed in an unseemly hurry.

We too hastily gathered Nahid and bustled out. For we discovered that the dance, so cathartic to the dancer, habituates the viewers, lulling them to sleep.

Twice more after that first time we accompanied Nahid to this house. Sparkling with wit and endowed with the wisdom of generations of women, the sheikha explained that there were many houses like her own. "They are much the same, with the exception that men dance in other places as well. Zairan enter all who are oppressed," she smiled. Then, thoughtfully she added: "The weak, controlled by others, succumb to the power of jinn."

Now that we were involved in Nahid's struggle, our sympathies were aroused and we followed the developments of her loveless marriage with a falcon's eyes. It was apparent that easing Nahid's malady necessitated expensive treatment, but we noticed that whenever Ibn Majid caused Nahid grief, her illness grew worse. Aggravated by his abusive habits her symptoms lingered for two years, yet none of us thought the inevitable would happen.

One day Nahid's foreign jinn went too far. After a tumultuous scene, caused by a drunk, violent Ibn Majid, the jinn urged the poor woman to leave her home and her children. Angry, defiant Nahid obeyed the jinn, and accompanied by a servant, she went to the sheikha's house where she danced for two days.

Meanwhile, Ibn Majid's curses could be heard throughout the house when he discovered that Nahid had left.

"That's the last time that this jinn from the Jewish Gehenna dominates my life," screamed Yussuf's brother. "From now on the damned jinn can dance in the village with every black shawatin haunting the dark."

And with this terrible curse he ordered Nahid's belongings packed. The day following her return he sent her back to the village with his children and a servant. I was trembling when I heard the news, and flew to Sophia's flat. Sophia was angry, but neither astonished nor shocked. "You see," she said, smiling bitterly, "how quickly a woman who protests can be silenced. She is put into the living coffin—the village. Now no one will hear her pleas for help as she lives neglected and dishonored."

"What protests, Sophia?" I asked. "It was this male jinn who caused her to act. He made her ill. It is unjust that her husband should banish her. What will happen to her in the village? The jinn will surely kill her if he is not placated, as you well know. Cast out as she is she will have no means to do his bidding. She can't afford silk suits and shirts, and Ibn Majid will just ignore her."

"Darling," Sophia said, laying a calming hand on my arm, "I don't think she will die. Oh, her suffering will be heartrending and real, but I think the sheikha in the village will help her. Above all she has young children to care for. Mothers of young children resist the death threats of jinn remarkably well. So she will live, but she might wish that she were dead."

For days afterwards Sophia's words haunted me. Somehow a subtle message had been conveyed. After days of puzzling, the meaning of her subtle message became clear: Sophia did not believe in jinn. She had called Zairan possession a protest. With a strange new clarity I understood this was a protest against the husband. Moreover, I understood that our belief in red jinn gave women a small outlet—a miniscule opening—through which they indirectly pointed fingers at the inequities and torments of their lives.

I shook with the importance of my discovery, for now I understood the fundamental law of our society. It was based on inequality. It allowed us to be the property of our fathers, brothers and husbands. It was this epiphany that destroyed my peace of mind. Wherever I sat or walked, whether I nursed a baby or lay with my husband, thoughts about our laws, about women's duties and their minimal rights tormented me.

Sophia had shown me pictures of the bound, mutilated feet of Chinese women. To me, these crippled, painful feet became the symbol of women's torment without representation and defense. Who spoke for the Chinese baby girls when their feet were bound? No one! Who spoke for the young girl, Amina, when they mutilated her?

Sometimes I silently berated Sophia for having poisoned my mind with bitter drops of clever knowledge. But mostly I gratefully admitted that painful knowing was better than ignorant contentment.

My brooding days were forcefully interrupted by sad news—my father was dying. On one of his journeys far up the Blue Nile, a treacherous fever had taken hold of him. No one, even the Western doctor they consulted, could cure him. Bit by bit the hotness burned and ravaged his body until he knew he couldn't last much longer. Now he had asked for me to come to his side.

"No," Yussuf said, dismissing the notion. "You can't go. You are almost ready to deliver my child, and therefore you must stay. Nothing must interfere with the birth of my future son."

"Please, Yussuf," I pleaded, taking his hand in mine. "Let me go. What can happen? I am healthy, and the delivery is a full month away. He was the best of fathers, and I shall forever mourn him if I cannot see him one more time. Let us ask Marie Latourelle. Let her be the judge. If she thinks that I could endanger the child, I shall not go."

Thus I pleaded, and at last he agreed. Marie Latourelle was consulted. At first she worried that my father's fever might be contagious. Yet since no one else had contracted his disease she reasoned that the illness must not be infectious. "Stay a few feet away from the bed, and wash well when you come from his room," she admonished.

Provided with ointments, solutions for decontamination and tablets to purify water, I set out for the village by car. At the last moment Yussuf decided to neglect his business and come along. We travelled in the huge, black Mercedes driven by the family's chauffeur. Every square inch of space was filled with gifts—the many items I knew they lacked in the village. Crowded among our belongings and baby necessities, I rode, holding Hassan on my lap while he surveyed the scenery rushing past with great solemnity.

It was the season of ayam el tahur. The hot sun fevered our skin, our blood and our minds. From the desert punishing winds carrying fine sand sharp as splinters, blew across the silently suffering landscape. It seemed that to the hot, driving wind our car was an inconvenient boulder that had to be punished for impeding its progress. Screeching, it etched its sandy fury into the car's glossy finish. Whenever the abrading sounds reached their crescendo, I heard Yussuf groan.

"What folly to travel to see a dying man," he complained loudly, competing with the rushing, hissing sounds of the wind. "He might be dead before we arrive. The car will be ruined and Zajid will be furious that it will need repainting. Why in Allah's name did I join you in this folly? All the shawatin knew this was wrong, and they punish me now."

In this way he continued to complain until I softly said, "Yussuf, not long ago it was you speaking with compassion and great love of filial duty to our parents. Like my own father, you loved best the Qur'an's passages on obedience to one's elders. What has changed your mind?"

"Be quiet woman," he countered. "Save the drops of saliva that still remain in your mouth. Soon, the wind will have us dried as mummies. Nurse my son, so at least he will not suffer dehydration."

I could not understand my husband anymore. Once, not so long ago, he had been patient, kind and understanding. Now, I barely knew the man that sat beside me. What had changed him? Turned him against me? I didn't know, and he wouldn't tell. So we sat in silence. Yet, even I had to admit that the journey was fraught with misery. If every window in the car had been closed, we would have died of heat stroke. So we compromised by opening the windows alee, which also invited the drifting sand inside the car.

Sweat never had a chance to form fully on our skin before being whisked away by the wind. I had covered Hassan's head with a gossamer fine shawl that needed shaking every few minutes. Yussuf wore native white clothes, and, like me, kept most of his face covered.

Our chauffeur, Abdul Hakim, a most patient man, wore goggles and a scarf covering his nose and mouth. He calmly steered along a path only he could see because most of the road had vanished beneath the fine, treacherous gift of el-khalla, the emptiness. From the chauffeur's hand hung a string of worry beads, gliding through his fingers while he steered the heavy car. He belonged to the brotherhood of Sufi, and meditated and prayed with the help of these beads whenever he could withdraw from the world. As long as he gripped the wheel of our car, I felt safe. I watched his motionless back and thanked the Almighty for the gift of Abdul Hakim's protection.

Stiff, dehydrated and deathly tired, we tumbled at last from the car when we reached my family's compound. My brothers surrounded Yussuf and carried him off in triumph, for he was a great man in the village. I was glad that I wouldn't be troubled by him anymore for the duration of our stay. The chauffeur carried my cases and presents to the door of the women's hosh, where my mother and aunts gathered me up along with my belongings.

Mother, looking bent, slight and creased, allowed me time to wash and change my tob. I was astonished that she had aged so rapidly. She left me no time for reflection, but hurried me off into my father's presence. There was cause for this haste, for he was extremely weak and had asked incessantly to see me and his grandson, once more.

They had laid him on a fine bed in the middle of the men's common room, with clean white garments covering every inch of his body. Here he could still be an integral part of the household. In the face of birth and death, rules are broken and laws amended, and so it happened that my mother led me straight into a room that was otherwise forbidden to women. Across from me, behind my father's bed, stood my oldest brother Khalid. He'd grown even more since his wedding, and had broadened about the shoulders, so that now, his face glowering, he looked to be a most formidable adversary.

From the moment I entered, he watched me coldly, his eyes as venomous as cobra spit. His hands played with the cord encircling his long robe as if he were fondling a dead snake. For a moment I wondered whether my brother's intense hate for me was a measure of his love for our father or only a boundless disdain for femaleness. My heart skipped, for with Father's death he was, after my husband, the executor of my fate. For one moment his eyes held me captive, as the snake holds captive a fearful bird, but then, my father's eager gaze claimed my attention.

"Father, I came as fast I could," I cried. His eyes clamored to see the grandson I carried in my arms, so I knelt beside his bed, holding the child before me.

"Say 'Salaam, Grandfather,'" I coaxed. Hassan obliged nicely.

The salaam my father offered his grandson came from the depth of a parched, rumbling throat. It was apparent that he spoke with great effort. He forced himself to form words until I understood his bidding.

"Recite Al Takwir."

I stood so he could see my face and began:

> *"When the sun*
> *(With its spacious light)*
> *Is folded up;*
> *When the stars*
> *Fall loosing their luster;*
> *When the mountains vanish*
> *(like a mirage);*
> *When the she-camels,*
> *Ten months with young,*
> *Are left untended;*

When the wild beasts
Are herded together
(In human habitations);
When the oceans
Boil over with a swell;
When the souls
Are sorted out;
(Being joined like with like);"

On and on I recited. Al Infitar, Al Mutaffifin; Al Inshiqaq. The prayers befitting one who is to leave this world and about to be judged by his creator.

"All mystery, fair or shrouded in gloom,
Will vanish when the full Reality
Stands revealed. If this life is but Painful
Toil, there's the hope of the meeting with the Lord!
That will be bliss for the Righteous,
But woe to the arrogant dealers in sin!"

At these words my eyes strayed to my brother's face. Khalid's eyes thundered anger in my direction. At last Father, soothed by the sweetness of the verses, motioned me to stop. He had never touched me for as long as I lived, except once, to lift me onto the ox cart when I was ill after the ritual excision. He did not touch me now. But straining, he whispered, "You were a gift to me from Allah and I bless you for all your life."

He closed his eyes and moments later the harsh, rasping sounds of breathing ceased. Weeping, I realized that this had been our final moment together, more, I knew that he had loved me. In fact he had chosen to elevate me above his sons by using his last breath to bless me.

Before it had seemed that there were only three people in the room: Khalid, Father and I. Now I was aware that my mother, brothers, Yussuf, my sister and a few of my uncles were also present, standing in segregated groups along the walls. Nearest, at Father's feet, knelt Hamida's father, who had been his companion and partner on many trade journeys.

Hassan, as if understanding the importance of this moment, had remained standing quietly in front of me. I gathered him up and fled, while behind me a wailing sound rent the air. The mourning had begun. I rushed to the women's sleeping quarter, rocking in sorrow my child who was frightened by the sounds of wild despair filling the house.

Over the next days Yussuf's eagerness to return to Khartoum was tempered by his wish to negotiate my part of the family fortune. A'isha, Hamida's mother and blessed gossip, informed me that Khalid, treacherous as always, had bargained away my small fortune for a piece of Yussuf's business.

"This is bad for you," warned A'isha, "for your father told Khalid to keep full control of your part of the family wealth, so that you might have something to fall back on if things went badly with your husband. Yet now, with your father barely cold, Khalid disobeyed him. Keep your eyes open because he can't be trusted."

"What can I do?" I asked. "There is no one to plead my cause. The haboba is dead and Mother is weak when dealing with her sons. Fortunately, I trust my husband and shall not fare badly."

As soon as I spoke these words, great doubt assailed me. All of Yussuf's strangeness of late came to mind. I felt uneasy. Yet, having no other reason to distrust him but my instincts, I shrugged off my concerns and went about my business.

Before I left Khartoum Sophia had requested that I look after Nahid. I had planned to go visiting her with Mother and A'isha as my chaperones. The old Nasredi haboba had died two years earlier and Amna, who should have assumed her position, could not be prevailed upon to return to the village. By default, the women's quarter was ruled by a mild, unsure woman in her thirties, yet the ancient compound seemed to be the better for her attentions.

The cobwebs were gone, the kitchen was clean, the hosh was swept and the griddle gleamed from heavy use and polish. I had met Bashira, the young matriarch who had found it impossible to adjust to the city, on my previous visit. Insecure of her own position in the household she relied heavily on Nahid's support, and both women benefitted.

Nahid confided, when during our visit we had a moment alone, "At first I thought I'd die of boredom, and the jinn was angry and nearly killed me with his unceasing demands." She continued, "But then I realized that I had needy children. Life would continue for them and for me wherever we were. The village sheikha assured me that most husbands regain their wits when the drives of the penis lessen. 'There is hope,' she said, 'as long as you live, there is hope.'"

I conveyed Sophia's greetings and concerns. Yet Nahid assured me that she didn't need our help.

"I thank you both for your kind thoughts, but I have found ways to survive."

Extremely pleased with my visit, I reported to Sophia that her evaluation of Nahid had proved correct. To ensure Nahid's continued success, I charged A'isha with the task of looking after her, to ensure that she was not lacking for support. This A'isha promised. Three days later we were back in Khartoum.

• • • • •

My second son, Fahim, was born two weeks after my father's death, pulling me out of my mourning with his healthy squalls. Complications from sporadic bleeding kept me confined to the foreign hospital for a few days, where I eagerly practiced my French by conversing with Marie Latourelle and the nurses.

Yussuf came twice for short stays to see us, and Sophia, Amna and Madam Thibodeau visited bearing gifts. Sophia told me that the kind wife of the French Ambassador had taken a great liking to me, a claim I believed because she presented me with the most charming silver baby bowl, fork, spoon and cup.

Since males—with the exception of husbands—could not visit a woman in a hospital, it was days later when I presented my second son to Zajid, who burst with pride that his eldest son produced such robust offspring. I blessed his maleness too, but for other reasons. I knew whenever I recalled Khurshid's tiny corpse, that I would never permit genital excision to be practiced on a daughter of mine. I prayed every day that I would never have to battle the family in a fight for a daughter's right to remain whole.

Yussuf was well pleased with his second son, allowing me to spend plenty of money on the children and myself. Secretly, I hoarded away a good part of this allowance. He also gave me free rein to spend time with Amna and Sophia away from the house. Amna's slow, plodding mind was a blessing in disguise. She never suspected that Yussuf might object to our meetings with foreigners, and so we met, with impunity, all of Sophia's foreign acquaintances— the Air France flight crews, American and English Embassy employees, and a few Germans who spoke French. Since Amna didn't speak French we conveyed our little secrets in this tongue.

Looking back upon this time, I surmise that Yussuf salved his conscience lavishing money and certain freedoms on me, in order to feel unfettered by scruples when engaging in the forbidden with his circle of friends. He met me with either paternal condescension or unwarranted anger, neither in the intimate mode of earlier times.

Besides taking good care of my children, I continued my French, math and geography lessons with Sophia. Yussuf spent little time with me. Often, I never heard him come home at night and so I had much time to read.

At first, I grieved when he neglected me, but there was nothing I could do. Even gentle probing sent him into fits of anger. I took comfort from my ever-philosophical Sophia who counseled me, "His anger is an admission of guilt. Why should he be out of sorts if he had reasonable explanations for his absence? You could divorce him, but it would mean going home to the village, and there your brother would be awaiting you. No, you are better off here, enjoying relative freedom. Wait it out. Sooner or later they get bored with their hussy toys and return to the family fold."

Heeding her words, I worked harder at my studies, for the new world that opened up before me compensated amply for my grief. Imperceptibly, I began understanding many different social concepts, cultures and customs. The more I learned about other people, the more I understood about my own world. Knowledge and Yussuf's indifferent treatment changed my formerly humble soul imperceptibly, until I could rationalize my clever little lies and omissions. Furthermore, my days were filled with the countless tasks of motherhood. Hassan spoke well and asked a hundred questions in an hour, often leaving me helpless because I had no answers for my grand inquisitor. There was so much more for me to learn.

Three months after Fahim's birth it was time once again to visit Hofryat. It suited me that we stayed at the Nasredi house with Amna and Zajid. Since the death of my father, I felt not only like a stranger in our home, but unwanted as well. Khalid had somehow pushed aside my uncles and assumed the position of patriarch. Everyone marvelled at this astonishing feat. A'isha came to visit Amna and me and reported the domestic changes. Her husband, although a slightly foolish man, had been in line to head the family, yet had been brutally shouldered aside by Khalid.

"Your mother is haboba now, Amina," A'isha told me. "Yet, I will say this, it is your brother who speaks through her mouth. Unlike your grandmother, she is a weak haboba and never stands up to Khalid for our interests. She thinks him infallible." A'isha sniffed disgustedly, her face a moon of scorn.

"It's hard to watch how she fawns over him, and you are well off out of his reach. He seems to envy you, even hate you, and no one knows why."

Dear A'isha, I wouldn't enlighten her, for how could she comprehend his jealousy of my ability to recite? I was glad to hear that Hamida, my childhood friend, was the mother of five, four boys and one girl, and therefore well respected in the house of the Mahdi. For a fleeting moment I wished that my life could be as simple and serene as Hamida's—that I was bereft of the knowledge and the troubling thoughts I had found in the city—that I was just a village woman again. But the thought passed, like a spasm passes through the body.

A'isha brought sad news as well. "I know that you liked Sasat," she said, reaching for my hand. Her small hands had grown plump and were soft and comforting to touch. "She lives no more. Something went wrong with her last pregnancy. They whisper in the hosh that Hadija was at fault because Sasat wasn't cut open early enough for delivery." While speaking, A'isha's eyes were directed at the dirt floor. Sensing my hurt, she could not meet my eyes.

"She labored too long, unable to expel her fruit. Hadija could not be found until too late. They say when finally Hadija cut her open the baby was dead and Sasat died shortly thereafter."

The grief encompassing me turned to hate. Two of the people who I had loved best were dead because of our brutal customs. Not enough that they'd killed the girl with the gory practice, they'd killed her mother as well. How fortunate I was. I acknowledged owing a tremendous debt to my husband for sparing me. I mourned Sasat and resolved to be more conciliatory, patient and understanding toward my husband.

Back in Khartoum I devoted even more time to my children and studies. Shopping had become boring because I saved my allowance and lived frugally. I enjoyed my children's progress, but Fahim's behavior troubled me. He seemed very relaxed sometimes, but filled with agitation at others. His small frame shook with frustration when his hands failed to grasp an object, and developing rapidly, he was determined to keep up with Hassan, an impossible task for one so young. A camel fashioned from hide and stuffed with hair had become the object of Hassan's affection. Large enough and solid on its feet, it was a true steed. Mounted, toy sword in hand, my little boy became a warrior. Both camel and sword were Zajid's gifts in the warrior tradition of Islam.

A few months passed and then, unexpectedly, I found myself pregnant again. This must have happened during one of the few nights Yussuf had spent with me. From the beginning, this pregnancy was different than the previous two. Morning sickness plagued me and my cravings for odd foods drove Aziza to distraction. Often, I discovered I did not want a particular dish anymore when it was finally served, having replaced this craving already with another. It was annoying to be so burdensome, but I couldn't help what was happening in my body.

"I felt miserable like you when I carried daughters," said Sophia. "Conversely, I always felt well carrying sons."

"Two of my sons affected me like this, so don't pay attention to Sophia's remarks," commented Amna, who would have been thrilled with another grandson.

Fate chose an unusual day for the arrival of my daughter. For days storm clouds had gathered until they looked like black, angry, bloated jinn, amassing over the convergence of the Blue and White Nile. Thunder and lightning, fearsomely portending catastrophe, woke me hours before dawn. Coinciding with nature's display of primordial might, pain racked my body announcing my child's arrival.

I left my bed, calling for help. Somehow I knew that there would not be much time, and I was afraid to be alone. No one heard me. I knocked on Yussuf's bedroom door. No answer. Anxiously, I fled down the dark corridor to Amna's apartment. I knocked, and moments later she opened her door looking voluminous, dressed carelessly in folds of her tob.

"The baby is coming. I need help," I cried.

"Where is Yussuf?" she asked, peering over my shoulder into our darkened apartment.

"I don't know. I knocked on his door, but there is no answer."

Angry clouds outside, angry clouds on Amna's face. She was obviously displeased with her son's absence, and it was apparent that she didn't know what to do with me. Zajid, appearing old and dishevelled, shuffling in slippers, came to the door and peered myopically at us.

Although he seemed sleepy, almost drugged, he understood my plight before we had time to explain. No doubt troubled his mind but one: that no child should be born in his presence. He sharply ordered Amna to take me to my bedroom and he'd see to the rest. Within minutes he had the car waiting for us with Sophia, the intrepid one, at the wheel. Minutes later we sped through the predawn streets to the clinic.

Despite savage labor pains ripping down my back making sitting unbearable, I still had lucid moments witnessing Sophia's heroic effort to ferry us safely and quickly to the hospital. Overhead the thunder roared, echoing off the buildings. Bright, blinding light flashes were interspersed with total darkness feebly pierced by the headlights of our car, while torrential rain deluged streets unaccustomed to such volume. Soon, they became rivers and lakes with their own rules and treachery. The moist air smelled sharply of sulphur and left an acrid taste in my mouth.

Through all the terrors bestowed on the city that night, Sophia steered our car undaunted, never concentrating on the terror outside, but only on my condition.

"Breathe deeply, Darling, and recline as much as you can," she advised one moment, only to call moments later, "Hold onto the baby a moment longer, we are almost there."

That night I came to highly value the placid Amna. She supported my body and, being totally calm, diffused the panic that threatened to drown me. Murmuring both the most sublime and the most banal moments of mother-hood, she distracted me, causing laughter and easy tears. At last we arrived. Supported by the women, who half-carried me, drenched by the downpour, at times cast into darkness and into unbearable brightness thereafter, we staggered from the parking lot to the entrance.

My daughter was born thirty minutes later with my friends holding my hands. Amna became my friend that night, because I finally could see, beneath placidity and mental laziness, her inherent goodness.

After such travail the delivery was easy, and I felt so well afterward, that I begged to be released. Marie Latourelle obliged and hours later I relaxed in my own bed. Aziza flew happily about because she loved children and now, besides her own brood, she could mother one more of mine.

From the beginning, the mental and emotional connection with my daughter differed from what I had experienced with my sons. To begin with, she was a much smaller baby at birth than the boys had been, and so my protective instincts were more intense. There was a daintiness, a delicacy, about this child, something totally different from my boys' robustness. Even her cry for attention was less demanding and lusty than her brothers.

For these reasons, I held her lighter in my arm, used a softer voice and cuddled her more. Like Hassan, she was contemplative in demeanor. From the moment her eyes focused, she was easily entertained watching new and different things, whether pictures or objects. She was easy to love, for she had an endearing smile, and seldom cried or fussed. She was a pleasure to raise and we were greatly attached to one another.

It had been my wish to name her Khurshid, in memory of the little girl-bird who had died. In fact, she often she reminded me of her, but Yussuf decided her name should be chosen by consulting the Qur'an. For this ritual the family gathered in Amna's flat. We all sat, some settled on modern seats, but most of us on pillows on the floor. For some reason we had chosen to dress in white from head to toe. Covered in tobs and sheaths, we looked like a convention of ghosts. I held the sleeping baby in my lap. A name means nothing to a child, except for the fact that someone loved it well enough to choose. To remain nameless means to be unclaimed, therein lies the importance of the ceremony.

Zajid entered the family circle carrying the silk-wrapped Qur'an. He prayed, unwinding the fabric covering the Qur'an, and held the Holy Book aloft. Yussuf, standing beside him, proffered a stiff paper, which the old patriarch, eyes closed tightly, inserted between the pages of the book.

Opening his eyes he looked around, pausing to pronounce the significance of this moment. Then, he opened to the page indicated by the marker. He was quiet for a moment, then, visibly taken aback, he said, "Her name is to be Maryam as is indicated in Surah 19."

And then Zajid read with reverence the famous words of the angel: "Nay, I am only a messenger from thy Lord, to announce to thee the gift of a holy son." To which Mary answers: "How shall I have a son, seeing that no man has touched me, and I am not unchaste?"

Hearing this, we rejoiced. Such a distinguished name for our child. The prophet Jesus' mother, Maryam, greatly influenced the Muslim concepts of filial duty, for her son showed her kindness and respect, shielding her from the abuse of her people. Such deeds are looked upon favorably by Allah and held up for all to emulate.

My daughter was presented to the village when she reached the end of her first year. Yussuf had decided that we should celebrate Ramadan in Hofryat, where, as he said, one felt the holiness of the season with greater intensity because of the poor surroundings. The weather was mild, and strangely, I looked forward to spending time with the women in the village, especially my mother. Perhaps such feelings arose in me because I had borne a daughter and looked for a deeper connection with my own mother.

I knew why I wanted to spend time in the village, but I could not fathom what motivated Yussuf. With the exception of feasts and weddings, he avoided the village, and so we only went there once a year for the required return. Trying to understand what drove him to Hofryat, I queried Sophia who laughed and replied in French, "Perhaps his cleric exhorted him to greater piety, and this is a journey of atonement." Then, becoming poetic, she waxed, "Verily, thereafter he might change his ways. Thou shalt see him a chastened man in the future and model husband."

Her lighthearted remarks were the closest I came to understanding his motives.

The visit I had anticipated with such emotion soon felt like drinking vinegar. For all time, I shall remember the sour taste lingering for the entire length of the visit. It contracted my mouth with harshness from the moment I laid Maryam in my mother's arms. She never saw the baby as a person in her own right, with her own unique qualities, but compared her from the first to her larger and more vigorous grandsons. She spoke straight over my Maryam's head about the boys' virtues without even glancing at her a second time.

And so it was wherever we went. Compliments were heaped upon the boys, while the little girl, so precious to me, was coldly ignored as if she did not exist. Hamida was no exception. She favored her boys outrageously, paying no mind to the sweet girl innocently hiding behind her tob, which had become quite voluminous around her rear.

It was A'isha who removed some of the bitterness from this visit. She'd noticed my silent rage, and asked for its cause in her usual ungarnished manner.

"It infuriates me to see my boys elevated, but my daughter relegated to nothingness! She might as well be a baboon, for all they care. Even my own mother frets like a camel-mare over the boys while blatantly disregarding my beautiful daughter. It irks me, for without females to bear them there would be no men, and yet, a girl's presence is not even acknowledged."

A'isha's little raisin eyes were filled with amused malice. "I've had those same thoughts myself," she said. "Of course, I'd never state them to anyone here. You must remember how I pushed for you and Hamida to marry well. That was because I determined early on that of my children Hamida was the best and brightest. May Allah forgive me, but I thought that my boys would not amount to much, and they didn't. It was Hamida who fulfilled my ambition to be the grandmother of a flourishing, wealthy and great family. I know how you feel, but you best not vent these feelings in public."

I was truly astonished. A'isha, flighty, gossipy A'isha, had become philosophical about the female condition. Talking to her relieved some of the oppressive feelings that had gathered within me. Still, I was thankful when after a lunar month we were on our way back to Khartoum. I had missed Sophia more than I ever thought I'd miss anyone. With her usual stubbornness, she had refused to leave Khartoum, although Zajid and Yussuf pressured Abdullah to join us.

Sophia asked Abdullah, "Why do you think I would return to Hofryat when I wouldn't even go to Mecca or Medina?" and then she persuaded him to spend Ramadan with her in Alexandria where she had friends.

Back home, I easily fell into my chosen routine, which seemed precious and light compared to the dullness of the village's daily blather.

Maryam grew into a charming, dainty child, who despite her delicacy, was brimming with energy. Early on, I observed that she was very intelligent. She was bright like Hassan, but her intellect was heightened by a great degree of cleverness, perhaps necessitated by her position in the family. To be the youngest, overshadowed by two or more siblings, requires an easy disposition and a clever brain to deflect intrusions, because the rights of the youngest siblings are easily abridged, their feelings trod upon.

However, Maryam was not to be trod upon. She was about two years old when I first noticed her clearly using reversal of mood to win skirmishes. Hassan could always be prevailed upon to be gentle with Maryam or to relinquish a toy, but Fahim was less cooperative. Once my back was turned, he'd snatch away her toys or pull her hair to let her know how unwelcome she was. Obviously, he had never quiet forgiven her for claiming part of my attention. Although he loved her and he could be very tender, other times it pleased him to tease and vex the little mite.

In the beginning of these torments she would wail in her misery, which only filled him with open glee. Then one day, to my astonishment, I saw her smiling brightly into his face after he tore the rag doll I had made for her from her hands.

"Take it," she said, and she turned and walked toward me. I picked her up and congratulated her on being a good girl who knew how to share, while Fahim dropped the doll as if seared by a flame.

"She is supposed to cry—she doesn't play fair!" he cried, outraged.

"The game is changed," I laughed. "Play by new rules. When you play with her you must share."

Again and again he tried to coax her into feeling vulnerable and frustrated, but even when he pinched her or pulled her hair she would just smile and leave. Fortunately—for all of us—Fahim didn't suffer from deep-seated malice and so eventually adapted to his role as an older brother. Astoundingly, for she was so sweet, Maryam developed a taste for deception as she grew older. Without confiding in me or fussing, she hid those treasures that she did not want to share or see destroyed by her wild brothers. I found her favorite books, beaded bracelets, and pictures under my mattress, a place secure from boys. Sometimes, when they had been especially bothersome, she even hid her brother's best loved toys there. I admit, I never let on that I knew.

I marvelled at my girl and was thankful that it was up to me to help her develop her gifts. When I read she'd often come to me questioning what I was reading. Without intent, more placating than teaching, I pointed out letters and explained their meaning, and then, as if without effort, she was reading. When I sat over my meager accounts (I had managed to deposit a small sum into an account, procured for me by Sophia and Madam Thibodeau in a Parisian bank, where it drew higher interest than I could get in Sudan), she showed the same curiosity, an almost physical need to understand the secret behind numbers.

She was only three years old when her ability to calculate small sums and subtractions outstripped even Hassan's accomplishments. While teaching her geography I found the secret of her speedy memory. It was her way of perceiving things whole rather than stringing learned bits and pieces into a fabric at a later date, as most of us must do. She saw connections between separate things.

We were looking together at a map of Egypt and Sudan. Just for the fun of it, I told her about El Bar en Nil the way I had told the boys.

"El Nil, at its beginning, sleeps in two different beds far apart from each other. One bed is blue, the other is white, and so we call his beginnings, the headwaters, the White and Blue Nile."

As before, I then pointed at Lake Tana saying, "Above this lake, in the highland, lies the blue bed in a land we call Ethiopia." Then, tracing with my finger the curves of the Blue Nile, I outlined how the river flows through Ethiopia, creating an enormous swamp land, entering into Sudan, where, at Khartoum, the White Nile joins it to form the mighty river, which hindered by cataracts, bisects Sudan and all of Egypt, ending in an enormous delta.

When next I questioned her about the river she astounded me with her recall. Her brothers had been older than Maryam when I taught them, and I had been gratified that they'd learned the rudimentary facts of the Nile and Sudan. Only by repetition did they learn the greater detail.

Why I should have been given such a mysterious child—a child of uncommon intelligence—was beyond my understanding, but I felt blessed.

Time, once flowing with viscosity, now stepped out with the speed of the racing camel. I was busy all the time, as the children fed on my meals as well as on my mind. The boys were insatiably demanding of my attention. So much so that I had to limit their access to give Maryam her due.

To the family we presented a most pleasant picture. We were a beautiful, healthy, growing family. But those who knew me well knew the picture was false, that my smile and patient forbearing hid shadows and nebulous threats. Yussuf was absent more often than not, and the responsibility of raising the children fell entirely on me. He was only home on weekends and holidays for an appearance of family unity, and during most of that time he slept.

Long ago, I had stopped trying to understand what might have driven him away from me. I admit that the nagging question of what had stolen his love for me and his children and bit by bit imperceptibly fashioned him into this stranger, had long ceased to interest me. Resigned, for I could do nothing, I steeled myself against pain and self pity, and worked on what I could influence.

My boys were bright and I taught them well: reading, writing, Arabic as well as French, math and geography. The rest they picked up in school with ease. Their school reports gladdened my heart and pleased Zajid extremely. Yussuf also was pleased, for this he was grateful, but his attitude toward me had become neglectful, even hateful. He respected me, even found me formidable, but he came to my bed no more.

Throughout this time, a period often fraught with pain, anger and sometimes despair that my paragon of virtue had become even less of a husband than most others, Sophia and Amna stood by me and helped as much as they could. Amna understood nothing about Yussuf's behavior. On one hand, he was still her adored son, yet on the other hand she was wounded that by his continual absence he deprived her of more grandsons. Sophia knew I had dreamed of spiritual alliance, of true companionship; my high expectations had turned to dust. I was to discover the secrets that were destroying my marriage shortly before Maryam's fifth birthday.

CHAPTER *Eight*

W oe was me and shame, for I was almost twenty-four and had to my credit only three children. Yet, as everyone in the family knew, it couldn't be helped since my husband was absent most nights. Although I felt I was truly blameless for my empty womb, I knew that blame was not only heaped upon my husband, but on me as well, and that spiteful whispers circulated among the family.

I imagined that they speculated that if I only pleased him more, he'd stay, or if I tried harder, begged him a little, or wasn't so lazy in bed, he'd surely stay home instead of spending time among the whores.

Verily, I knew it wasn't so. I could do nothing because it was as if Yussuf was bewitched. Imagine my shock then, to hear our servants discussing our marital horrors. They were well versed in the tawdry doings of my spouse while I, besides guessing wildly, walked about like one blind.

One day approaching the kitchen, when they assumed I was gone, I heard the whole miserable, degrading tale. Besides Aziza's familiar voice, the low-pitched murmur of the houseboy's wife, Seria, penetrated into my bedroom. It was she, who most times carried the market's purchase to our kitchen and stayed for tea with Aziza. I had encountered them often while they were shelling peas or cleaning vegetables, chatting companionably. So, heedlessly, I was about to enter the kitchen, when a phrase caught my ear that lamed my feet.

"Master sees her every night, and has lost all shame."

I froze behind the door. Like a thief stealing valuables from the pockets of his victim, I snatched bits of information from the women.

"Poor lady. She is kind. Her children are well mannered and no trouble. Never have I heard a cross word from her for my master, Yussuf. But he treats her with contempt and neglect." That was Aziza's voice.

"And she is generous," came Seria to the fore, building up my character.

"Where did you hear these things?" asked Aziza, and Seria answered, "From the chauffeur. You know he is almost holy, he prays so much. How could he keep such secrets any longer? He told his wife, thinking to ease his burden, and she told me. He thinks it's wrong that the master practically lives with an uncircumcised infidel."

My head jerked back as if I'd been slapped. Moments later the heat of shame, humiliation and anger filled me until I thought I'd burn to death. So this was the drug that he held dearer than all else. How could he be possessed by an infidel, like our women by jinn? I could not understand him. Even less could I believe that he, raised with the spirit of adat, would break the bond that bound our families.

But what I thought mattered little. This was my reality. Now I knew that he was drawn like a moth to a woman like Sophia—a woman totally intact. For his wife he chose me, the traditional sacrifice, yet he chose to sleep with a woman whose femininity had not been cut away. How could I compete with her? I was mostly numb during the sexual act because although I was somewhat restored, no surgeon could replace what had been torn away. None of my tenderness, attempts at passion or whispers meant to reassure his masculinity could compare to her.

At hearing the servants conversation something crushingly painful happened inside me, as if my heart was wrenched from its place. I knew not why, but the pain carried with it the need to assume blame for our failed marriage. And so, I assumed the full blame without a thought.

With my last strength, I closed the door quietly and threw myself across my bed, weeping inconsolably. Perhaps I had not heeded the good advice on how to behave in my marriage bed.

"Moan," said the women back in the village, "they like that. Try not to show pain, but pretend that you are pleasured."

Had I been inept and clumsy? There were no answers echoing from the walls, and when I heard the children's voices I roused myself. I washed my eyes with cold water and went to meet the boys, avoiding their questions about my reddened eyes.

Morning found me despondent. Outside brilliant sunshine brightened the world, spreading its heated message to live, to act, to enjoy. I shut my fancy drapes against its lures. My world was empty and I hurt as only the used and scorned can hurt. I found a stark, black tob embroidered with yellow thread, which suited my mood. That, I wound carelessly about me and presented myself moments later at Sophia's door. Not long thereafter I was settled in one of her graceful, but comfortable chairs, sipping a tea, which she insisted would calm me. It didn't calm; instead it allowed me to release the dammed up poison that promised to destroy me.

"What shall I do? Apparently I don't have the most powerful weapon at my disposal, having lost it to the knife. So tell me, what can I do?" I asked Sophia with great bitterness. I was consumed by childish, hateful thoughts. At that moment, I hated even my beloved Sophia, for Sophia too was one of them.

Yet, angry as I was at her, and all other foreign devils, I needed her counsel and advice. Alternately, I was awash in bitterness, jealousy, anger and despair. My jealousy, since I could not vent it on the cause of my grief, was directed at her. Finally she had enough of my accusations and anger. She drew herself up haughtily. "First you must collect yourself. I have never seen you like this before, Amina, and it is not becoming."

She calmly drank her tea while her eyes, greenish-gray in the morning light, were thoughtful and intent. When she spoke, it was if she immersed me in an icy bath, so cool, deliberate and logical was her analysis of my situation.

"Don't believe for one moment that your circumcision is the reason for your problem," she began. "True, it is an important factor, it is a symbol of your life, of your condition. Now perhaps you can understand fully why women succumb to Zairan jinn. Better to be possessed then living zombie-like—better to whirl in ecstatic dances, then to repress the last shreds of self."

Sophia was wrapped in a becoming silken Western robe, and although concealing, the robe, unlike the tob, gave the wearer a shape, an identity. She gracefully poured more tea for us, and continued.

"It doesn't matter whether the woman he sees is intact or not, but it matters whether she indulges in perversion," she reasoned. I dared not consider her words, so I only listened. "Apart from this, much more might be involved. Obviously he cherishes the forbidden aspect of this relationship, and one also might speculate that wine or intoxicants are involved."

She looked at me, inner tension revealing her age with fine lines I had never noticed before, and continued with bitterness in her voice: "But whatever the reasons for his behavior, it is wrong and it should be stopped. Yet it has been allowed to continue for a long time. You must have noted that no one in the family wants to address his failings and correct the situation."

With her words I reflected that Yussuf had become exceedingly powerful. Zajid, his own father, dared not touch on the matter, too afraid to alienate his oldest son. I knew that after Maryam's birth he confronted Yussuf and raged at him that he'd left me alone the night of her birth.

"It is time you mend your ways and study the Qur'an again," he'd said to Yussuf. "For you are remiss in your duties—on a fast way to dissolution, dishonor and shame."

Sophia, too, remembered his words as she sipped her tea. In her eyes I glimpsed remembered unpleasantness, a sentiment confirmed by her next sentence. "I never want to see Yussuf again as he looked then. I imagine shawatin to look like this. I expected him to explode in his father's face, but he controlled himself, and just said 'What is between my wife and me is my business, and although you are my father, the Qur'an gives you no rights in my marriage.'"

In the same manner, he ignored Abdullah's rather gentle admonitions, as well as the sermon of the Imam. According to Abdullah he convinced the holyman that his evenings out with his friends were harmless entertainment. Why look askew at him, he who never raised a hand against his wife and never cried out in anger?

"Of course he doesn't have to raise his voice," I exclaimed when Sophia mentioned this. "It's enough to make me freeze in my tracks when he measures me with a bloodcurdling look. So you tell me that I must live without hope; that I am to live, without complaint, without recourse except to seek divorce, face the loss of my children, and live as a servant to my relatives in the village."

"That is the verdict of the world we live in," the words fell heavy from her lips. "Nothing can be done, for he is your husband. So you must try to live in this house, as well and with as much dignity as you can muster."

"That's easy for you to say—all is well in your life," I struck at her with childish anger.

"Listen, Amina dear, when I married Abdullah I gambled with a freedom greater than you can imagine. But I also knew that bad marriages, poverty and every other ill can occur no matter where you live or who you are. Over time, I have come to believe that only financial security ensures a woman of a decent life. So I advise you to hold still. Meanwhile, gather as much wealth as you can, and learn, learn, learn. For you are the mother of a daughter, and it is for her that you must provide a better future."

"What about the boys? Am I not to care about them?"

"Never mind their fate. They are the privileged ones. Everyone will look after them, coddle them, spoil them. Yet the very same people will neglect your daughter."

And so, in the crucible of my unhappy marriage, my pain and anger was eventually burned away leaving me with a clear resolve. I would follow Sophia's dictates and bend to the inevitable.

• • • • •

According to my new tenets, I lived a new life. At twenty-five I was resigned to monastic celibacy, dedicated to the rearing of my children. Only Sophia made the humdrum of my days bearable. Without her, and the visits to her foreign friends, I should have become lost and bitter, perhaps dull and unattractive. But the irrepressible Sophia kept me laughing, kept me thinking, kept me neat and clean as an ostrich egg, even on days when I felt like a drudge.

I've always dreaded the season of ayam el tahur. Nature and humans conspire to make it a season of torment. We assiduously avoided the village during this season, choosing to visit during balmier, less stormy days. So imagine my surprise when Yussuf confronted me in my bedroom and told me to prepare our children's belongings during the next three weeks, for at least a month of visit.

"But why?" I questioned. "It's miserable in the village when the sand blows in from el-khalla."

"Has the city removed you so far from adat and religion that you forget our duty?" he asked, his face black with scorn. "Did you forget that Hassan is almost nine years old and uncircumcised? Do I have to remind you of your duties as a mother? It will be done. All at once. The boys, the girl, at the same time. We shall have a great feast for the boys. The family shall rejoice and be happy in our good fortune."

If he had taken a wooden club, and hit me over the head, I could not have been more stunned. I had tried to forget that these circumcision rituals were hanging over us, as the legendary sword hung over Damocles of Greek myth. I could almost contain my feelings when it came to the snippet of foreskin the boys would lose, although I felt as if run through by a sword when I thought of Hassan and little Fahim standing there being cropped by the knife in their most sensitive place. Yet, I could suffer that. But what was in store for my little one—that I could not bear.

I felt poignantly with my entire being that nothing could force me to render my small bird to Hadija's knife. Nothing—no husband, no family, no cleric—would make me betray the trust that my happy, delightful child placed in me. I would die first. I became agitated with emotion.

"Uh, Yussuf, please, not Maryam. She is much too young. She is barely five. Please let us wait a year or two until she is stronger." By now I cried. "Please. Do remember that I told you about the girl, Khurshid. She was older by two years, and yet she bled to death. Remember that I was nine and nearly died of infection? Oh please, please let us wait. I'd rather we would not do this at all to our children."

"Are you insane, woman?" he shouted. "What are you saying? That we deny our culture? Our customs and religion? That we become outcasts in the family? In our country?"

My fear and anger gave me strength to stand up against him.

"Why not?" I shouted back and saw his shock at my raised voice. "Abdullah's and Sophia's girls are not circumcised. Why not my daughter?"

"Because their daughters live in Paris, you imbecile," he replied, his words like ice. "They had to send them away because here they would never have been accepted. My daughter is going to get married. Here in Sudan. Where I can control whom she marries, and what kind of children she breeds."

Allah in heaven. *Aiiiah!* What had happened to the man I married? The nice man, the feeling one, who loved poetry, and was concerned with women's plight? Somehow, that man had vanished, as completely as moisture wiped of a mirror. Zajid and Abdullah, the mild-mannered examples of manhood in the days of his youth, had been replaced by the fast, hard new crowd he was running with now.

"You have three weeks to get your affairs in order," he said as if the matter was settled. "So don't waste time—start planning now. You will need gifts for the circumcisers, for grand-parents and the women of both families. The gifts for the men and the boys shall be my worry. I want this to be a grand feast, so don't spare any expense."

With that, he threw a hefty wad of bank notes onto my bed, and without giving me another look, he left, closing the door with a resounding flourish.

My body's fiber melted and I sank onto the cold marble floor, hugging my legs to my breast, shrinking my body to the size of my diminished state. What kind of mother would I become if I could not prevent my child's pain, or worse, became accessory to it? And yet I had no power to shield her! I had no power to shield my boys, or myself for that matter, from whatever edict whether evil or good, the family headed by the men would enact and enforce.

I could do nothing, except commit suicide to protest. Were I to rant and rave, they'd simply lock me away until the deed was done. Then I'd be a non-person unable to do anything for my children. A ghost whose voice would never be heard, who remained unseen, except when orders were to be given. Examples made of obstinate women had left an indelible impression, and I believed myself too weak to bear such ostracism.

However, the more I thought, the more long-abated anger rose up throughout my being. I resented that I had no voice in the matter of my own body, my own destiny, my children's lives and their well-being. A horrible thought occurred to me. I had no destiny. Nothing more was in store for me, unless I bore more sons. I was just a vehicle for the family to carry on its line of male successors. Unconsciously I had been rocking back and forth. As my rage grew, I rocked even harder. Then, suddenly, I was struck as if by lightening. A powerful force entered my body suffusing and dominating me. A raging scream escaped my throat, rattling the window panes in their metal frames.

That roar wasn't my scream, for I would never scream like this—could not. But whatever possessed me could. I needed no sheikha to tell me that I was possessed. I knew, without doubt, that a most fearsome jinn controlled my body. The jinn rent my tob asunder, tore my hair out from its pins and stamped my feet.

The jinn screamed again and again in his loud male voice that sent Aziza running into my bedroom.

"By the prophet in heaven, what is going on here?" she cried.

"What has happened to you, lady Amina? You look as if evil has befallen you. Who did this violent deed?"

"No one," screamed the jinn in his obnoxious, raucous male voice.

"I am just angry. *Aiiiiii!* Furious. *Awwwwwiiiiii!* I won't be treated like this anymore. *Uhh, Ouwah, ouwah,* I want out!"

I heard the jinn screaming and tried to calm him, forcing my own voice through his screeches, but against his power, I could not prevail. Against my wishes he used my voice, powerfully distorting it to scream obscenities and gibberish until I fell to the floor, exhausted. Then, mercifully, I fainted.

Vague babble reached me through blackness. Nothing made sense. Babble, babble. Baby gibberish. Louder now. Annoying. Stop it!

Painfully annoying. Bah, bah, bah...Know that voice. Amna. Other voice, Sophia. Deep voice, Zajid. Zajid? Another pitch. Aziza. Words. I understood the words.

"Look at her! By all that is holy. Her eyes are white. Lord in heaven what happened?" Amna's frantic voice asked.

"Her eyes rolled upward. I've seen this before in men with terrible injuries." That was Zajid. In his younger years he'd seen war. Aziza's voice, keening with funereal zeal, tried to explain the little she understood while distancing herself from any trouble that might ensue.

"I just don't know what happened, "she wailed. "Lady Amina had a fine day. She played on the roof garden with the children. She came to the kitchen for the children's lunch, and they ate in the living room. Then Mr. Yussuf came and spoke to her for a minute, and when he left I heard these screams. Terrible, terrible screams."

Go away. All of you. I am not opening my eyes. In my mind I am saying words that can't be heard, for I cannot speak.

"Did you hear what Mr. Yussuf said?" That was Zajid's voice.

"Nooo."

Zajid coaxed, "Aziza, good woman, don't be afraid. I know the kitchen door is not solid. One hears things, whether one wants to or not. So what did you hear?"

I should open my eyes and end this right now. Try as I might, I can't. I heard Aziza tell our conversation.

"Why would she carry on like this?" asked Amna her voice filled with wonderment. "A feast, a big celebration is to happen, and she screams?"

"No, no," interjected Aziza, "those weren't her screams. Those were screams of a devil. Curses and gibberish—not her voice. Just look at her. Have you ever seen her in such disarray? No, someone did her violence."

"Amina. Poor little one. My poor friend," murmured Sophia never adding another word. She knew.

At last I could open my eyes. I saw them standing above me, their worried faces bent over mine. It felt like I was caught in the circumcision ritual all over again—faces looking down on me while they cut—and I began to shake uncontrollably.

"She is ill," said Amna authoritatively, "She has a fever and we must get her doctor."

"Before we do that, let me take care of her for awhile. I will try my special tea and see if I can get the fever down." The voice of reason was Sophia's. Accustomed to her command, no one, not even Zajid, dared object. To the contrary, Zajid remarked that this was valuable advice because no one could have entered the flat. Therefore he reckoned that I probably suffered from some female hysterical upwelling that could be soothed with tea.

To my considerable relief he succeeded in ushering every one out the door leaving me alone with Sophia.

"Can you hear me?" asked my friend with clear, clipped enunciation.

"If you can hear me, but can't speak, press my hand with your fingers."

She held my hand in her own. Since I still could not muster my vocal cords I pressed her hand. Her elegant, sweet-smelling hands rubbed my arms while she murmured, "Relax, relax. All will be well. I promise. Your body is as rigid as a board. Try to close your eyelids."

I concentrated. All my will power went into this simple endeavor, but finally I succeeded in shutting my eyes.

"Open your eyes," commanded Sophia, and when I did my vision had returned.

"You have eyes again," smiled my friend. "Now see if you can speak."

After awhile I managed to form words. At first, I spoke haltingly and broken. I told her everything—the circumcisions, my fury, my vow not to sacrifice my daughter, and how the jinn entered my body.

"For the moment, forget about the jinn. You said you have three weeks to make a plan and see it through," said the intrepid one, unhesitatingly.

"What plan?" I asked, frantically. "What can I do? I can kill myself in protest." In my agitation I had become rather loud.

"Calm down and lower your voice," commanded Sophia, and so I continued quietly.

"Where could I hide from him? Where can I run to? My own brother would deliver me and my children into Yussuf's hands the instant he saw us—all of my family would, for that matter."

"What are you prepared to do to keep your daughter safe?" Sophia asked, looking deep into my eyes as if to plumb the depth of my soul.

"What are you willing to sacrifice? And sacrifice you must. You won't get to keep all you will want to keep. So think, and think deep."

I thought. Entertaining treasonous thoughts often enough before, I spoke quicker than she expected me to. I sat up straight, and pushed my body back until I felt the wall behind me. Looking straight into her eyes, I said with my new jinn voice, "I'd give up everything to save her—Yussuf—my sons—my life—if it would free her, save her, I would do it."

Sophia never ceased to amaze me, for she smiled a secretive smile which expressed that she'd known my answer all along. How could she have known what I had never acknowledged to myself?

"Good. If you feel this way I will help you. We know powerful people who like you. Madam Ambassador, for one, air line stewardesses, and the American lady archaeologist. How much money do you have in the bank?"

With renewed energy I jumped out of my bed. The slap of my naked feet striking the marble floor startled us, disturbing the secrecy of our whispered conversation. From the hiding place in my clothing chest, I pulled out my bank book, where it lay between the folds of gold-brocade.

I handed the book to Sophia who found the last entry. She glanced at me with astonished admiration. "*Mon dieu*," she exclaimed spiritedly, "you have done well. You must have bought almost nothing for yourself. I am amazed that Yussuf never noticed your frugality."

"He notices hardly anything that concerns me," I cried resignedly. I had saved, over a period of nine years, fifteen thousand dollars.

"How clever that you converted the money to American dollars. This will be exceedingly helpful. Of course, once out of Sudan, fifteen thousand is nothing. You will have to find work."

"What are you saying? Do you mean there is a way for me to get away?"

"Yes. I have planned for this day since your marriage turned sour, when you became unhappy. I was not going to sit idly by and see you destroyed. So I cast out my net. I found that things can be done to spirit you and Maryam away. The boys must stay. For were you to take them, Yussuf would hunt you to the end of the earth."

Dizziness addled my brain. I had to lean back because the room swirled around me. I was shaken by Sophia's revelations, by the matter-of-fact manner with which she disposed of Hassan and Fahim. A terrible pain shot through my breast. How could I ever leave my boys?

"Why did you never say anything to me about this plan? Why the secrecy?" I asked when my head cleared.

"This thing is dangerous. I had to be sure that you were truly ready to take such a step. You have to be willing to sacrifice your life, or else there would be no reason to jeopardize good people by involving them."

The hope of saving Maryam gave me courage, emboldened me. Excitement fevered my blood. My cheeks were glowing as if I'd spent hours in the hot sun. My pulse was racing. This was my destiny—to leave and save my child—to tell the world what is done behind the walls of the hosh. The sheer boldness of the undertaking made me shudder. I knew I could be as brave and steadfast as the women I had read about. I would succeed, I would survive, and, best of all, my child would grow up free.

Before Sophia left me that fateful evening she warned me: "Don't let Yussuf find out that you think a jinn possessed you. Do you hear? He would love to have an excuse to banish you. If they question you about the earlier commotion, say you fell, hurt your head and fainted dead away."

Any woman who had vicariously shared in the fate of the unhappy Nahid, as she was banished by her husband, would have understood the gravity of Sophia's warning. I couldn't appear sick, possessed or troubled. Mine was to be the image of contentment, of rejoicing compliance with my husband's wishes. I deeply hated deception, but even dumb, yoked oxen sought relief from drudgery by pretending to limp. I could do as much.

For hours I lay without sleep until finally retreating into restless slumber. With a start I awoke, my heart pounding, sweat beading my forehead, moistening my palms. The darkness around me was impenetrable. I strained listening for sounds. Slowly the memory of my dream returned: As in a shimmering, softly vibrating Fata Morgana I again saw the picture of a woman. Wearing a black tob, the woman stood, harshly outlined against the sands, in the vastness of the desert, her upturned hands stretched out. In one hand the woman held a thumb-sized miniature of Maryam, in the other the equally small figures of Hassan and Fahim. Before her, nebulous in the shifting sands, danced a red jinn like the flickering flames of a fire, his face filled with laughter and amusement. Beside him a fearsome, black-maned lion, with Yussuf's face, stood poised to spring at the woman.

"These are your choices," smiled the jinn. "Give him the children," he pointed at Yussuf the lion, "and he will carry the boys on his back, and devour you and the girl. Give me the boys, and I will obscure his vision with my sorcery, so you and the girl can escape."

I watched as large, crystal clear tears fell from the woman's eyes, watched how she tenderly nestled the miniature children against her cheeks, watched how she kissed them, held them before her to look at them again and again. I watched as she suddenly tossed the boys to the jinn and ran. The jinn, as he had promised, spread his flaming body before the lion, and mother and daughter escaped.

Was the dream a portent? Surely I was the woman in black. In the dream I gave the boys away, but could I leave them in the light of day? I was to find no rest that night and on many yet to come. When my brain, fevered by trouble, allowed me no respite, I read. Concentrating with all my might I was able to withdraw into a structured, logical world, untouched by emotions. Whenever the thought of my boys haunted me to the point where I thought I could not do the deed, I withdrew into ancient times. I studied the history of the Nile and its people that I might take with me part of my roots.

CHAPTER  Nine

During the next days I performed specific functions, dictated to me each morning by Sophia. One day I had to shop with Amna and Sophia, while another was to be spent sewing, mending and tending the children on the roof garden of the house, while yet a third day was spent lunching with Sophia's friends from a foreign embassy. All the while she never told me how our flight was to be accomplished.

"I can't tell you anything, Darling," she explained. "The less you know, the better you can act. When the day comes I will tell you what you must do, and it will be done in a great hurry. Meanwhile, enjoy your children as much as you can. Pretend to be very happy. Have a very few, necessary things for yourself and Maryam in a large handbag ready at all times. Two handbags, at most, will be all you can take with you. But you won't need much."

When I plagued her with questions she cut me short, "Trust me. That is your only choice."

My days were filled with bittersweet emotions when I played with my boys. Often I felt a sickish, stomach-cramping excitement, mixed with the fear of detection. Each look at the calendar confirmed that before long, my test of courage would come due. Mornings crept along, while afternoons and evenings passed with the quickness of water evaporating in the hot sun.

With every fiber of my being I tried to convey to my precious boys how much I loved them. I told them a hundred tales of sweet, loving mothers who had to leave their children in my effort to prepare them for the shock they were to receive. In one tale the mother threw herself into the mouth of the Crocodile-God who menaced her children, so that they might live safely.

In another fairy tale, a mother and her three children were swept down the river. With her strong arms, she pushed her boys onto a rock, yet was herself carried away, their small sister clinging to her neck. Saved, a long way from home, she could not return, and was never to see her boys again. Yet every evening, when the stars shimmered in heaven, the mother and the small sister would be looking at the sky and pray for the boys. And, by a miracle, the boys would always be moved at the same time to stand under the stars and think about their mother and sister.

With my stories I tried to help them understand what lay ahead, sowing seeds in their minds that they might know later that they were not carelessly abandoned. Whenever my sadness consumed me, I burdened Sophia with my worries and tears, and she promised that she'd keep my memory as a good mother alive in the hearts of my boys. Such promises always soothed my conscience. Perhaps I should have prepared Maryam in some way, but I could not for fear she'd give us away.

Throughout this time, Yussuf's presence was hardly felt. Twice he looked in to see the boys before their bedtime and joked with Maryam since he was in a good mood. He had a childish way of tickling her, making her laugh while telling her a riddle or making a play on words. Never once did he notice that most times the child smiled only to please him, not because she enjoyed his riddles and games. Her understanding of language was much more advanced than his childish exchanges, yet for some reason, she never once allowed him to see her intelligence. Instead, she indulged him with smiling patience as if he were the infant.

Once I inquired into her habit of concealing her intelligence from her father, and with touching purity she answered, "It's a game, Mamina. Dado," (a name she'd invented for Yussuf which stuck, and was also used by the boys), "wants a special little daughter, and I make-believe that I am that daughter."

How glaringly her remark made me aware that already she had learned in small increments, through his reactions, that his boys must be superior in every aspect of development, therefore she played the role of a simpleton for him.

How much of my mind had been suppressed? I would never know the full extent of my deprivation. Worse, without Sophia's interference I would have never known that I had a mind capable of learning a multitude of subjects.

On a Friday, six days before our departure for the village, I was cooking the children's favorite chicken dish. No one in the family could cook like my mother, and she'd taught me well. She was a sorceress when blending her spices, gifted with deft hands, gifted with the right touch. Unerringly she detected the missing ingredients in a dish; without fail she knew when a dish was seasoned to excess. Needless to say, I could never match her art, but my children, and even Yussuf on occasion, liked my dishes better than Aziza's.

I was spooning yoghurt spice chicken onto saffron rice when Aziza announced Sophia. I left the children who had waited patiently to be served with Aziza, asking her to bring us tea, and joined Sophia in the sitting room. Greeting me with her usual warmth she caught my eye and pointed a finger at my bedroom.

"I would like to see your new robe," she said for Aziza to hear. "Would you try it on for me?"

"Of course, I would like nothing better," I retorted.

We retreated to my bedroom where we could not be overheard. Whatever Sophia would tell me was important. We sat in matching chairs separated by a small table, and made small talk. For nothing significant could be said before tea was served and all chances of divulging a secret had passed. I tapped my foot nervously, hardly able to wait for the tea, but Sophia sat with collected grace.

It seemed to me that Aziza took forever to fill two dainty cups and take her leave. The moment the door was firmly shut, Sophia exhaled loudly, as if she'd held her breath for a long time and said, "Be ready on Wednesday. I don't know precisely at what time it will happen, but Wednesday is the day. I would like for you and Maryam to be alone at home that day. When I come for you, we must leave immediately."

My heart pounded. I heard the blood sing in my temples. My fingers assumed a life of their own arranging and rearranging the folds of my robe in precise rows. Yes, I was ready and prepared, but I was also frightened. Could I do this thing? *Yes, I could.* If I were to be caught would he kill me for this affront? *Yes, he might.* No one would object to having a wife, absconding with his flesh and blood, put to death in a fit of anger. Still, I would go. I would take my chance—the only chance for Maryam to stay whole.

Sophia could always read my mind. She reached for my hand and I realized that she was shaking. "You think that Yussuf is capable of killing you if he were to find out." Her breath came in little bursts as she spoke.

"Yes. He's become even stranger lately, sometimes he walks to his room like a zombie, and his eyes are bloodshot and unfocused. There are times I am afraid of him."

Sophia pressed my hand in hers and said with assurance, "Not long now. Prepare."

"Depend on me. I shall be ready," I whispered to Sophia. She hugged me to her breast with great emotion, then searching my eyes, she left well convinced of my resolve.

Sunday night my bedroom door flew open, and Yussuf loomed in the frame. His face was flushed crimson. He was bursting with importance.

"Sheikh Hafiz Mahmood Ibn Saud, of the royal house of Saudi Arabia, is in town and has accepted my invitation to the boys' circumcision feast. We have to leave immediately, for I will have to make many preparations before the village compound is ready for his Highness. I've sent out envoys to begin the preparations, but we best be there ourselves to see that all is perfect."

I staggered under the sudden blow. When I found my tongue I queried, "Do you mean this minute? I have worked hard, but have not finished all my preparations. Quite a few gifts must still be purchased, and although I mended and sewed for days, the boys' garments for the ceremony are not completed."

"You fool! Of course, I didn't mean this minute. But Tuesday morning after breakfast we shall be off. I will brook no tardiness or malingering. I want everyone ready at my command." These words he spoke convincingly, slamming the door with great force.

He left me shattered. We were foiled. He had ruined our perfect plan by one day. One destiny-shattering, terrible day. I began to cry, silently. I believe my hopelessness would soon have transported me into loud lament had it not been for my daughter's soft hand on my back. I had forgotten that she was in the room. Hassan and Fahim were with Zajid. He loved to talk with his grandsons in the evening while he drank his cup of strong coffee.

"Mamina, don't cry," she offered, her small face earnest and concerned. "Let us visit with Aunt Sophia. You never cry when you are with her."

I hugged and kissed her and complimented her on being the brightest child that ever was. We told Amna where we'd be and set out for Sophia's flat. Fortunately Abdullah was absent, and so no time was wasted on formalities and explanations. Cleverly, Sophia enticed Maryam to peruse a stack of picture books. The moment I had Sophia's attention my despair poured from my lips as water cascades from the cataracts of El Nil.

"He is carrying us off to the village Tuesday morning," I wailed. "Some Saudi sheikh is in town and will do Yussuf the honor of attending the circumcision feast." So far I had spoken composedly, but overwhelmed by my bad fortune, I began to sob. "What am I to do? What now? I will die if they hurt Maryam. I know I shall die."

Sophia looked troubled and thoughtful. Her eyes, green, stormy pools, were fastened on my troubled countenance. When I finished, she said nothing. We just sat there in silence, and it was as if every cell in her body became thought.

At last she said, "Where is Yussuf?"

"Out to dinner with his friends, and the sheikh, I assume."

"I must ask you to take a risk tonight. Should you be caught you must tell them a believable set of lies. I will go out now and visit with those who are part of our plan. We shall see what can be done to remedy this disaster. Abdullah will be out until after midnight. So, shortly before midnight, you must sneak down to my flat for the news I will bring you. Should anyone detect you, be bold and say you were ill and needed me to drive you to the doctor. Will you do that?"

"I will."

Shortly after returning home I put Maryam and the boys, who had returned in high spirits from Amna's flat, to bed. They were unruly and noisy. Stirred by Zajid's stories of horse- and camel-mounted warriors fighting in the vastness of the desert, they pretended to be such warriors by whacking each other with sticks, which their grandfather had thoughtfully provided them.

The self-control available to me was barely enough to keep from screaming at my sons. I needed to be alone. I needed time to think. My soul begged for peace, and I could not endure their rowdiness. Yet I could not leave them with the picture of an angry mother in their hearts; so I contained myself. At last, my beloved tormentors settled into their beds, and after telling them more tales of unfortunate mothers and children, at last I could retire.

I felt as nervous as a gazelle stalked by a hungry lion. To calm my racing heart I entered the kitchen to make some herbal tea. Hours ago Aziza had left for her own home, leaving the kitchen neat and clean. The black slab of granite on which she kneaded the dough for the sweet, yeast rolls Yussuf and the children so loved, sprang to life when the light struck its surface. Speckles and veins of gold, silver and beige reflected the light and sparkled like jewels.

The modern electric stove, her pride and joy, gleamed antiseptically white. I prepared my tea things at the stove, filled the water pot and set it to boil, measured tea into my favorite China tea pot and prepared my cup.

I sat on the modern couch, my legs folded under my body, and sipped the tea. My ears and senses were tuned to catch the slightest sound in the house. I heard the elevator rise and then stop on the third floor. Thereafter all was quiet. I tried to read, but my pounding heart overpowered the words that my mind tried to digest.

Trying to find comfort I disassembled my packed handbags, rechecking each item for its perceived need, only to stuff everything back impatiently before I was finished. Of what use could such perusal be to me? Had I not searched and worried over the contents a hundred times? Why should these items grow more useful or less so, for that matter, in the space of one night?

I paced the flat with impatience. I checked Yussuf's doors. Still locked, as always. I looked in on my sleeping children. God's angels could not be more perfect than my children, I thought. I knew my heart would break the day I could not see my sons' faces anymore. There they lay. My exhausted little warriors. With black hair, black, long, silky eyelashes and almond skin, they were more beautiful than the *putti* in the Renaissance paintings, which Sophia treasured. They were as innocent as their softly rounded faces proclaimed.

Standing in their doorway I reflected that only once, for an enchanted moment, are we allowed the childhood glow of innocence. Fleeting as the morning mist, it departs the very moment the world touches our souls with hurt and common crudity. Then, like summer sun burns cherry blossoms, life's harshness supplants the soft-rounded appearance of innocence with a leaner look in preparation for future struggle. I searched Hassan's face for common touches, but Allah be thanked, his face was still good and pure.

Bitterly I realized that I would be the to first mark his soul and his sweet face through my desertion. With my act his innocence would vanish, swept away by the hurt and bitterness which the abandoned feel. My heart ached so much, that I felt I would die. And yet, what was I to do? If I left the boys, they would feel mental anguish, but they would live and prosper. If I stayed,

Maryam would feel physical pain as well as the emotional hurt of betrayal. Above all, there was always the chance that she might die. If she lived, her health and her happiness would be forever bound up in the complications caused by the monstrous intrusion into her body.

Midnight approached. Draped in black and barefoot, I crept through the darkened, narrow tunnel which led to the elevator. Since my first day in Khartoum, I had hated this passage, afraid of its deep shadows. They had built this miserly, windowless corridor to save space, adding insult to injury by using only a few overhead lights.

In the back of the house, behind Amna's apartment, there was a staircase to be used in cases of electrical outages and as a fire escape. It was darker, more lonesome even than the hallway I had to traverse each day. Parts of it were open to the air allowing pigeons and bats to make gruesome homes in the ceiling. In all my city days, I had walked its narrow, winding steps only once, in the company of other women, when the elevator failed. Now, in the depth of night, the staircase looked fearsome and threatening. Cowardly, I chose detection above safety and called for the elevator.

Fortunately for me the elevator rumbled upward, but lightly. I slid inside, and as the door closed behind me, I prayed that the light might not die, as it had on previous occasions. My knock on Sophia's door was answered at once. Sophia seemed—in contrast to me—not nervous at all. She answered my whispered Salaam in her everyday voice, and bade me to come and sit in the most comfortable chair of her living room, a chair normally reserved for herself. The significance of this did not escape me. I felt myself tensing even before my fate was announced.

"You shall leave tomorrow morning. Ostensibly, you will take Maryam to see Marie Latourelle for her booster shots. I will go with you, and carry your second bag. I won't tell you more of the plan. It would only worry and confuse you. You must both be ready by nine o'clock. I shall order the car."

For a long time that night we talked. Throughout our planning stages it had never occurred to me that Sophia might place herself in the gravest danger. Now, when the day of reckoning was upon us, I could see Sophia's exposure.

"I dare not think of what they will do to you, should they suspect you of engineering my flight," I fretted.

"Don't worry your poor head with unfounded suppositions," soothed Sophia. "I will deal with whatever happens at the given time."

"They can imprison you," I wailed, desperate for her to acknowledge her own danger.

"I hope my Abdullah will protect from such a fate."

"Perhaps he can't? Should Yussuf press charges against you, the court will decide."

"I know," Sophia said with great calm. "I am well aware of the danger. Yet all of us must decide what is important in life. It is more important to me that Maryam remains unharmed than to guard myself against some evil that might befall me. I hope we can help you and still avoid danger, but we shall see what the future holds."

When I left that night it was as if I was parting from her forever. Perhaps I sensed the things that were to come; perhaps I was imagining the worst scenarios based on overwrought emotions, but it was hard for me to let go of my friend. Again and again, I thanked her for having befriended me, taught and molded me, and allowed me to grow, to know, and therefore, ultimately, to decide my fate for myself and for my daughter.

At last she gently unwound herself from my embrace, ushered me ever so kindly out the door and admonished me to rest. The elevator swallowed me and carried me upward to my bed.

Despite my worries, I fell asleep almost instantly. I slept soundly until kitchen noises awakened me. Instantly, I was aware of the day's importance. In my robe I went to the kitchen for coffee, a drink I had come to cherish in the city although I never tasted it in the village. I thought I should faint, for there, leaning against the counter, stood Yussuf drinking coffee, in his hand one of Aziza's sweet rolls.

"Salaam, Yussuf. You are about early today," I exclaimed, my voice high with surprise and dismay. I knew well enough that he got up before dawn each morning to chant the proscribed prayers, but usually he was not about at this hour. After his prayers he usually crawled back into bed for more sleep, as do most men of his class. Laborers begin work after prayers, or have already been at work, stopping to pray when the plaintive call emanates from the mosque.

"Salaam, Amina." He measured me from top to bottom and wasn't totally displeased. Suddenly his mood changed, and fleeting anger furrowed his brow.

"The chauffeur tells me you ordered the car for today," he complained. "That won't do because I need it. Sheikh Hafiz Mahmood Ibn Saud is my guest and I shall take him about in the car."

If a thunderbolt had struck the house that instant I should not have noticed. For my mind was impaired by his horrid news—impaired, as if I'd received an electric, stunning jolt. He didn't seem to notice my shock. I fought for composure. Finally a sound approximating the croaking of a frog escaped my mouth.

"But, forgive me, I need that car today. It is for Maryam." I was thinking fast.

"She must have these shots before we depart for the village. The doctor is quite adamant that I bring her. Especially before something so monumental as circumcision." At that point I broke out in tears. My desperation crumbled all resolve to be firmly reasonable. "I don't want her to die the way I saw Khurshid die. She is our child, and I want her to live." Something of the old Yussuf showed itself in the softening of his face. His eyes peered at me with a mixture of warmth and desperation at women's folly.

"Take a cab," he ordered. He opened his wallet and put some bills on the counter. "Who is going with you?"

"Sophia."

"No," he cried out, as if firing a shot at me. "You are much too often in the company of that woman. She puts ideas and notions into your head. You shall go with my mother. I will tell her to be ready."

I thanked him for his kindness and returned half dazed to my bedroom. I realized the plan could still work with a cab, maybe even be better than with our chauffeur. But Amna? What to do with Amna? I needed Sophia. I heard the apartment door close behind Yussuf. As if a burden was lifted from me, his leaving freed my thoughts.

"Watch the children for me, just an instant. I need to talk to my mother-in-law," I cried to Aziza, leaving her with my sleeping brood. Hurriedly, wrapped in my tob, I flew down the hall. I dared not take the elevator, since at this hour any of the men leaving the house might encounter me. I preferred to remain unseen by all. Nothing must connect me to Sophia today. The iron door to the fire escape squeaked complainingly when I pushed it open. Seldom used, the rusty hinges noisily resisted my efforts. I hadn't noticed the squeal before and it sent me into a panic. Surely everyone in the house must have heard this grinding sound.

Frozen, I listened for a reaction to my commotion, but nothing moved. Leaving the door slightly ajar, I dashed down the narrow steps, imprinting my foot clearly in the dust and grime, offerings from the city's air. A pigeon, disturbed by my hasty movements, flew up, brushing my cheek. Thank heaven my scream was swallowed by deafening traffic noise, as strong up here as in the street. I stumbled, barely catching on to the parapet, otherwise I'd have pitched head first down the stairs. I counted, stopping at the third metal door downward. Gently I pulled the door toward me, but it would not budge. Why did all unhappy occurrences have to coincide and plague me, in the space of a few days? The final evil touch vexing me to the point of madness was this stubborn door.

I pulled and pushed until my face dripped with perspiration. By now the sun had risen. The temperature rose with the passing minutes. I had to get to Sophia, fast. I gave up my useless pursuit, and raced back up the stairs. When I tried the next door up it opened instantly, and I slipped into the darkened hall. In the flat at the very end of the darkened corridor I heard a girl wailing. Soon the wails turned to screams following a loud smack. Hearing the slap substantiated my understanding that it was a girl crying, because no mother dared slap her sons.

I stood in front of the elevator, biting my fingers, that I might not scream if the arriving elevator had passengers. But except for the sobs of the girl all was silent. The elevator doors opened and I entered hastily. Moments later I knocked on Sophia's door.

Her maid, a magnificent, tall woman of the Dinka tribe, resplendent in a colorful, long, loose-fitting dress, answered the door. Since she was not a Muslim she could dress as she liked, as long as she kept to the dictates of modesty. I whispered that I urgently needed to see my friend. Her face was a study of chiseled, polished blackness. She looked at me, shooting venomous arrows from large, expressive eyes. For although she was bright, well-trained and served Sophia with devotion and skill, she hated interruptions of her routine, and looked upon guests as plagues.

Perhaps my helpless, frazzled look tugged on her motherly sensibility or perhaps she wanted to expedite my leaving, but suddenly her face softened and with a sweeping gesture, she invited me in. She ushered me into her kitchen when I indicated that I'd rather avoid the living room. She poured a cup of her incomparable coffee for me, and left to find Sophia. A moment later my friend was with me. She listened closely, and then gave me instructions.

"You must take Amna in the cab with you," she began reassuring me. "Give the driver the address of the hospital, but, before you get there make him stop at Martimex where we always shop. Tell Amna to wait in the cab for just a minute because you must purchase Maryam's shoes which she needs to try on for size. Therefore she must go with you. If Amna objects, you must quickly leave with the girl, and hurry into the store. Go straight to the back entrance where there is a big door which is always closed. Today, it will be open a fraction. Glide through this opening as inconspicuously as possible, and push the door shut. On the other side you will find a huge key in the lock. With it you must lock the door securely. You will be in the warehouse, where someone will be waiting for you."

I had never seen Sophia so intent, so serious, and yet so frail. Her eyes held mine, commanding me to remember her words. We had been standing under bright ceiling lights in her kitchen, which revealed unmercifully the ravages time had wrought upon her lovely face. I noticed tired, woefully deep lines around her mouth, indicating unimaginable suffering, and the hateful wrinkles that ruin women's eyes. We had been holding each other's hands. Now the pressure of her fingers grew almost painful on mine as she continued her instructions.

"Don't run," she warned. "You don't want to attract attention. But move as fast as possible."

A terrible thought occurred to me. "What if we make into the warehouse and no one is there to guide us further?" I asked her.

"I can't foresee such failure, for the people helping you are the best there are. But should no one come for you, you must continue straight down the alley between the merchandise. There will be another door leading out into the street. Look for a black Mercedes, and get into the back seat. The driver will say: 'Are you the chosen one?' and you must answer: 'Yes. I was chosen.' You can trust him explicitly. He will take you to your first destination."

Never before had I noticed that my friend had aged during our almost nine-year friendship. Magically, she had managed to project through the years a picture of mature, graceful beauty. But on this early morning, without her careful, daily preparation, and distraught by my problems, she looked her true age. It pained me to leave her behind now that she seemed so vulnerable and frail, the one who had always been invincible as polished granite.

Yet there was no time to dwell on my worries and fears, for she turned me around with both hands, pushed me toward the door, and said, "Time is rushing like the river, and you have no time to linger. Farewell. May God protect you and keep you safe. Remember always that I love you like a daughter." I turned my head and saw tears streaming down her face. I could not help but turn and embrace her.

In her embrace I was strong, decisive and sure. In the face of my strong friend's temporary weakness I gathered courage, for once she too needed assurance and hope. I wiped her tears away with a corner of my tob and kissed her on the forehead.

"Don't worry. We will be fine. Thanks to you, we will triumph. We will lead free and wondrous lives. Rejoice, for you set us free."

It was time. I smiled at her with all the confidence at my disposal, then I turned and left.

• • • • •

A warrior left Sophia's apartment that day—a fighting creature had awakened. I clenched my teeth with the certainty that I would kill to protect my daughter.

No creeping up the dirty staircase for a warrior, for no one knew where I came from. I went up by elevator, strode down the dark hall in long strides and closed the door with a thud. Then I prepared for flight.

We were a bit crammed in the back seat of the taxi because I had gained weight since this morning. Unable to carry a second handbag without raising suspicions, I had carefully fastened and strung the contents of the second bag about my body. These items, like real body weight, had found a natural resting place about my middle, hips and bottom.

I wore Maryam's shoes, some of her clothes and underwear and, for some inexplicable reason my ceremonial shawl. I had no idea why I felt a need to take the shawl. Perhaps it was to forever remind me of the reason for my escape.

As we arrived at the Martimex I ordered the driver to stop and silenced Amna's complaint with my new commanding voice. Maryam safely in my grip, we strode into the store. Swiftly, holding myself erect, I parted the crowd moving purposefully to the back of the store.

No one seemed to pay us any mind. I knew, of course, that in a country as poor as ours, a person would betray a trust or confidence for little money. And so I kept my eyes open for anything out of the ordinary that could spell treachery. The metal door was slightly ajar, as promised, and we slipped through the small gap. Then I closed the well-oiled door and remembered to lock it with the large key.

The storeroom was bathed in perpetual twilight and stacked with crates and boxes. A path led through the rows of goods, yet to my dismay the promised guide was nowhere to be seen. For just a moment, the old Amina was back in charge. She faltered long enough to allow fear to creep in, but my blessed child awakened the warrior once more.

"Mamina, I don't like this place. Let us go back to the lights and toys," she suggested.

"No, Dear, " I murmured, "today we are playing a game. First, we must find a path through the boxes and things. Then, I will take you to a place of joy."

Willingly she trod beside me, moving her small feet as fast as she could, as I pressed on not waiting for the guide. We had passed the middle of the storeroom when I heard voices.

"One person," Sophia had mentioned. Yet I heard two or three men speaking. Ill boding for us. I quickened my step and whispered to Maryam that we had to be absolutely silent.

"It's part of the game," I whispered, finger to my lips. Delighted, she winked at me. Now we could hear the men's footsteps. I pulled Maryam with me between two huge crates because the men's voices were growing closer. No doubt these men were searching for something. After a moment of heart stopping fear I realized that they were looking for part of a shipment. Breathless, pressing Maryam's face against me so she couldn't cry out, I saw the men pass near our hiding place. Moments later, arguing as they walked, they entered the jungle of crates on the other side.

Quickly we squeezed through the narrow passage between crates and walked stealthily down the main isle. Precious time had been lost. Would the car be still waiting when we finally arrived outside? I saw the door ahead of us, and we almost flew the last feet toward it.

Someone had locked the door, but the key was in the lock. I removed our last barrier. A grave sense of danger made me take the key, and lock the door from the outside.

The car described by Sophia wasn't far. By now we were running. Hastily, I threw the back door open. Before we were safely inside we heard sharp, metallic clanking and banging on the warehouse door, followed by loud, angry voices.

I was still pulling the car door shut when the car sped away. Finally, safely submerged in traffic, the driver spoke. Smilingly he turned to face me and asked, "Are you the chosen one?" I answered him, "Yes, I was chosen."

He'd asked the right question, but doubt had crept into my mind. Things had gone too smooth. My escape couldn't have been that easy. Could this perhaps be Yussuf's driver? If he'd discovered our plot, it possibly could be. The usher in the store room, who never came to help us, could have sold us for thirty pieces of silver. But I had seen our driver's face and decided to trust my feelings and allow myself to feel safe.

The driver said no more. The road with its terrible traffic demanded all his attention. We couldn't afford to be involved in an accident. Besides cars, trucks and buses, thousands of bicycles were abroad. Caravans entered the roads, small, colorful three-wheeled jitneys weaved in and out of lanes, men, their heads loaded with goods, crossed the streets almost at will.

Once we left the proximity of the Martimex I was lost. Streets and buildings looked strange, unfriendly, and so I withdrew into the interior of the vehicle and concentrated my attention on Maryam. So far she found the game we were playing quite comical, whispering and giggling in answer to my questions.

A hundred times I was tempted to ask where we were going, and just as often I stopped, for it mattered not. Wherever destiny led us had to be a place of safety—nothing else mattered.

Suddenly I became alert as we approached an area I recognized. I became excited. Before us was the ornate gate and the lovely palm-edged drive which I had committed to my heart's memory, for I loved it so. Then I knew we were safe—safe with Madam Thibodeau.

However, we were not to enter the house. Instead the chauffeur led us speedily across the lawn toward the back of the estate. "Until you can leave the country safely you will live in the garden house," he explained. "No one must know you are here. Knowledge of your presence could result in the most dire consequences for Madam and the Ambassador. So we must secret you away, even from our own trusted servants."

"What about you?" I cried. "Wouldn't a large sum make a difference in your life?"

With the hauteur of a prince he countered, "I cannot be bought at any price. I'd die for Madam."

He said no more. Although he aroused my curiosity, I was unable to extract other confidences from the man. As he moved lightly, seemingly effortless, and always slightly ahead of us, I fully took his measure. He was tall and his powerful wide shoulders bespoke great strength. He had picked up Maryam, who had been unable to keep up with us, and carried her with the ease a child carries a doll. He was coal black, with a nose as the beak of the harpy, prominent and strong. His lips were thin, dividing his face as if slashed by a knife, a face, that gave me no clue of his tribal origin. There was an air of ferocity about him that I could not explain, yet I trusted him explicitly.

When he smiled, as he did now, his narrow lips became full and generous, and his face shone with goodness.

"It was clever of you to have locked the door back at Martimex. We should have been caught had you not done so. Our man in the warehouse must have been in trouble."

"I am glad you waited. We were very late."

"I shouldn't have been there much longer. Yet, I had promised Madam to do my utmost."

I had been wondering how to address this man who had played such a crucial role in our escape. It felt uncomfortable to speak to him impersonally. "What shall we call you? It seems we will be seeing much of you, and I'd like to know your name."

Evasively he answered, "You can call me Nuredin, the prince of tales." He laughed loudly, amused by his own witticism. In the following weeks we did, indeed, come to think of him as our prince. Bantering, we arrived at the charming garden house, its many windows and shaded veranda overlooking a fragrant garden. Inside, besides a bedroom, there was a pretty sitting room, a kitchen niche and a shower with a lavatory.

Painted a dark green that blended with its lush surroundings and trimmed in white, the octagonal pavilion had been built with weary travellers in mind. People needing to refresh their bodies and minds would find peace amid the serene setting. Every window opened onto another enchanting vista. We could see the main house shining through green foliage from one of the windows. Yet Nuredin assured me that the pavilion was invisible from the house.

From a canvas satchel stowed under his free arm, our gallant driver removed a variety of items important to our stay. Nuredin put a container of milk and another filled with fruit juice into a water-cooled box and left a supply of fruit, bread, jam and tinned meat on a plain, wooden sideboard.

"As soon as it is dark, warm food will be brought to you. So don't worry. All is well. In here are books, and toys for the child." He pointed to a large leather trunk. Then he left us to rest. In the bedroom I found a grand, soft bed of European styling and we stretched our bodies between crisp white sheets. To my great surprise, for I thought my fevered brain couldn't rest, we fell asleep almost instantly.

Madam kept us hidden and safe for three weeks. Day by day, we were looked after by the much-trusted Nuredin. On a few occasions, whenever she managed to be unobserved, Madam came to visit us. Kindly and patiently, she informed me of any intelligence she had gathered.

Through her I learned that Yussuf had offered a reward of $10,000 for the return of his wife and child. The sheer largess of the reward took my breath away. All roads were blocked, all cars were checked. That was an easy thing to accomplish because there was only one road for such undertaking leading to either Ethiopia or Egypt. Madam also told me that at the airport and the train station women with children were subjected to the most undignified searches. I marvelled that one unimportant woman and an insignificant girl could cause such fervor. Somehow I was reminded of the story of the starving, neglected camel that escaped into the desert and, henceforth, was pursued by his owner with fevered relentlessness.

We spent a quiet comfortable week, wrapped in the experience of new sensations. I dared not worry about things I couldn't control. In hiding like an escaped convict, I was as helpless as a child. Not that I had ever had much control over my life or destiny, but it had seemed to me, when deceiving Yussuf, manipulating him so I could learn with Sophia, that I had some control.

At night the devils came. My dreams were of blackness pierced by my sons' voices, of headlong flight, clutching Maryam while black-shadowed shawatin pursued us. And then there was the dream of the red jinn. Again and again I relived the desert scene with a Yussuf-faced lion and the dancing, burning jinn, and over and over I handed my boys to the jinn. I dreaded sleep, and in sleepless hours I pondered why the jinn dream haunted me so, until one night the dream changed. Once again I stood in the desert, but when the lion came, my persona split. I became the red jinn, burning and dancing, but I also stood there as Amina holding my tiny children in my hands.

When I awoke, I knew. I, the red jinn, was the warrior, maker of harsh decisions, sparing the other Amina an enormous guilt that would have surely crushed her. Strangely, the thought of another persona comforted me and allowed me to sleep.

At dawn and dusk we strolled in the garden behind the pavilion. Nuredin, who had become our friend, was always in the lead. Always he carried a long, sharp, sword-like weapon, for poisonous serpents sought out the quiet richness of the back garden. Once, with a mighty stroke, he dispatched a large cobra he had antagonized by striding into its space. On these walks Maryam asked a thousand questions, which he tried to answer truthfully.

A child less perceptive, less intelligent might have been easier to placate, but she would also have been less of a companion in our shared danger. Somehow my little one understood that my strange actions were based on weighty reasons, and she trusted me implicitly, yet she also needed explanations to make sense of her world. Some of her questions were heartbreaking. I cried inconsolably when she asked if she would ever see her brothers again, showing me thereby that she fully understood that we were not playing a hiding game.

As usual, we were sitting after dusk on the veranda. She was settled in my lap with my arms around her. Lately she had a need to nestle with me often because the world she knew was no more.

"Look up to the stars," I encouraged, "and remember the story I told the boys—that they should gaze at the stars at this hour. They are thinking of you now." And then I decided to explain frankly that it was for her own safety that we had escaped the family. That girls and women were treated harsher than men, and deprived of their freedom in our society.

"Is that why you must cover your head and lower your eyes when men are around?" she asked, her small face earnest.

"Yes, that's why."

Then she surprised me. "Mother, what do they do to the girls during the purification rite?"

I shuddered. Maryam was much too young to know about such painful things. But then I realized, that had we stayed home, not only would she know about the pain, she would excruciatingly feel its agony. So I lowered myself facing her, resting my bottom in village fashion on my heels, and, eyes level with hers, I began to explain the horrible rite.

I began by recounting the moment when they'd come and taken me away.

How they'd pushed me onto the angareeb on which they would moments later perform their painful deed. I told her how they held me, how they spread my legs and shrilled their song, while Hadija the exciser cut from my body what God had placed there. Unbeknownst to me tears flowed as I recounted the ancient hurt.

"That's why we needed to leave when we did. Next day your father would have taken us to the village to have this done to you."

Maryam took my face between her small hands. "Don't cry anymore, Mamina," she said, stroking my cheek. "I am glad we left home. I don't want this done to me." For a moment her eyes grew thoughtful, her gaze seemed to move inward. "What about the boys?" she asked. " Do they hurt them too?"

"Yes, they do. But not nearly as severe as what they do to girls." I explained about the snippet of foreskin that's left to the knife, which the grandmothers so proudly wrap around their fingers. And, of course, I spoke of the feast the boys are given. I was gratified, for my bright girl understood the injustice instantly.

"Oh," she pointed out, "for so little hurt they are given a feast, and the poor girl just gets to have tea."

At the end of the week Madam Thibodeau came unexpectedly to our hideout.

One look at her face told me that she was bringing bad news. Her blue eyes were troubled and red-rimmed in her otherwise perfectly made-up face. Not a hair was out of place, and yet I read the signs of fear and suffering. She didn't prolong my agony of suspense. Holding my hands, she gave me the truth bluntly, after she made me sit down.

"Darling, I have but one way to tell this. Our beloved Sophia is dead. Your husband killed her." Madam covered her mouth with her delicate hand to stifle her sobs, while her tears ran thickly down her cheeks and over her fingers. At first, her words did not reach me, then, when I finally understood, my mind revolted against the horrid truth. It couldn't be. Dead? Not Sophia! My invincible, intrepid, resourceful, beloved Sophia. I realized at that moment that I could have accepted anyone's death, but hers. She was my life, my brain, my blood. Without her, I too was condemned to die. Through the dullness of my denial I heard Madam speaking once more.

"After you left, your husband raved for days. He said that it was Sophia's fault that you escaped," she explained. "He bellowed—the whole house heard him—that his wife and child were his possessions like the furniture, and that no one, but no one, could steal what belonged to him." Madam dabbed at her cheeks, trying to stem the flood, and continued her horrible report.

"The thought, that you—forgive me, but he called you a dumb village mouse—duped him maddened him until he sought revenge. Last night he entered her apartment and stabbed her to death. Abdullah came too late upon the scene to aid her. She died in his arms."

Madam now sobbed unashamedly. Her white, porcelain makeup, which usually gave an illusion of translucent pearliness to her face, dissolved, exposing fine mottled skin beneath. She suffered intensely, yet she pulled herself together with great self-control so I would hear the rest.

"Her death seems to have driven Abdullah mad. It must must have been a horrible scene. Sophia, stabbed in the throat, could not speak to him. She just looked at him with those incredible eyes—while the blood he tried to stop and could not gushed from her wounds, and so she died. When they pried her dead body from his arms, reason left him. Since that moment he sits inertly in his darkened room, and stares into space. The house is divided against itself. Many voices speak of Yussuf's use of hashish. They say that his indulgence of this drug changed him profoundly and caused the rift in your marriage. They say it was the cause for his troubled relations within the family."

Yussuf? Hashish? I had heard of men who loved this drug, believing it to make them more virile, lending them strength and endurance. I had also heard that indulgence by the hashish eater led to violence and cruelty. Somehow this would explain the gradual change in my husband that had caused me such pain. In our country the dried flowers of the hemp plant are boiled to concentrate the hashish into a most powerful substance, which ingested by mouth turns the eater into an all powerful being. Everyone knew that angry hashishin could kill their own family.

Suddenly the misery of it all overcame me and I cried out, "I must go back. Oh, God what have I done?" My outburst stopped Madam Thibodeau's tears. Her voice became instantly sharp and commanding.

"Don't think it, and don't say it. Sophia was my best friend. We were like sisters. She lived and died for the things that she so fervently believed. She believed in you, and took an incredible chance so you could live with your convictions. Now you must carry on. It is not up to you to change the course of what she set in motion. You must be strong and follow the course she laid out for you."

Madam paused and caught her breath. "Apart from that, don't think for a moment that your return could solve anything. To the contrary—you'd make everything worse a hundred-fold. Must I remind you that, despite Sophia's death, they'd still circumcise your child? What do you think would be in store for you? Your husband might kill you, too. At the least he will banish you, or cast you out into the street. Sophia is dead. You can't change that."

We had forgotten about Maryam, who was silently playing in the next room.

Now she crept forward. She was pale, and her small body trembled with fear. She cried in a pitiful voice, "Mamina, Mamina, I don't ever want to go back home. I never want to see Father again. Please, please let us stay here and never go back."

I hugged her to me. How could I have forgotten, even for a moment, that she was present, able to hear the monstrous tale? Looking into her pale, small face I promised, "We shall never go back."

CHAPTER *Ten*

Like ghosts and owls we moved at night. At dusk and dawn we walked the gardens. During the day we stayed indoors, avoiding the prying eyes of gardeners and servants, but when the shadows grew enormous, blanketing open spaces with gray diffusion, we crept outdoors. Our souls were also shadow-filled—our life-lights diffused, as the night world around us. Most times our grief for Sophia overshadowed our fear of detection, numbing us to our own precarious situation.

Thus, for a couple of weeks we lived in a timeless vacuum of existence. We walked, we spoke, we read. But our actions seemed unreal, unconnected to the world, meaningful only to Maryam and myself. We lived with shared grief, for Sophia had been a teacher to both of us. Alternately I was comforted, almost grateful to have this time to grieve, then again frightened that we were still within reach of Yussuf and the family. I believe that Maryam dealt with the loss of father, brothers, family and home by suppressing all thoughts and feelings. Once to my amazement she pitifully defended Yussuf by announcing, "He just couldn't think right."

Later in a reversal, she speculated, "He mustn't love us if he killed her because he knew we loved her so much." From snippets like that I watched her puzzle out the events in her life, which had been the most peaceful, uneventful existence up until that time. Best as I could I tried to explain what had taken place and why.

Our secluded peace ended in violent upheaval. Three weeks into our stay we were jolted awake one night by pounding on the front door, resounding through the pavilion, portending danger. Frightened, we clung to each other, kneeling in our bed until I comprehended that whoever sought entry must be a friend because an enemy would have broken the slight door at once.

For the first time, a lifetime of Islamic modesty was stripped away by the more powerful fear of survival. Clad only in my nightshift I flew to the door, which I opened without question. Nuredin almost fell through the opened door. He had been leaning against it, one ear pressed to the wood to hear if we were awake.

"Quick," he shouted, "dress and gather all you need." He pushed a package of European clothes at me and told me to put them on.

"We have to leave at once. Your husband's family has convinced the authorities that Madam shelters the two of you. The premises will be searched in minutes. Already they are knocking at the front gate. Madam's butler is stalling them, but how long can that last?"

I asked no questions, leaving every decision in his hands. While Nuredin excitedly broke this news, he began to pick up our things, which he stuffed into a valise. We turned off the lights in the front room. Hastily and breathlessly we somehow dressed, gathering our things, removing as best we could all traces of our stay. I cringed to think that once again a dear woman would have to suffer the consequences of my actions.

Flashlights searching for a path to the pavilion came dangerously near when finally we fled through the back door into the garden. Nuredin carried Maryam and the valise; I carried my oversized, stuffed purse and some odds and ends that I thought might come in handy bundled into a shawl.

I rejoiced, for the night was as dark as black velvet, the moon invisible, the stars feeble in their effort to light up our world. Nuredin moved silently, like a lion stalking prey. I followed closely, breathlessly, afraid of pursuers and night creatures alike. Haste drove us into obstacles—brushing the shrubbery we awoke mournfully complaining birds. Small noises, magnified in our minds a thousand-fold, were sending us into throws of worry.

Yet we made progress. A few times Nuredin stopped to listen in the direction from which the agents pursuing us were expected, yet he never heard a sound. Our progress over the grounds was finally halted by a high, stone wall. There, without hesitation, Nuredin turned to the right, following the wall. Not long thereafter he found a rusty iron door which he opened with a small, ornate key.

We slipped through the narrow opening. To my surprise we stood on a narrow path between fields, such as one finds in rural communities. Not far from the gate the outline of a vehicle sent chills through my body. I whispered to Nuredin that the enemy had already found us.

"No. This is ours," he reassured me, and bundled us into the car. This car, which he called a Land Rover, was most wonderfully suited to flight, and probably saved our lives as we fled toward Egypt. It carried us with the same efficiency used to speed along a paved highway, through fields, barrens, deadly stretches of desert and dry, stony wadis.

"As the bird flies it is only about 400 miles to the Egyptian border, but we don't have the luxury of flight. Another impediment is our inability to use the road that runs alongside El Nil because it is well watched. We cannot use the bridge to cross the Atbara River, and must travel through the desert to stay out of sight." With these words Nuredin prepared us for the hardships to come.

Without Nuredin, the marvelous vehicle would not have been enough. Only through his perseverance, vast knowledge of the desert and his driving skill did we survive this most gruelling flight.

Nuredin, like the legendary prince, magically overcame the greatest dangers. Obviously, we could not drive into the few villages and towns along the road to provision ourselves with food and gasoline. Yussuf's spies had broadcast his lucrative offer of reward weeks earlier. Therefore, when need overcame us, Nuredin sought out large depressions in the desertscape, a dip between dunes caused by run-off from flash floods—anyplace at all to hide the conspicuous Land Rover. He'd leave us there at sunset, setting out on foot for the village.

On these excursions he always wore a white, somewhat shabby burnoose, which provided ample shading for his head and face. Before leaving us, he pulled from below the drivers seat his deadly accurate Beretta and a shiny Smith & Wesson .22 caliber revolver. He carefully checked them before handing one of them to me, with the same warning each time: "If anyone comes within shouting range, tell them to leave. If they approach anyway—shoot. Aim for their chest and kill them, for if they get away, it will be our death."

I promised to do as told, whereupon he left us to our lonely vigil. He'd given me a quick course in the use of his weapons, as well as driving lessons, and had been pleased with my hand-eye coordination and the sureness of my aim.

My deftness with the weapons reassured him that for a lowly woman I had some courage and capability, and yet he felt it necessary to remind me anew at each of his departures, "If I am not back at the appointed hour, something's amiss and you must leave following the map I gave you."

There came the night of his third foray to one of the square, squalid little farm compounds that we had spied from afar with his strong binoculars. He had left us as before in a sandy depression, a soft spot amid the moonscape of rock and gravel. We'd chosen to leave the confines of the Rover for awhile to stretch our cramped limbs. A few hours had passed and we still sat hungry, thirsty and cold on a tarpaulin wrapped in our blankets. The deep, inky dark that follows the sunset had given way to a clear sky. Enough light from the almost full moon fell upon the desert to grotesquely lengthen the shadows of boulders and dunes, making me think I had died and now lived forever in the valley of dread. Without my child I should have perished or been consumed with terror.

"Do you think he will find us again?" worried Maryam.

Whispering, I answered honestly, "I do not know. He might be captured and can't come back." I looked at the Land Rover, shadowy on a patch of gravel, and thought that we had stretched our bodies enough, that it was time again to return to the safety of the vehicle, when I heard a high, cackling sound. The same instant I saw a moving shadow. A hyena. I had never seen or heard this animal before, but Nuredin had described it with such accuracy that I knew instantly what was before us.

"They are as deadly as lions," he'd admonished, "but there are few in the desert and you might never see one."

I threw our blankets off and grabbed my gun. Then, I saw a second shadow. Longingly, I looked to the Land Rover, but I knew we were cut off from its safety. One of the animals was only feet from the vehicle. Again, we heard the chilling cackle. Maryam, gripping my thigh, made a strangling noise and then whispered, "Will they eat us Mamina?"

"No, they will not," I said grimly. I concentrated on the bolder, larger of the shadows coming toward me from my right. I knelt. I remembered that the gun fired low. To hit accurately I needed to aim high. In unison, the hyenas attacked from different angles. For the moment I ignored the smaller one. It was farther away, coming from my left, attempting to attack us from the rear. I fired at the large animal. The shot went high and the brute kept coming. I fired again and the beast dropped. Maryam's scream made me turn in time to fire at the second animal ready to spring at her.

The force of the bullet hurled the beast away from us, but, amazingly, it recovered its feet, staggered, and with bloodcurdling screams and yips, managed to gallop away. Too stunned and shaken to move I allowed the animal to get away. The shots echoed in my head, my hands shook from recoil and excitement. I knelt beside my child, holding her, reassuring her that all was well, and all the while I shook like a leaf in the wind.

I had kept an eye on the animal I thought was dead, and it never moved. Certainly, I had neither the will nor the courage to ascertain its condition. Murmuring to Maryam I began to gather our belongings so we could return to the Land Rover, when I saw yet another shadow approach. I dropped the blankets and reached for the gun in one fluid motion. Again I dropped on my left knee and aimed, but Nuredin's cry stayed my trigger finger.

"Do not shoot me. By all that's holy, do not shoot," he kept calling as he approached. Our happiness to see him knew no bounds. Maryam hugged him and finally, I allowed myself to cry away the fear and tension of the last hours.

"I thank you for those shots, Amina." His words interrupted our joyful outpouring. "I would have never found the camp without your shots. I missed the marker I had left for myself, and was walking away from this area when I heard you. I never heard such a wonderful sound," smiled our friend.

"Oh, Nuredin, my friend," I began to explain, "you should thank the hyenas because they were the reason for the commotion." When he had heard the full story of our frightful adventure, he dutifully examined the dead hyena, shining his flashlight over it from head to tail. He tested its condition with a swift kick, declaring it demised. Bending over the animal he examined the wound and commented on my good luck. Stirred up like beehives, we told him in turn about the one that got away. Sagely, he nodded, and then he praised me for being brave and trustworthy. I became silent and suddenly felt shy.

Later, we devoured the meat and bread he had procured and refreshed ourselves with draughts of good, cold water, and prepared for rest. We spread the
tarpaulin on the sand because Nuredin felt we were safe and did not need to
sleep knotted up in the vehicle. Trusting the seclusion of our camp, he made a
small fire with a few sticks and camel dung he had brought. We gloried in the
small pile of light and warmth, growing mellow and prayerful, falling asleep
when it died down.

Emboldened by Nuredin's kindness, I dared ask him a few nights later to
tell me about his life. That night it was bitter cold. Wrapped in every shred of
clothing available, we huddled under the tarpaulin, not daring to light a
warming fire for fear of drawing enemies.

Perhaps it was our physical closeness—or perhaps a desire to lighten a
long-carried load of hurt—but he began recalling his childhood as the beloved
son of a chieftain of the Dinka. He was raised with pride and care by a
powerful father. Through his sparse words shone his love for his people in
their desperate struggle for existence.

Their life was harsh. His people were dependent on the cattle they
herded on the edge of the great swamps in Southern Sudan. Plentiful rain in
their region allowed good fodder to grow. Yet the goodness of rain was offset
by mosquito and insect plagues.

With other boys his age he herded cattle, fighting off predators looking
for an easy kill. When he was thirteen, straight, tall and well-muscled, his
father charged him with the responsibility for their entire herd. Four other
boys were charged to work under his lead. For the month that followed no
losses occurred and he was praised for the faithful execution of his duties.

"But," he said, "the peace was shattered one day at noon. They came under
the bright light of the merciless sun. Arab slavers from the north. Since ancient
times they were a scourge upon my people, and also the Nuer, our neighbors.
Determined to lay Islam on our backs and find slaves for their farms and cities,
they came and stole our young. They raped and pillaged as they had always
done. Those coming without soldiers were too cowardly to challenge the
warriors; they'd snatch children instead."

He had spoken forcefully, with ill-concealed anger. But now his mood
changed. He grew pensive and sad. "We were far from our village; no sound
would alert the men. We were strong boys, between eleven and thirteen—not
afraid to set our spears against lion and hyena—yet against guns we were no

match. It was over in a minute. They'd cleverly come upon us with the help of one of our own turned traitor.

"The moment they saw us, their guns barked, although we held no weapons in our hands. In an instant we were surrounded. They were careful not to hurt the merchandise. My best friend had a flesh wound in his thigh. They took care of it. After a small struggle they had overpowered us. What could we do? There were too many. They strung us to together like beads on a metal chain and moved us out of the area. We were herded into trucks when we came to a road and driven far away from home."

Overcome by his memories he remained silent. I thought of the young man's heartache when they tore him away from his village. The knowledge that he was to become a slave must have galled his soul. Suddenly, I remembered that the slavers from the south were Muslims, like our family. Why would he help me—a Muslim woman? My curiosity got the better of me.

"How did you meet Madam Thibodeau?"

"It was she who bought me and gave me my freedom. She saw me one day in the city. I was carrying a heavy, badly stacked load of tile for the man I'd been sold to. A few tiles slipped from the load and broke. In a fit of anger, the man beat me with insane zeal. Madam, a Christian, made her driver stop him. She haggled with the wretch for an hour because he did not want to sell me. In the end he let me go for a small fortune. You have experienced her concern for people yourself, and so you can imagine how it was.

"Madam was kind to me. She clothed me, fed me and taught me. She sent me to see my family, and told me I could remain at home if I liked. But the village had become strange to me. I'd seen too much to ever be happy in the village again. So Madam took me back and had me trained as her special envoy, her man behind the scenes, and that's how I like it."

"So why help an Islamic woman after the harm that Muslims did to you?"

"Madam said you are as unfree as I was when I was a slave. That's good enough for me."

I remembered that Sophia's maid came from the Dinka tribe. Had she also been enslaved I wondered. Nuredin knew her well, and said she had come to Khartoum as a free woman.

CHAPTER *Eleven*

A lexandria, Egypt

In the end, we reached Alexandria, Egypt, desiccated, burned and lean, but otherwise unscathed. Safely immersed in a soothing bath, I remembered my childhood dreams of el-khalla, and the hypnotic attraction of the place. Thankfully, I reflected upon the fact that our most fanciful wishes are never granted us. Now that I was acquainted with her emptiness, I had new-found respect for the daring intrusions into the interior of the desert by the caravans of yore.

Our flight only skirted the edge of her deathliness. For that is what I came to think of her as we moved in and out of her realm as need dictated. At times her vast chasm sheltered us from our pursuers, other times she did her best to sear the life from our bodies.

Through our travails, Maryam never complained. She knew that when there was water, she drank, and if there was none, we thirsted. She had noted that we reserved for her the greater part of our water and our food rations. With an earnestness beyond her years she told us that she could do with less. Her touching wish to share in our deprivation brought tears to my eyes. Nuredin told her she made him feel proud.

"You are a worthy cause, Maryam," he complimented and she bathed in the warmth of his affection.

Each morning, long before the sun rose, we began to travel. We rested in the shade of a canvas tarpaulin rigged to the roof of the Land Rover when the sun blazed overhead and travel became unbearable. When the greatest heat subsided, we were off again until total darkness drove us to rest.

For the crossing of the Atbara River, Nuredin hid us under the tarp in the back of the vehicle, among the gasoline cans and the provender. For Maryam and me it proved to be the worst hour of our trip. We lay cramped and wedged together, jabbed by sharp-cornered crates and tools beneath the heavy tarp that increased the heat a hundred-fold, nearly suffocating us. I heard Maryam gasping. Feeling gently for the edge of the tarp with her small fingers she created the slightest of openings enabling us to breath.

As we lay there huddled and dripping with sweat, we overheard Nuredin negotiating with the man who was to ferry us across the river. I suddenly realized from the tone of their negotiations, that the ferryman with the intuition of one who sees many different people—often in calamitous straits—sensed the clandestine nature of this crossing. People such as he profited from other peoples' misfortunes and calamities. Sure enough, he hinted how unusual it was to see such an expensive, almost new vehicle, crossing the Atbara at this remote point. Then he followed this remark by quoting a sinfully high price for his service.

"You should thank Allah the Great, Ferryman," Nuredin boomed with easy laughter, "that he sent someone into your miserable corner of the world who can pay your exorbitant fee."

The ferryman, appreciating Nuredin's open acknowledgement of his cunning and greed, joined in the laughter breaking the uneasy spell. Moments later, I felt us rolling onto the rocking floor of the flat boat.

On the Atbara's opposite bank, out of sight of the ferry boat, we were released from our steaming prison.

Just in time, I thought, because I knew we couldn't have endured much longer. Maryam's color was a dangerous deep scarlet. We moistened her face and body with precious water, fanning her while holding her upright.

After five days we crossed into Egypt. Yet, even though we had crossed into a different land, Yussuf's agents were still active in this region, and we had to proceed with extreme caution. We stayed away from Lake Aswan, travelling instead through the Eastern desert. It is a most fragmented, rocky, barren, virtually uninhabited territory that blankets the land between this man-made water and the Nile River below, and on its other border, the Red Sea. We never strayed too far into its interior.

When we reached Luxor, a most beautiful city that would remain for me the most wonderful of all cities, Nuredin boldly mingled the Rover with the traffic, and we became invisible in the throng of vehicles and people. It was here that we reached Madam Thibodeau's contacts, found shelter and sustenance.

Tearfully, we said good bye to Nuredin, who left, having delivered us safely to friends. What could we say to him? How could we thank him for risking his life for us daily for many weeks? Words failed us. My daughter, who hugged and kissed him tenderly, expressed her feelings much better than I who was bound by culture and tradition. Then, like a dream, he was gone from our lives and we felt orphaned, vulnerable. After two day's rest, Madam's friends ferried us to Alexandria where we were welcomed into the house of a French doctor.

EPILOGUE

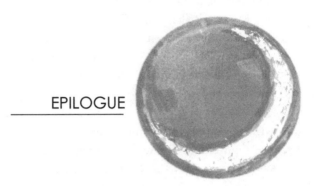

Today, I walk along the beautiful River Seine in Paris. The sun shines brilliantly, making the flowers of my silk dress come alive, warming my bare arms, teasing my eyes with shades, dapples and dazzles. It is my thirty-fourth birthday. The handsome, dark-haired man on my arm beside me is Etienne, my husband of nine years. He is taking Maryam and me to one of the *bateaux*, which float like swans on the river, for a dinner celebration of my special day.

The splendid young woman on Etienne's other side is Maryam, who at fourteen has blossomed into a poised, fine-featured girl with the promise of great future beauty. When I look at her my heart sings. She strides along freely, unencumbered by a nine-meter tob. Her long, silky hair is stirred by the breeze—no head cover for her proud mane. Her feet are comfortably and elegantly shod, and her body is enhanced by the pretty, blue sheath dress she is wearing.

She carries her head high and her demeanor is free and easy as she debates with Etienne whether France should become a part of the European Union or stand proud and alone, a nation unto itself.

But that is only what one discerns on the outside. I know her to be brave, dependable and ready to bear hardship, worthy of every measure of the terrible sacrifices I had to make to change her fate.

"So, Mademoiselle," teases Etienne, "what did you learn in anatomy this week? What does your pretty head remember about the arm?"

"Too easy, Papa," cries Maryam with mock disdain, and then recites in sing-song fashion humerus, ulna, radius, carpals of the wrist, metacarpals and phalanges.

"*Bon*, Maryam, you will become a doctor, yet," smiles Etienne, well pleased with her quick response. Etienne is the reason for Maryam's wish to become a physician. From the beginning, Etienne treated Maryam with respect. He often talks to us about his cases and problems in the hospital where he works. Maryam, who adores him, remembers well how she had besieged him with questions when they first met—questions which he had answered patiently, and in depth. Later, discerning that her interest was genuine, he allowed her to follow him around when he visited hospital patients, and sit in on his lectures at the Sorbonne.

Rising in the morning, I bless the day, every day, and I give thanks for my little family. Etienne is the spring of my well-being, the calm, quiet, undemanding love of my life. He is different from other French doctors who see themselves as all-powerful god's of healing. Doctors—what an important part they have played in my life. In my mind I see a bridge spanning from the red-headed, freckle-faced saviour of my childhood, to Mary Latourelle, to our friend in Alexandria, the doctor granting us shelter, to Etienne and, perhaps one day, Maryam. I am humbly grateful for their skills and mercies

For the first two incredible years after our escape I suffered pains that only mothers can feel who have lost their children. Guilt lived in my heart and our home. Guilt so crushing that for the longest time I could not eat without tears. For it is sustenance that a mother provides for her children and I was not feeding my boys. Guilt and tears returned at night when I put Maryam to bed. It was then I'd see the boys' heads on their pillows. Many a night we stood outside under the stars and sent wishes into the darkened firmament in the hopes they too might look up into the heavens and feel our thoughts.

Could I ever forget my dear friend Sophia? Sophia—my supreme martyr—lives forever in our hearts. We will never forget that she died for our precious independence, for Maryam's bright future.

Why did she have to die? In my mind I have played the scenes vividly a thousand times over trying to detect where we went wrong. What was the awful mistake that led to her death? One unforeseen factor emerges again and again. None of us knew that Yussuf's apparent sophistication was only skin deep. Apparently, submerged once more in our culture the veneer imperceptibly rubbed off until he reacted like many scorned men. To this day unanswered questions return, begging to be answered.

Some time ago Maryam appeared in the kitchen. On her face was the special look portending discovery of interesting news. She handed me an article copied from a medical text book.

"Did you know that the word assassin stems from the word hashishin, user of hashish?" she asked me, and I replied that I hadn't known. "Look at the example they give in their discussion of this drug: Nizar ibn al Mustansir, around 1090 wanted to become caliph. To accomplish this goal he used the support of a Muslim religious order spreading terror throughout the Muslim world with cruel, murderous attacks and assassinations. These men fired their fighting fervor by ingesting hashish until they became insensible against pain and emotional terror enabling them to commit the most monstrous acts." Maryam paused and favored me with an expectant look.

"Now you see that you can't blame yourself any longer for the act of an assassin. For that's what Father became, blaming Sophia for all the evil and problems in his life."

In such ways she tried to relieve me of my guilt. Over time I have come to forgive myself. So much has happened since that day of horror. Of course, time is the greatest healer of all. In time, bits of information trickled through to us gently healing my wounds. I could forgive myself—because others forgave me.

Our protector in Alexandria, the doctor, had flown us to Paris as soon as he had proper documents for our departure. Somehow, I fear, these documents were not quite official. But it's not for me to examine the gift of a camel for flaws in its hump. We arrived in Paris in a round about way via Germany.

The good doctor found us a small apartment, well situated by the Bois de Boulogne, and much too expensive for us. But we made do, since he also found a job for me teaching geography and Arabic at a lycée soon after I passed my examinations. Shortly thereafter he introduced me to Etienne, a doctor. We fell in love and got married. Of course, my first marriage had ended the moment I left my husband's house. Under Islamic law one only has to proclaim thrice: "I divorce thee, I divorce thee..." and the marriage is dissolved.

For the first time in my life I feel that I am an equal partner. When

Etienne and I looked for apartments, it was I who chose the one in the Rue de Civry Neuf. In this quiet, quaint, brownstone complex arranged around a courtyard, I found the perfect place for us to reside.

Across the street is a creamery, which is almost a necessity because of Etienne's typically French daily indulgence in a large variety of different cheeses. The "Bois," which I have come to love and walk in daily, is only minutes away by foot, and I am close to the lycée where I teach.

Here, in this peaceful, bourgeois hideout I overcame my guilt of leaving my boys motherless. Here, Sophia's girls come to visit, and to reassure me. Not long after our arrival in Paris I contacted Sophia's daughters to tell them of their mother's bravery, her ingenuity in weaving our escape plan. I cried bitterly, recounting our last meeting, painting a picture for them to remember their mother by. I told them of the day Madam Thibodeau stunned us with the harsh news of her tragic death.

I begged them to forgive me, because I was the cause that set the tragedy in motion. At first the young women, who prefer to be called by their French names, Claudine (the older) and Estelle, were cold and distant. Devastated by their mother's death it was hard for them to think of another's feelings and understand my overwhelming guilt. But, being Sophia's true daughters, they understood in time that I needed absolution.

Their family connections bring me good news about my boys, abating some of my guilt. It is now apparent that the family never understood that we fled because genital mutilation threatened Maryam. In their minds the concept is so ingrained that they can't consider it as a reason for flight. No, quite to the contrary, they chose to believe Yussuf's hashish use—with its harsh and strange behaviors, a strangeness they had experienced themselves, was the cause for our escape.

Amna, unflappable as always, moved the boys into her own quarters when my defection became clear. She never speaks of me at all, as if I never existed. But Zajid has been heard to tell the boys that I had been a good mother, that his own son frightened me into leaving.

Abdullah, Sophia's husband, freed himself of the abysmal depression that immobilized him. To immortalize his wife's life and her beliefs, and in utter defiance of family, tradition and culture, he sold his part in the family enterprise and left Sudan to reside with Claudine and Estelle in Paris.

Reading, learning every day more about the world, my eyes are opened to many forms of constraints laid upon women all over the world. I see a long litany of different forms of female mutilation. Female genital mutilation is not only practiced by Africans. Asian peoples have different forms of the practice in their cultural heritage as well.

Chinese culture mutilated women's feet, Indian culture committed wives—and in some places commits them to this day—to die upon the husband's funeral pyre in the practice of suttee. Thai parents sell small daughters into brothels to pay off debts, while the fashion industry of industrial countries pushes women to have their breasts reduced, or enlarged, their hair dyed, their skin bleached, and their fat suctioned off in a neverending competition for elusive security.

I am amazed how many countries document the possession of females by spirits. I remember, vividly, how close I came myself to becoming possessed. I know it wasn't possession by a spirit—it was hopelessness itself that claimed me. Long ago, Sophia had correctly determined the reasons for Zar possessions: possession gains for the disenfranchised women a small measure of power, relief from control, without changing their position.

I would like to see true changes in women's lives, not the ecstatic dance of temporary transformation.

I am reminded that in my culture female circumcision is enforced by women with much more fanaticism than by men. This makes me determined to become a powerful force capable of changing this mind set in my country and all over the world. To this effect I write articles, teach and give lectures on the subject. And perhaps one day little girls the world over will be left whole.

•   •   •   •   •

And as I sit, considering these facts, I also contemplate how strange a thing the human mind—for though I'll never see my home again, it always lives within. There are the nights when I can hear the wind telling the desert tale in the reeds of the roof, nights when the haboob showers sand in my bed, when the smell of kisra permeates my dreams, and soft voices murmur in their sleep. And then I walk the earthen floor again, feeling the smooth, cool clay beneath my naked feet, I smell the water in the zirs, and hear my father's voice. Yet even in my dream I feel the pulling of the tob; I hear the shrilling voices at ayam el tahur and then...I run into the desert.

REFERENCES

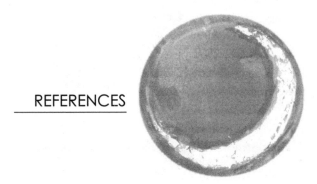

Apena, Adeline. "Female Circumcision in Africa and the Problem of Cross-Cultural Perspectives." *African Update* 3 (1996).

Boddy, Janice. "Spirits and Selves in Northern Sudan: The Cultural Therapeutics of Possession and Trance." *American Ethnologist* 15 (1988).

Boddy, Janice. "Womb as Oasis: The Symbolic Context of Pharaonic Circumcision in Rural Northern Sudan." *American Ethnologist* 1 (1982).

Emiagwali, Gloria T. "Female Circumcision in Africa." *Africa Update* 3 (1996).

Iweriebor, Ifeyinwa. "Black Women in Publishing." *Africa Update* 3 (1996).

Kaster, H.L. *Islam ohne Schleier*. Gutersloh: C. Bertelsman Verlag, 1963.

Lewis, Bernard. *What Went Wrong: Western Impact and Middle Eastern Response*. New York: Oxford University Press, 2002.

Lewis, I.M. *Ecstatic Religion: An Anthropological Study of Spirit Possession and Shamanism.* New York: Routledge, 1989.

Matias, Aisha Samad. "Female Circumcision in Africa." *Africa Update* 3 (1996).

Ong, Aihwa. "The Production of Possession: Spirits and the Multinational Corporation in Malaysia." *American Ethnologist* 15 (1988).

Walker, Alice. *Possessing the Secret of Joy.* New York: Harcourt, Brace, Jovanovich, 1992.

"FGM in Eastern Africa: Development Issues and Recommendations for Intervention." December 1994, Population and Human Resources Division, Eastern Africa Department, Africa Region.

To order additional copies of:

ESCAPING THE

Twilight

ISBN 0-9726535-5-4

send $15.95 plus $4.00 S&H to:

Arnica Publishing, Inc.
620 SW Main, Suite 345
Portland, OR 97205

To order by phone, call (503) 225-9900
Order online at arnicapublishing.com